U0136599

2011 不求人文化

2009 懶鬼子英日語

2005 意識文化

2005 易富文化

2003 我識地球村

2001 我識出版社

寫給過了 30歲才要開始 好好學英文的你我

[邁向雙語國家的成人英文基礎課]

User's Guide
使用說明

Point 01

8個篇章，40個主題

涵蓋生活的8大情境，從就學到就職、從升遷到退休、從日常到意外，全書細分成40個主題單元，詳細介紹日常應用得到的英文單字與會話金句。

UNIT 01
A Reservation for Dinner Tonight
預約今晚的晚餐

♪016-01 Can I make a reservation for dinner tonight?
我可以預約今天晚上的晚餐嗎？

♪016-02 Do you take reservations over a week from now?
你們接受一週後的預約嗎？

♪016-03 Can you put me on the waiting list?
你能幫我放在候補名單上嗎？

♪016-04 I need a table by the window. 我需要訂一個靠近窗戶的桌位。

♪016-05 It's under John. 以約翰的名義。

♪016-06 I'd like to make a reservation for four people.
我想要預約四人的位置。

Point 02

6大學習技巧

- 用主題帶出短句——初步認識單元主題。
- 用標題帶出單字——心智圖延伸單字，更隨機補充相關單字。
- 用故事帶出情境——帶領讀者用四個關鍵問句來還原模擬情境。
- 用情境帶出對話——建立好情境之後順水推舟地帶出對話。
- 用對話帶出文法——利用相關的對話句介紹句中文法。
- 用學習單來複習——利用學習單來進行快速簡單的單元複習、完整完成學習步驟。

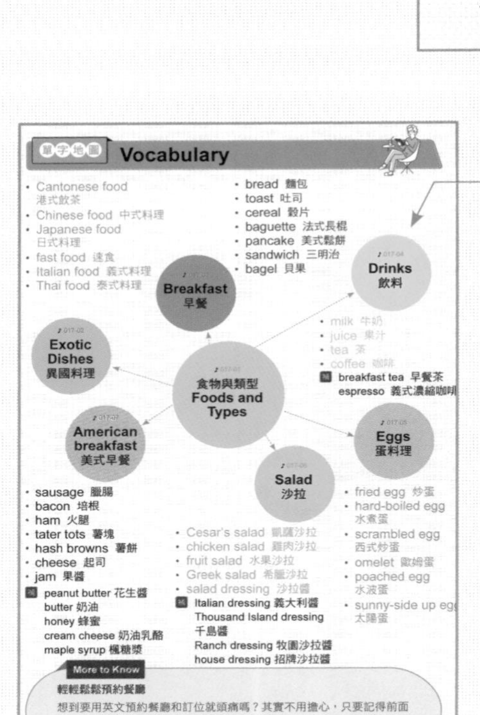

單字地圖 Vocabulary

食物與類型 Foods and Types

Breakfast 早餐
- bread 麵包
- toast 吐司
- cereal 穀片
- baguette 法式長棍
- pancake 美式鬆餅
- sandwich 三明治
- bagel 貝果

Exotic Dishes 異國料理
- Cantonese food 港式飲茶
- Chinese food 中式料理
- Japanese food 日式料理
- fast food 速食
- Italian food 義式料理
- Thai food 泰式料理

Drinks 飲料
- milk 牛奶
- juice 果汁
- tea 茶
- coffee 咖啡
- breakfast tea 早餐茶
- espresso 義式濃縮咖啡

American breakfast 美式早餐
- sausage 臘腸
- bacon 培根
- ham 火腿
- tater tots 薯塊
- hash browns 薯餅
- cheese 起司
- jam 果醬
- peanut butter 花生醬
- butter 奶油
- honey 蜂蜜
- cream cheese 奶油乳酪
- maple syrup 楓糖漿

Salad 沙拉
- Cesar's salad 凱薩沙拉
- chicken salad 雞肉沙拉
- fruit salad 水果沙拉
- Greek salad 希臘沙拉
- salad dressing 沙拉醬
- Italian dressing 義大利醬
- Thousand Island dressing 千島醬
- Ranch dressing 牧園沙拉醬
- house dressing 招牌沙拉醬

Eggs 蛋料理
- fried egg 炒蛋
- hard-boiled egg 水煮蛋
- scrambled egg 西式炒蛋
- omelet 歐姆蛋
- poached egg 水波蛋
- sunny-side up egg 太陽蛋

More to Know
輕輕鬆鬆預約餐廳
想到要用英文預約餐廳和訂位就頭痛嗎？其實不用擔心，只要記得前面

Point

03 兩段式錄音 Ft. 美籍老師 Ft. Youtor App

- 兩段式錄音：對話分成兩種聆聽模式可以選擇，有正常版和模擬對話版。
  正常版——可以選擇語速，也可以邊聽邊暫停，練習跟讀！
  模擬對話版——對話中挖空角色對話，請化身角色，和美國人來場模擬對話！
  ※ 延伸學習：也可以善加利用 App 中「暫停」與「語速調整」的功能喔！
- 每單元對話頁中的最後一個音檔，就是你大展身手的機會！掃描對話頁的 QR Code，每一句對話皆會對應一個音檔，而該頁的最後一個音檔，則是將角色挖空的完整對話音檔！將自己帶入對話中，看著書中對話句子，練習開口說！
- 美籍老師親自錄製全書英文單字與英文例句。
- 紙本結合數位，用手機一掃，就能聽音檔，超便利學習！（詳見 P.005 說明）

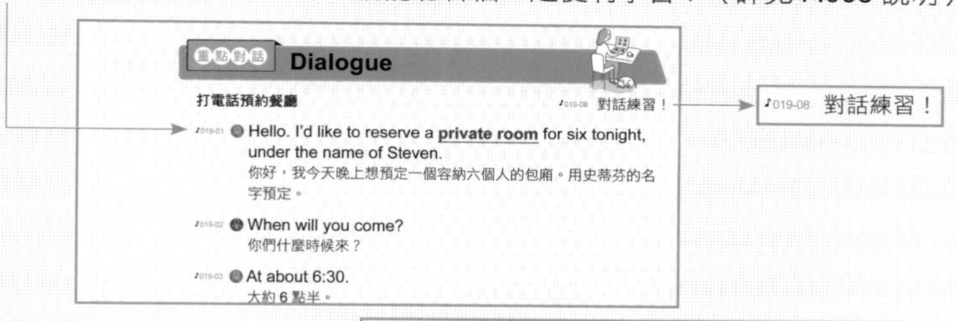

Point

04 做事用方法，學習見成效！

How to Say
聽懂服務生的回應！
- I'm sorry, but we're fully booked. 真的很抱歉，但是我們都預約滿了。
- I'm sorry, but we don't accept any reservations in advance.
  不好意思，我們不接受預約喔。

- 全書運用 6 個學習技巧串連而成，更加入了多種學習幫助專欄，適時補充英文相關用法或是美國文化資訊。
- 運用目錄加以認識內文章節，目錄中還有使用者專欄，方便掌握自己的學習進度（請見 P.007-P.014）。

目錄專欄介紹：

篇章導引——分為三步驟，按照步驟更加認識學習內容。

你將學會——介紹單元將學到的相關資訊，還可以先挑選有興趣的單元來學習。

檢視成效——有小方框可以做記號，記錄自己是否按照步驟進行學習。

重點對話 Dialogue

Chapter 01 美食佳餚

和服務生點餐

♪025-05 對話練習！

♪025-01 Would you like to order, sir?
要點餐了嗎，先生？

♪025-02 **I would like to have a steak, please.**
我想要點一份牛排。

♪025-03 Anything else you want to order?
請問還需要其它的嗎？

♪025-04 A glass of red wine.
一杯紅酒。

Point 05 努力，還能更省力！

- 整本書放大字級──讀起來不吃力，才是真正的省力。
- 句子不再落落長──用短句做為學習開端，不再害怕看到長句。
- 用法解釋最簡化──整理表格、範例、相關用法，一目了然。
- 單字延伸心智圖──聯想單字，才是記得單字的正確方法。
- 利用音檔跟讀法──三段式錄音，完美掌握聽力與口說練習。
- 補充文法小講堂──補充 6 個文法重點講堂，建立基本文法觀念！
（詳見 P.271-P.286）

「聽．說．讀．寫」全面掌握，幫你在努力之餘省點力！

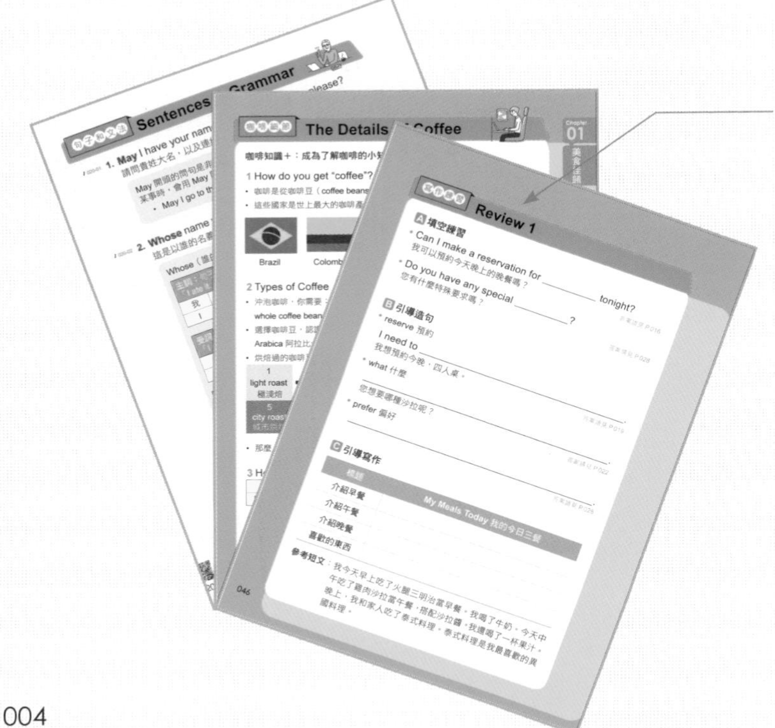

Point 06 不是歸零，是校正回歸。

不再是「student 學生」、現在已經是「manager 經理」；不再喜歡「basketball 籃球」、現在喜歡「golf 高爾夫球」；不同人生階段，為您更新不同的英文學習內容。吻合自己的人生程度，才是正確的學習程度。

線上下載「Youtor App」（內含VRP虛擬點讀筆）

為了幫助讀者更方便使用本書，特別領先全世界開發「VRP虛擬點讀筆」（Virtual Reading Pen），讓讀者可以更有效率地利用本書學習、聽取本書的音檔。讀者只要將本書結合已安裝「Youtor App」（內含VRP虛擬點讀筆）的手機，就能立即使用手機掃描書中的QR Code聽取本書的中英單字與英文例句。「VRP虛擬點讀筆」是以點讀筆的概念做開發設計，每次重新啟動時需要再次掃描QR Code。

Youtor App
（內含VRP虛擬點讀筆）
下載位置

「VRP 虛擬點讀筆」介紹

❶ 讀者只要掃描右側QR Code，將會引導至App Store / Google Play免費下載安裝「Youtor App」（內含VRP虛擬點讀筆）或是於App商城搜尋「Youtor」即可下載。

❷ 打開「Youtor App」（內含VRP虛擬點讀筆）後登入。若無帳號請先點選「註冊」填寫資料完成後即可登入。

❸ 進入首頁後請點選右上角的QR Code掃描鍵，掃描書中的QR Code下載音檔，再次進入首頁即會出現「VRP虛擬點讀筆」。進入「VRP虛擬點讀筆」後可至熱門排行中篩選或搜尋想尋找的書籍，將音檔一次從雲端下載至手機使用。

❹ 當音檔下載完畢，讀者只需要開啟「Youtor App」就能隨時掃描書中的 QR Code，立即播放音檔（平均 1 秒內），且離線也能聽。在下載完成前，請勿跳出下載畫面，避免音檔下載不完全。（若以正常網速下載，所需時間為 3 至 5 分鐘。）

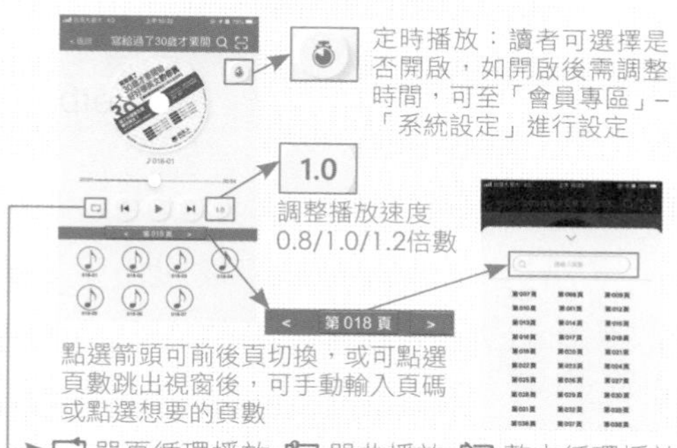

❺ 若擔心音檔下載後太佔手機空間，也可隨時刪除音檔，當書籍同時有多冊時，能分冊下載及刪除，減少 App 佔用的儲存空間。購買本公司書籍的讀者等於有一個雲端櫃可隨時使用。

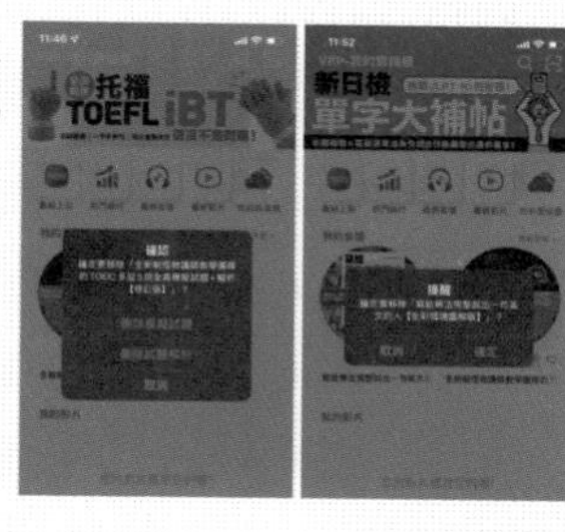

★「Youtor App」（內含VRP虛擬點讀筆）僅提供給「我識出版教育集團」旗下「我識出版社」、「懶鬼子英日語」、「不求人文化」、「我識地球村」、「字覺文化」……等出版社具有【虛擬點讀筆】功能的書籍搭配使用。

★「Youtor App」（內含VRP虛擬點讀筆）僅支援Android 6.0以上、iOS 9以上版本。

★ 雖然我們努力做到完美，但也有可能因為手機的系統版本和「Youtor App」（內含VRP虛擬點讀筆）不相容導致無法使用，若有此情形，請與本公司聯繫，會有專人提供服務。

首先，很高興再次與懶鬼子出版社合作，感謝出版社總是和我討論這些有趣且寓教於樂的英文教學書，讓我的教學過程中多了一些探討的樂趣和來自讀者的反響，而這本是我和出版社一起討論過的書籍中，第一次挑戰寫給不一樣年齡層的書籍，因此，我也感到非常興奮。

回顧我的教學路，這十多年來，的確大多時候都面對著年輕的臉孔，鮮少能以其他不一樣角度去思考的時候。這次承蒙出版社邀約，著手進行這本給 30 歲大人的英文書，是一次具有挑戰性的寫作過程。為此，我和出版社多次書信往來，討論架構與面向，花了一年才讓這個不具形的點子，蛻變成現在你們手中的書籍，與你們相見。

在進行本書的期間，我參考了許多以往寫過的書籍，翻閱了英文教學路上前輩們的心血和作品，發現其實學習總是大同小異，只要用對方法，都能夠事半功倍，不論學習什麼都是一樣的，最重要的，就是學習方法！本書結合 Youtor App（內含虛擬點讀筆），只要用手機掃描，就可以用手機聽音檔，難道不是最方便的一個學習方法嗎？另外要感謝出版社，願意配合我的想法，將音檔以兩段式的方式呈現，讓學習者能夠以不同的學習方式，去練習開口說英文。

一如以往地，我要感謝廣大的讀者們，不論是你們的回饋還是建議，我都確實地收到了，因為有你們的支持，才有《寫給過了 30 歲才要開始好好學英文的你我：邁向雙語國家的成人英文基礎課》這本書的誕生。希望這本書也能帶給大家一次美好的學習經歷，由衷期許能夠讓想學好英文的你，不論年紀，都能享受學習的樂趣。

Raymond Tsai
2022.09

Contents
目錄

Chapter 01 Cuisine and Dishes 美食佳餚

篇章導引

Step 1 引發興趣，可先上網搜尋相關資訊。
例如：美國用餐禮儀、餐館小費等。

Step 2 了解學習主題，翻開書中單元頁。瀏覽單元標題與各單元單字。

Step 3 Critical thinking 反思：
異國美食該怎麼說？
正餐與點心怎麼說？
到餐廳吃飯怎麼描述用餐座位要求？

你將學會

- ☐ 向服務生點餐
- ☐ 詢問餐點特殊要求
- ☐ 替換餐點選項
- ☐ 各種異國美食說法

檢視成效

- ☐ 聽 聽美籍老師說給你聽
- ☐ 說 用跟讀法練習口說
- ☐ 讀 閱讀英文與中文內容
- ☐ 寫 提筆練習寫學習單

Contents
目錄

Chapter 02 Daily and Public Transportation 日常與大眾運輸 047

篇章導引

Step 1 引發興趣，可先上網搜尋相關資訊。
例如：美國地鐵路線圖、美國火車票價。

Step 2 了解學習主題，翻開書中單元頁。瀏覽單元標題與各單元單字。

Step 3 Critical thinking 反思：
地鐵與火車的差異是？
開車時遇到意外狀況該怎麼說？
我該怎麼描述車子要加的油種？
捷運是地鐵的一種嗎？
充電站有分種類嗎？

你將學會

- □ 搭乘大眾運輸的說法
- □ 詢問票價或時刻等資訊
- □ 回答他人對大眾運輸的問題
- □ 為車子加油／充電的說法

檢視成效

- □ 聽 聽美籍老師說給你聽
- □ 說 用跟讀法練習口說
- □ 讀 閱讀英文與中文內容
- □ 寫 提筆練習寫學習單

Chapter 03

School Life 學校生活 079

篇章導引

Step 1 引發興趣，可先上網搜尋相關資訊。

例如：美國學年制度與臺灣的差異。

Step 2 了解學習主題，翻開書中單元頁。瀏覽單元標題與各單元單字。

Step 3 Critical thinking 反思：

每個國家的學年制有差異嗎？

美國大學中哪些課程是臺灣沒有或較少見的呢？

在美國住宿要花多少錢？

你將學會

- ☐ 課程的名稱與修課的說法
- ☐ 準備考試的方法與說法
- ☐ 學校處室的說法
- ☐ 宿舍與宿舍相關事務的單字

檢視成效

- ☐ 聽 聽美籍老師說給你聽
- ☐ 說 用跟讀法練習口說
- ☐ 讀 閱讀英文與中文內容
- ☐ 寫 提筆練習寫學習單

Contents
目錄

Chapter 04 Workplace 職場 111

篇章導引

Step 1 引發興趣，可先上網搜尋相關資訊。
例如：美國的求職網、美國平均薪資。

Step 2 了解學習主題，翻開書中單元頁。瀏覽單元標題與各單元單字。

Step 3 Critical thinking 反思：
怎麼說服面試官你的錄取理由？ 如何向人資部描述你的離職理由？

你將學會

- ☐ 面試時相關的自薦金句
- ☐ 離職的理由與委婉的說法

檢視成效

- ☐ 聽 聽美籍老師說給你聽
- ☐ 說 用跟讀法練習口說
- ☐ 讀 閱讀英文與中文內容
- ☐ 寫 提筆練習寫學習單

Chapter 05 Go Shopping 去逛街 161

篇章導引

Step 1 引發興趣，可先上網搜尋相關資訊。
例如：美國知名品牌、連鎖超市等。

Step 2 了解學習主題，翻開書中單元頁。瀏覽單元標題與各單元單字。

Step 3 Critical thinking 反思：
美國的 outlet 和臺灣的 outlet 有差異嗎？
outlet、shopping mall、department store 的差異是什麼？
maker、supermarket 的差異是什麼？

你將學會

- ☐ 商品尺寸、顏色等細節的說法
- ☐ 詢問店員欲購買的商品
- ☐ 購買與拒絕的說法
- ☐ 從首飾到服飾再到鞋子的描述

檢視成效

- ☐ 聽 聽美籍老師說給你聽
- ☐ 說 用跟讀法練習口說
- ☐ 讀 閱讀英文與中文內容
- ☐ 寫 提筆練習寫學習單

Contents
目錄

Chapter 06 Health & Medication 健康與醫療 193

篇章導引

Step 1 引發興趣，可先上網搜尋相關資訊。
例如：美國醫院看診費用、臺灣健保制度。

Step 2 了解學習主題，翻開書中單元頁。瀏覽單元標題與各單元單字。

Step 3 Critical thinking 反思：
想在美國看病，有哪些分類？ doctor 泛指全部的醫生嗎？
在異地感到不舒服時，該如何幫助自己？
常備藥品應該要有哪些？哪些是需要醫師處方籤的藥品？

你將學會

- □ 藥劑、藥丸等相關說法
- □ 聽懂用藥的指示
- □ 主動描述不舒服的症狀
- □ 理解醫療相關的基本單字

檢視成效

- □ 聽 聽美籍老師說給你聽
- □ 說 用跟讀法練習口說
- □ 讀 閱讀英文與中文內容
- □ 寫 提筆練習寫學習單

Chapter 07

Daily Situation 生活情境 219

篇章導引

Step 1 引發興趣，可先上網搜尋相關資訊。

例如：美國最大的銀行、跨國轉帳手續費。

Step 2 了解學習主題，翻開書中單元頁。瀏覽單元標題與各單元單字。

Step 3 Critical thinking 反思：

怎麼描述自己想要辦理的銀行業務？

如何詢問銀行不同帳號的差異？

如何向客服人員描述自己遇到的問題？

你將學會

- ☐ 描述提款與領款的說法
- ☐ 與銀行帳號及帳戶相關的說法
- ☐ 電影場次、票價等的相關說法
- ☐ 描述問題給客服人員聽

檢視成效

- ☐ 聽 聽美籍老師說給你聽
- ☐ 說 用跟讀法練習口說
- ☐ 讀 閱讀英文與中文內容
- ☐ 寫 提筆練習寫學習單

Chapter 08 Traveling 旅遊 245

篇章導引

Step 1 引發興趣，可先上網搜尋相關資訊。
例如：跨國機票的費用、轉機時刻。

Step 2 了解學習主題，翻開書中單元頁。瀏覽單元標題與各單元單字。

Step 3 Critical thinking 反思：
到機場報到的說法和到飯店報到的說法一樣嗎？
如何回答海關一些簡單問題？
抵達時刻該怎麼描述？

你將學會

- □ 描述機票上的資訊
- □ 說出在機上的請求
- □ 描述自己的行李與隨身物品
- □ 描述出發和抵達的用法

檢視成效

- □ 聽 聽美籍老師說給你聽
- □ 說 用跟讀法練習口說
- □ 讀 閱讀英文與中文內容
- □ 寫 提筆練習寫學習單

Chapter

01

Cuisine and Dishes
美食佳餚

UNIT 01

A Reservation for Dinner Tonight

預約今晚的晚餐

♪016-01 **Can I make a reservation for dinner tonight?**
我可以預約今天晚上的晚餐嗎？

♪016-02 Do you take reservations over a week from now?
你們接受一週後的預約嗎？

♪016-03 Can you put me on the waiting list?
你能幫我放在候補名單上嗎？

♪016-04 I need a table by the window. 我需要訂一個靠近窗戶的桌位。

♪016-05 It's under John. 以約翰的名義。

♪016-06 I'd like to make a reservation for four people.
我想要預約四人的位置。

How to Say

聽懂服務生的回應！

- I'm sorry, but we're fully booked. 真的很抱歉，但是我們都預約滿了。
- I'm sorry, but we don't accept any reservations in advance.
  不好意思，我們不接受預約喔。

單字地圖 Vocabulary

♪017-01 食物與類型 Foods and Types

♪017-02 Exotic Dishes 異國料理

- Cantonese food 港式飲茶
- Chinese food 中式料理
- Japanese food 日式料理
- fast food 速食
- Italian food 義式料理
- Thai food 泰式料理

♪017-03 Breakfast 早餐

- bread 麵包
- toast 吐司
- cereal 穀片
- baguette 法式長棍
- pancake 美式鬆餅
- sandwich 三明治
- bagel 貝果

♪017-04 Drinks 飲料

- milk 牛奶
- juice 果汁
- tea 茶
- coffee 咖啡

補 breakfast tea 早餐茶
espresso 義式濃縮咖啡

♪017-05 Eggs 蛋料理

- fried egg 炒蛋
- hard-boiled egg 水煮蛋
- scrambled egg 西式炒蛋
- omelet 歐姆蛋
- poached egg 水波蛋
- sunny-side up egg 太陽蛋

♪017-06 Salad 沙拉

- Cesar's salad 凱薩沙拉
- chicken salad 雞肉沙拉
- fruit salad 水果沙拉
- Greek salad 希臘沙拉
- salad dressing 沙拉醬

補 Italian dressing 義大利醬
Thousand Island dressing 千島醬
Ranch dressing 牧園沙拉醬
house dressing 招牌沙拉醬

♪017-07 American breakfast 美式早餐

- sausage 臘腸
- bacon 培根
- ham 火腿
- tater tots 薯塊
- hash browns 薯餅
- cheese 起司
- jam 果醬

補 peanut butter 花生醬
butter 奶油
honey 蜂蜜
cream cheese 奶油乳酪
maple syrup 楓糖漿

More to Know

輕輕鬆鬆預約餐廳

想到要用英文預約餐廳和訂位就頭痛嗎？其實不用擔心，只要記得前面這幾句話和單字，就能輕鬆預約！現今有許多餐廳也接受 E-mail 預約，甚至能在社群網站中預約，有些餐廳還有官方免費通訊軟體的 App 帳號。

情節故事 Story

Who You are making a reservation at a restaurant.
♪018-01 你正在預約一間餐廳。

Where You are on the way to the restaurant with your family.
♪018-02 你和家人正在前往餐廳的路上。

When It's five in the afternoon.
♪018-03 現在是下午五點。

What You will hear the server ask you:
♪018-04 "May I take your name and phone number, please?"
你將會聽到服務生問你：
「請問您的貴姓大名，以及連絡電話？」。

How to Speak

藉由四個問題（what——角色、where——地點、when——時間、what——做何事）來觸發想像，並可應用自己的經歷來構思出一段完整的短篇會話或故事。後面的篇章，會著重介紹相關的四個媒介問題，以啟發更多想像與相關的對話。

重點對話 Dialogue

打電話預約餐廳

♪019-08 對話練習！

♪019-01 Hello. I'd like to reserve a **private room** for six tonight, under the name of Steven.
你好，我今天晚上想預定一個容納六個人的包廂。用史蒂芬的名字預定。

♪019-02 When will you come?
你們什麼時候來？

♪019-03 At about 6:30.
大約 6 點半。

預約滿了，請放到候補名單

♪019-04 I need to reserve a table for four this evening.
我想預約今晚，四人桌。

♪019-05 Sorry, sir. All the tables have been reserved.
很抱歉，先生。餐桌預訂都已經滿了。

♪019-06 It's a pity. Could you put me on the waiting list?
太遺憾了。你能幫我放在候補名單上嗎？

♪019-07 No problem! I will call you if anyone cancels their reservation.
當然可以！如果有人取消訂位，我會打電話通知您。

More to Know

- 想要有隱蔽性，預約包廂的說法：
  make a reservation for a private room for six people 訂一間六人的包廂
- 想要單純訂位：
  make a reservation for six people 訂六人的位置

Sentences & Grammar

♪020-01 **1. May** I have your name and phone number, please?

請問貴姓大名，以及連絡電話。

May 開頭的問句是非常有禮貌的用法。通常要向別人請求或請問某事時，會用 May 開頭的問句。

- May I go to the restroom? 我可以去上廁所嗎？

♪020-02 **2. Whose** name will the reservation be made under?

這是以誰的名義預訂的？

Whose（誰的）是 Who（誰）的所有格。

主詞：句子中進行動詞的角色。
「I ate it. 我吃了它。」I（我）是主詞。

我	你／你們	他／她／它／牠	我們	他們
I	you	he / she / it	we	they

受詞：句中動作的接受者。
「I ate it. 我吃了它。」it（它）是受詞。

我	你／你們	他／她／它／牠	我們	他們
I	you	he / she / it	we	they

所有格：表示「所有權」。
「It is my book. 這是我的書。」my（我的）是所有格。

我的	你的／你們的	他／她／它／牠的	我們的	他們的
my	your	his / her / its	our	their

所有格代名詞：用來代替前文提過的所有格＋名詞。
「It is my book. That's yours. 這是我的書。那本才是你的書。」
yours（你的書）是所有格代名詞。

我的 ＋名詞	你／你們的 ＋名詞	他／她／它／牠的 ＋名詞	我們的 ＋名詞	他們的 ＋名詞
mine	yours	his / hers / its	ours	theirs

The phone is ringing

♪021-01 電話響不停！餐廳員工接起預約電話，並將資訊抄在便利貼上；掃 QR Code 聽聽看，這些便利貼上少的資訊是什麼呢？

Reservation!

- ✓ Andy Cheng
- ✓ 3 adults with ___ kid(s)
- ✓ Aug 24 18:00

Reservation!

- ✓ Ms. Watson
- ✓ A table for 6 people
- ✓ Time: ___________

Reservation!

- ✓ Mary Hsu
- ✓ ___ adults, ___ kid(s)
- ✓ Aug 30, 17:30
- ✓ Special Request:

____

Reservation!

- ✓ ___________

____

____

____

解答

1. Hi. This is Andy Cheng. I would like to reserve a table for four people. 3 adults with a kid. Time would be August 24th. 18:00.

2. Hi. This is Watson speaking. I want to make a reservation for six people. Time would be 19:00, date would be August 31st.

3. Good day, this is Mary. Mary Hsu. I would like to reserve a table for three people. 3 adults with no kids. Time would be August 24th. 18:00. Please call me back. Thanks.

4. Hi. This is Teddy. I would like to reserve a table for 16 people on 9/21. 12 adults with 4 kids. Can we sit indoors? Please call me back, thank you in advance.

UNIT 02

Order in a Restaurant

在餐廳點餐

♪022-01 **May I have the menu?** 我可以看一下菜單嗎？

♪022-02 Do you have a menu in English? 你們有英文菜單嗎？

♪022-03 Could you please show me the wine list? 可以看看酒單嗎？

♪022-04 What do you recommend? 你有推薦的餐點嗎？

♪022-05 I'd like to order a main course. 我要點一個主餐。

♪022-06 What kind of salad would you like? 您想要哪種沙拉呢？

♪022-07 I think I'll have beef instead of fish.
我想我還是不要吃魚，改吃牛肉好了。

♪022-08 Can I have the same dish as the lady?
我可以點與那位女士相同的餐嗎？

How to Say

特殊需求的說法：

- Do you have a vegetarian meal? 餐廳是否有供應素食餐？
  - religious meal 宗教餐點
  - dietary meal 病理餐點
  - non-beef meal 無牛肉餐點

Vocabulary

♪023-01 Foods and Types 食物與類型

♪023-02 Pasta 義大利麵

- farfalle 蝴蝶麵
- spaghetti 細長義大利麵
- penne 筆尖麵
- lasagna 千層麵
- capellini 天使細麵
- avioli 義大利麵餃
- rotini 螺旋麵
- conchiglie 貝殼麵

♪023-03 Cheese I 起司（一）

- Roquefort 羅克福起司
- Camembert 卡門貝爾乳酪
- Goat cheese 羊奶酪
- Feta cheese 菲達起司
- Mozzarella 莫札瑞拉

♪023-04 Cheese II 起司（二）

- Emmental cheese 艾曼達起司
- Cheddar 巧達起司
- Monterey jack 傑克起司
- Cottage cheese 茅屋起司
- Parmesan 帕馬森起司

♪023-05 Appetizers 開胃菜

- onion rings 洋蔥圈
- deviled egg 惡魔蛋
- smoked salmon 煙燻鮭魚
- chicken wings 烤／炸雞翅
- mozzarella sticks 起司條
- nachos 烤乾酪辣味玉米片

補 guacamole 酪梨醬
foie gras 鵝肝醬

♪023-06 Soups 湯品

- fisherman's soup 漁夫湯
- onion soup 洋蔥湯
- chicken soup 雞湯
- Borscht 羅宋湯
- tomato soup 番茄湯
- cream of mushroom 蘑菇濃湯
- cream of lobster 龍蝦濃湯
- cream of broccoli 花椰菜濃湯

♪023-07 Desserts 甜點

- doughnut 甜甜圈
- ice cream 冰淇淋
- macaroon 馬卡龍
- muffin 馬芬
- cupcake 杯子蛋糕
- sundae 聖代
- scone 司康
- Crème brûlée 烤布蕾
- tiramisu 提拉米蘇

More to Know

義大利麵竟然有這麼多種？

你知道義大利麵不只有常見的長麵條狀嗎？其實義大利麵有各種形狀，不同形狀也有適合的烹調方法和口味喔。看上方的義大利麵單字，去網路上搜尋看看這些義大利麵分別長什麼樣子吧！

情節故事 Story

Who You are a customer in a restaurant.
♪024-01 你是餐廳裡的一名顧客。

Who You are in an American restaurant with your best friend.
♪024-02 你和最好的朋友在一間美式餐廳裡。

When It's seven in the evening. Today is Monday.
♪024-03 現在是晚上七點。今天是星期一。

What You are ordering. You are wondering what to order.
♪024-04 你正在點餐。你正在煩惱要點什麼。

How to Speak

指定更換特定菜色，這樣說：

- I would like to have **fisherman's soup** for my set meal.
  我的套餐湯品想要漁夫湯。
  - cream of broccoli 青花菜濃湯
  - cream of tomato 番茄濃湯
  - vegetable beef soup 蔬菜牛肉湯

Dialogue

和服務生點餐

♪025-09 對話練習！

♪025-01 Would you like to order, sir?
要點餐了嗎，先生？

♪025-02 **I would like to have a steak, please.**
我想要點一份牛排。

♪025-03 Anything else you want to order?
請問還需要其它的嗎？

♪025-04 A glass of red wine.
一杯紅酒。

想要的餐點賣完了，換別種試試看？

♪025-05 Are you ready to order, madam?
女士，需要點餐了嗎？

♪025-06 I'd like a dhal curry and tomato soup.
我要一份扁豆咖哩和一份番茄湯。

♪025-07 I am sorry that tomato soup isn't served on Monday. I recommend mushroom soup. It's delicious, too.
很抱歉，星期一不提供番茄湯。我建議您點蘑菇湯，也很美味。

♪025-08 Alright.
好吧。

More to Know

想吃的主餐要怎麼表達呢？

- I'd like to have some **seafood**. 我想吃海鮮。
  - beef 牛肉 ▪ pork 豬肉 ▪ lamb 羊肉
  - chicken 雞肉 ▪ duck 鴨肉 ▪ surf 'n' turf 海陸餐

Sentences & Grammar

♪026-01 **1. What do you recommend?**

你有推薦的餐點嗎？

「What」是疑問詞，想要提問的時候，我們會用到的疑問詞有這些：

What	Who	When	Where	Which	How
什麼	誰	何時	哪裡	哪個	怎麼

♪026-01 **2. I'd like to order a main course.**

我要點一個主餐。

「I'd」是「I would」的縮寫，「would like to V」是個非常好用的句型，常用來請求別人協助，也是個比較有禮貌的說法喔！

- **I would like to** have this, please wrap it up for me.
  我想要買這個，請幫我包裝。
- **I would like to** share a story of my granny.
  我想要分享我奶奶的故事。

♪026-02 **3. What kind of salad would you like?**

您想要哪種沙拉呢？

kind 種類。

近義字：genre （尤指藝術的）類型、風格；type 種類。

♪026-03 **4. I think I'll have beef instead of fish.**

我想我還是不要吃魚，改吃牛肉好了。

instead of 的用法：

choose A **instead of** B 選擇 A 而不要 B

take A **instead of** B 買 A 而不是買 B

What's on the Menu?

打開菜單，映入眼簾的是——

-Menu-	－菜單－
Appetizer	開胃菜
Main Course	主食
Dessert	甜點
Beverage	飲料

來到點餐的環節，你想來份什麼樣的主菜呢？

Seafood	海鮮	Meat	肉類
salmon	鮭魚	beef	牛肉
shrimp	蝦子	steak	牛排
lobster	龍蝦	pork	豬肉
crab	螃蟹	pork chop	豬排
squid	烏賊	lamb	羊肉
octopus	章魚	chicken	雞肉

蔬菜和水果呢？

Vegetables	蔬菜	Fruits	水果
bean	豆子	strawberry	草莓
beetroot	甜菜根	peach	桃子
cabbage	甘藍菜	watermelon	西瓜
chickpeas	鷹嘴豆	orange	柳橙
carrot	紅蘿蔔	tangerine	橘子

來試試看用英文點餐吧：

I would like to have salad as an appetizer, steak for a main course, and a glass of orange juice. Thank you.

我想點一份沙拉當開胃菜，主餐要牛排，再給我一杯柳橙汁。謝謝！

UNIT 03

Go to a Steak House

到牛排館用餐

♪028-01 **How do you like your steak cooked?**
請問您的牛排要幾分熟？

♪028-02 How'd you like your beefsteak? Medium-rare, medium, or well-done?
你的牛排要幾分熟呢，三分熟、五分熟，還是全熟？

♪028-03 I prefer my steak done to a turn. 我喜歡牛排煎得恰到好處。

♪028-04 The steak is too tough to eat. 牛排太硬了，嚼不動。

♪028-05 The steak is so tender and juicy. 牛排鮮嫩多汁。

♪028-06 Do you have any special requests? 您有什麼特殊要求嗎？

How to Say

吩咐餐點的特殊指示可以這樣說：

- I am allergic to **ketchup**. 我對**番茄醬**過敏。
- I especially asked for **no chili**. 我特別吩咐過**不要放辣椒**。
- Don't put **garlic** into my meal. 我的餐點裡不要放**蒜頭**。

Vocabulary

In the Steak House 在牛排館裡

♪ 029-01

Tableware 餐具

♪ 029-02

- knife 刀子
- fork 叉子
- spoon 湯匙
- plate 盤子
- dinner plate 晚餐盤
- bowl 碗
- salad bowl 沙拉碗
- glass 玻璃杯
- cup 茶杯
- napkin 餐巾

Maturity Level 熟度

♪ 029-03

- blue rare 一分熟
- medium 五分熟
- rare 兩分熟
- medium well 七分熟
- medium rare 三分熟
- well done 全熟

Choice 選擇

♪ 029-04

- beef fillet mignon 牛菲力
- New York strip 紐約客牛排
- ribeye steak 肋眼牛排
- burger 漢堡肉
- sirloin 沙朗
- pork chop 豬排
- lamb chop 羊排
- leg of lamb 羊腿

Spices & Herbs 辛香料和香草

♪ 029-05

- salt 鹽巴
- pepper 胡椒
- basil 蘿勒
- rosemary 迷迭香
- oregano 奧勒岡
- sea salt 海鹽
- olive oil 橄欖油
- grape seed oil 葡萄籽油

Alcohol 酒

♪ 029-06

- red wine 紅酒
- white wine 白酒
- rosé 粉紅酒
- champagne 香檳
- cider 蘋果酒
- cocktail 雞尾酒
- sparkling wine 氣泡酒

Drinks 飲料

♪ 029-07

- ginger ale 薑汁汽水
- iced tea 冰茶
- soft drinks 汽水
- lemonade 檸檬汁
- juice 果汁
- sparkling water 氣泡水
- mineral water 礦泉水
- still water 無氣泡水
- fruit smoothie 水果冰沙
- mocktail 無酒精雞尾酒

More to Know

牛排館中較少有海鮮食物的選項，這邊補充介紹常見的海鮮單字：

- shrimp 蝦子
- lobster 龍蝦
- prawn 明蝦
- king prawn 大明蝦
- crab 螃蟹
- mussel 淡菜
- scallop 扇貝
- clam 蛤蜊

情節故事 Story

Who ♪030-01
You are going to have dinner with your partner.
你正要和伴侶一起吃晚餐。

Where ♪030-02
You are in a steak house. This is your first time to come to this steak house.
你正在牛排館。這是你第一次來這間牛排館。

When ♪030-03
It's eight. It's a little bit late for you to have dinner because you are very hungry.
現在八點了。現在這時間吃晚餐對飢腸轆轆的你來說有點晚。

What ♪030-04
You are ready to order. You are going to ask the server to come to you.
你準備好要點餐了。你準備要請服務生過來。

How to Speak

想要請服務生來點餐，你可以說：

- Hi, we are ready to order. 嗨，我們準備好點餐了。

Dialogue

在牛排餐廳點餐

♪031-09 對話練習！

♪031-01 Are you ready to order?
你們準備好要點餐了嗎？

♪031-02 Yes, please. I would like to have one New York strip and my wife would like to have a surf-and-turf.
是的。我想要一份紐約客牛排，我太太則想要一份海陸餐。

♪031-03 How would you like your steak?
您的牛排想要幾分熟呢？

♪031-04 Medium-rare, please.
三分熟，謝謝。

♪031-05 OK, sir. Do you want some wine? Many of the guests order our house wine.
好的，先生。要來些酒嗎？很多客人都會點我們這裡的特色酒。

♪031-06 What would you recommend?
你推薦什麼呢？

♪031-07 We have special prime wine from France that is now 10% off for the holiday.
我們有一款法國的頂級葡萄酒，現在因為節日的關係正在打 9 折。

♪031-08 Sounds great. I'll have two!
聽起來不錯，那來兩杯吧！

More to Know

牛排的部位要怎麼說呢？一起來看看，今天你想點哪種牛排？

- I would like to have a ＿＿＿＿＿. 我要點一份＿＿＿＿＿。
  - Ribeye 肋眼 ▪ New York Strip 紐約客 ▪ Sirloin 沙朗
  - Tenderloin (Fillet) 菲力 ▪ Short Rib 牛小排 ▪ T-bone 丁骨

Sentences & Grammar

♪032-01 **1.** What would you like to have for your soup? I strongly **recommend** our cream of lobster.
您要點什麼湯呢？我強烈推薦我們的龍蝦濃湯。

recommend 推薦、介紹、建議。
用法：

- recommend ＋名詞
- recommend ＋人＋ to ＋原形動詞
- recommend ＋ that 子句（that 可省略）：
  The attorney **recommends** the client **to** file a lawsuit.
  =The attorney **recommends (that)** the client files a lawsuit.
  律師建議客戶提告。

♪032-02 **2.** I am **on a diet**, so I only ordered a salad for supper.
我在減肥，所以只點了份沙拉當晚餐。

「on a diet」通常指以減重為目的的節食，通常前接 be 動詞。
diet 原意為某種特定飲食方式：

- The coach put him on a **high-calorie diet** for the upcoming ultra-marathon in Antarctica.
  教練讓他吃高熱量飲食，因應即將到來的南極洲超級馬拉松。
- No one likes to eat out with Karen because of her **restrictive vegan diet**.
  由於凱倫限制多多的純素飲食方式，沒人喜歡和她出去吃飯。

♪032-03 **3.** I don't eat foods with sugar **because of** diabetes.
我有糖尿病，不能吃有糖的食物。

「because 因為」的用法：

because of ＋名詞或動名詞 如例句	**because** 後接完整句子 例句改寫如下

- I don't eat foods with sugar because I have diabetes.

點餐 Let's order !

看完菜單，是時候向服務生點餐囉！看看以下的對話，請嘗試幫助這位女士點完她的餐點吧！

The server comes to you... 服務生朝你走來……

What would you like to order, lady? 女士，今天要點什麼？

I would like a ________________________. 我想點一份肋眼牛排。

肋眼牛排是以下哪個呢？

☐ beef noodles ☐ ribeye steak ☐ roast beef

How do you like your steak? 您的牛排要幾分熟呢？

Umm… I would like ________________. 我想要三分熟。

三分熟是哪個呢？

☐ blue ☐ rare ☐ medium-rare

Would you like something to drink? 您要喝點什麼嗎？

A glass of wine would be nice. 一杯紅酒就好。

解答

- beef noodles 牛肉麵
- ribeye steak 肋眼牛排
- roast beef 爐烤牛肉
- blue 一分熟
- rare 兩分熟
- medium-rare 三分熟

UNIT 04

Coffee Shop

咖啡廳

♪ 034-01 **Which kind of coffee would you prefer?**
你比較偏愛哪種咖啡？

♪ 034-02 I prefer a latte since it contains more milk than a cappuccino.
我喜歡拿鐵，因為它的牛奶含量比卡布奇諾多。

♪ 034-03 I like this kind of coffee because it is a blend of Java and mocha. 我喜歡這種咖啡，因為它是爪哇和摩卡混合而成的。

♪ 034-04 Americano, but I don't like Americano with ice.
美式咖啡，但我不喜歡加了冰塊的美式咖啡。

♪ 034-05 I like an Americano with no cream.
我喜歡美式咖啡，不要奶精。

How to Say

聽懂店員額外的問句：

- Do you want some sugar in your coffee? 您的咖啡需要加糖嗎？
- Would you like your coffee weak or strong?
  您想要淡咖啡還是濃咖啡呢？

Vocabulary

- espresso 義式濃縮
- café macchiato 咖啡瑪奇朵
- cappuccino 卡布奇諾
- dry cappuccino 乾卡布奇諾
- café americano 美式咖啡
- mocha 摩卡
- con panna 康寶藍
- café latte 拿鐵
- café au lait 咖啡歐蕾

- green 生豆
- light roast 淺焙
- medium roast 中焙
- dark roast 深焙

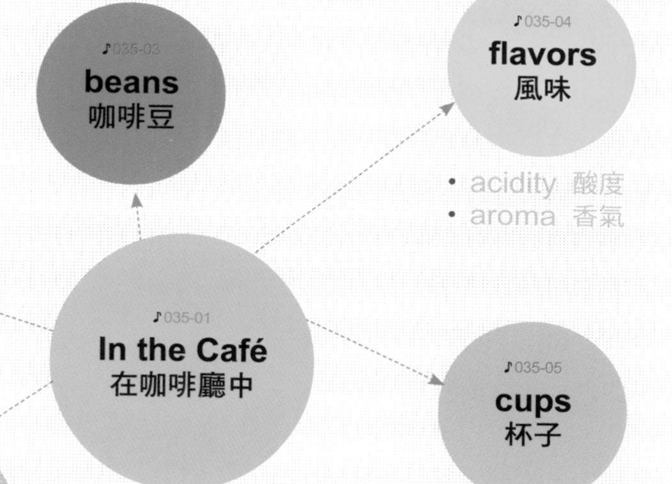

♪035-02
choices
選擇

- acidity 酸度
- aroma 香氣

♪035-07
require
要求

♪035-06
tastes
口感

- short 小杯
- tall 中杯
- grande 大杯

補 small 小杯
medium 中杯
large 大杯

- extra shot 加一份濃縮咖啡
- double shot 兩份濃縮咖啡
- triple shot 三份濃縮咖啡
- skim milk 脫脂牛奶
- low-fat milk 低脂牛奶
- soy milk 豆奶
- extra foam 多奶泡
- decaf 低咖啡因咖啡

- hot 熱的
- iced 冰的
- frappe 希臘法拉沛咖啡（冰沙）

補 smoothie 冰沙

More to Know

聽懂店員的問句！來到咖啡廳，選好要喝的飲料，店員會問你要內用還是外帶呢？

- For here or to go? 內用還是外帶？
- For here. 內用。
- To go. 外帶。

情節故事 Story

Who ♪ 036-01

You are a thirsty tourist, and you are ready to have a cup of drink in the café.
你是一名口渴的旅客，準備好要在咖啡廳裡點一杯飲料。

Where ♪ 036-02

You are in a famous café. This café has a long history and is famous for its coffee.
你在一間有名的咖啡廳裡。這間咖啡廳有著悠久的歷史，且這裡的咖啡小有名氣。

When ♪ 036-03

It's a sunny Thursday afternoon.
這是個晴朗的星期四下午。

What ♪ 036-04

You are looking at the menu, wondering what to order.
你正在看菜單，猶豫要點什麼。

How to Speak

想在咖啡廳點飲料，運用前面學過的「那一句」就可以點餐！

- I would like to have a cup of Americano. 我想要一杯美式咖啡。

重點對話 Dialogue

在咖啡廳裡享受獨處時光

♪037-07 對話練習！

♪037-01 What would you like for a drink?
您想喝點什麼？

♪037-02 I would like to have a cup of café macchiato.
我想點一杯咖啡瑪奇朵。

♪037-03 Sorry, we don't have any café macchiato here. Would you like some cappuccino or latte?
不好意思，我們這裡沒有咖啡瑪奇朵。卡布奇諾或是拿鐵可以嗎？

♪037-04 Well, then I'd like to have a cup of latte. Iced latte.
好吧，那我想要一杯拿鐵。冰拿鐵。

♪037-05 No problem. Miss, would you like some soda water?
沒問題。女士，您需要氣泡水嗎？

♪037-06 No, I'd like a glass of mineral water. And I would like to get an iced tea with lemon to go later.
不了，我要一杯礦泉水。另外，我待會想要外帶一杯檸檬冰茶。

More to Know

當店員向你詢問飲品的口感或回饋時，你可以這樣回答：

正面評價：

- It tastes good. I always enjoy the coffee of yours.
  很好喝。我一直都很喜歡你們的咖啡。

給予回饋：

- I don't like this coffee, it's too acidic.
  我不喜歡這杯咖啡，它太酸了。
- This cup of coffee tastes too bitter for me.
  這杯咖啡對我來說太苦了。

Sentences & Grammar

♪038-01 **1.** We only **have** espresso and skinny latte.
我們只有義式濃縮咖啡和脫脂拿鐵咖啡。

have 這個單字的意思很多，在此指針對販售飲品的「擁有」。也可用「sell 賣、offer 供應、provide 提供」來代替，句意相同。
have 的其他意思與用法：

擁有	I **have** a teddy bear. 我有一隻泰迪熊。
吃喝	I **had** dinner at seven tonight. 我今晚七點吃了晚餐。
做某事	I **had** done it. 我做完了。 I **had** a swim. 我去游泳了。

♪038-02 **2.** I would like to have **a cup of** latte with a double shot.
我要一杯拿鐵，兩份濃縮。

不論是可數或不可數物品，都可用可數單位表達。若此單位只有一份時，則以單數表示，如例句中的「**a cup of latte** 一杯咖啡」。

three **dozens** of eggs 三打蛋	fifteen **ounces** of melted butter 十五盎司的溶化奶油
six **glasses** of champagne 六杯香檳	ten **rows** of cheerleaders 十排啦啦隊員

♪038-03 **3.** There is a slightly **different** aroma between these 2 cups of coffee.
這兩杯咖啡有一個微小不同的香氣。

difference 名詞：

- People can clearly tell **the difference between** the two master theses.
  人們能明顯看出兩篇碩士論文的差異。

different 形容詞：

- Your facial features **are** no **different from** that woman's. Are you related to each other?
  你的臉部特徵和那女人的沒有不同。你們有血緣關係嗎？

The Details of Coffee

咖啡知識＋：成為了解咖啡的小知識家！

1 How do you get “coffee”? 咖啡從何而來？

- 咖啡是從咖啡豆（coffee beans）而來，咖啡豆長在咖啡樹上。
- 這些國家是世上最大的咖啡產地。看看這些國旗，你能答對幾個呢？

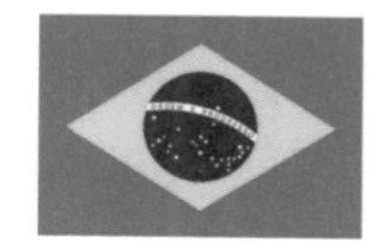

Brazil

Colombia

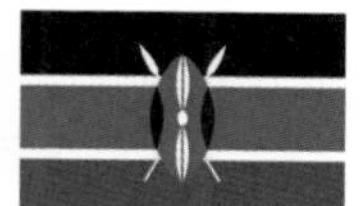

Kenya

Hawaii

Ethiopia

2 Types of Coffee 咖啡種類

- 沖泡咖啡，你需要：

  whole coffee beans 咖啡豆／ ground coffee beans 研磨咖啡粉

- 選擇咖啡豆，認識品種：

  Arabica 阿拉比卡／ Robusta 羅布斯塔

- 烘焙過的咖啡豆有以下幾種程度：

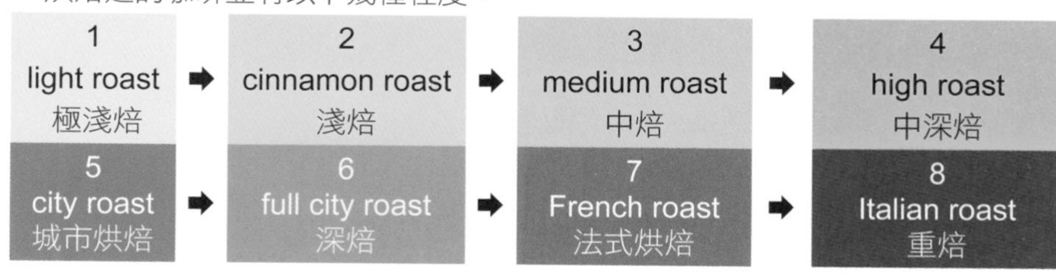

- 那麼，你知道未經烘焙的咖啡豆叫什麼嗎？＿＿＿＿＿＿＿＿。

3 How to describe? 為你介紹描述咖啡的用語！

acidity 酸度	aroma 香味	body 純度	aftertaste 餘味
balance 平衡度	mellow 香醇	mild 溫和	soft 柔順

解答

1. 巴西、哥倫比亞、肯亞、夏威夷、衣索比亞
2. Green Beans 生豆

UNIT 05

Traditional English Afternoon Tea

傳統英式下午茶

♪040-01 What kind of tea do you want, black tea, white tea, green tea, or oolong tea?

你想喝什麼茶，紅茶、白茶、綠茶，還是烏龍茶呢？

♪040-02 I would like to have a cup of Darjeeling black tea, thank you.

我想要一杯大吉嶺紅茶，謝謝。

♪040-03 Oolong tea with ice. No sugar, thanks.

冰烏龍茶，不要加糖，謝謝。

♪040-04 I would like scones with butter. 我想要司康配奶油。

♪040-05 I want some chocolate cookies. 我想要一些巧克力餅乾。

How to Say

想知道點的飲品或餐點是否可以做調整：

- 加料：a cup of________ with ________ 一杯加________ 的________
- 冷熱：a cup of hot / iced________ 一杯熱的／冰的________
- 搭配：a ________ with jam / butter 一份________ 配果醬／奶油

Vocabulary

♪041-01 In the Dessert Shop 在甜點店裡

♪041-02 snacks 點心

- waffle 鬆餅
- sandwich 三明治
- cinnamon bun 肉桂捲
- apple pie 蘋果派
- glazed doughnut 糖霜甜甜圈
- quiche 鹹派

♪041-03 cookies 餅乾

- chocolate chip cookie 巧克力豆餅乾
- chocolate s'mores 巧克力棉花糖夾心餅
- butter cookie 奶油餅乾
- macaroon 馬卡龍

♪041-04 cakes 蛋糕

- tiramisu 提拉米蘇
- red velvet cake 紅絲絨蛋糕
- pumpkin pie 南瓜派
- angel cake 天使蛋糕
- cupcake 杯子蛋糕
- Mille Crepes 千層蛋糕

♪041-05 sweets 甜點

brownie 布朗尼
mont blanc 蒙布朗
éclair 閃電泡芙
scone 司康
fruit tart 水果塔
custard tart 蛋撻

♪041-06 tea 茶

green tea 綠茶
black tea 紅茶
matcha 抹茶
milk tea 奶茶
white tea 白茶
Oolong tea 烏龍茶
herbal tea 花草茶

補 阿薩姆紅茶：Assam black tea
錫蘭紅茶：Ceylon black tea
大吉嶺茶：Darjeeling
（皇家）伯爵茶：Earl Grey
英式早餐茶：English breakfast tea

♪041-07 herbal tea 花草茶

- chamomile tea 甘菊茶
- chrysanthemum tea 菊花茶
- lavender tea 薰衣草茶
- jasmine tea 茉莉花茶
- peppermint tea 薄荷茶

More to Know

What is "Low Tea"？

傳統上流社會的英式下午茶就叫做「low tea」，low tea 並不「low」，而是上流社會在下午約 4 點的時候享用的午茶，因為是坐在起居室的矮桌上享用，所才會有「low tea」之稱。

Story

Who ♪042-01
You are a businessman who is tired and needs a rest in the café with desserts.
你是一個疲倦的企業家，坐在一間有甜點的咖啡廳中休息。

Where ♪042-02
You are in a café with desserts. The cookies and desserts in the café smell good.
你正在一間有甜點的咖啡廳中。咖啡廳中瀰漫著餅乾與甜點的香味。

When ♪042-03
It's 2 p.m. The cookies are just baked.
現在是下午兩點。餅乾剛烤好的時間。

What ♪042-04
You are going to have something sweet to get some ease.
你要點一些甜甜的東西，療癒一下。

How to Speak

認識更多甜點的說法：
- dessert 甜點
- bread 麵包
- pie 派
- Gelato 義式冰淇淋

重點對話 Dialogue

準備享受英式下午茶

♪043-09 對話練習！

♪043-01 Good afternoon. What can I do for you?
午安，請問您需要什麼嗎？

♪043-02 Yes, I would like to have a traditional English afternoon tea. Thank you.
對，我想要點一份傳統英式下午茶。謝謝。

♪043-03 No problem. Darjeeling black tea or Ceylon black tea?
沒問題。要大吉嶺紅茶還是錫蘭紅茶？

♪043-04 A cup of Ceylon black tea, please.
請給我一杯大吉嶺紅茶。

下午茶點餐

♪043-05 Sir, would you like some matcha?
先生，要來杯抹茶嗎？

♪043-06 No, I would like something else today.
不，我今天想喝別的。

♪043-07 Would you like some green tea today?
那今天來點綠茶怎麼樣？

♪043-08 A cup of green tea, please.
那麼請給我一杯綠茶吧。

More to Know

與甜點相關的用語：

- the icing on the cake 錦上添花的事情
  She won the scholarship and took the first place in the competition, just like **the icing on the cake**.
  她拿到獎學金，又拿到競賽冠軍，真是錦上添花。

Sentences & Grammar

♪044-01 **1.** She **is good at** baking. She brings cakes to me every month.

她很會烘焙。她每個月都帶蛋糕給我。

be good at 擅長某事物或技能。

表達正反面的不同用法：

be ______ at	
正面	反面
good 擅長的 excellent 優秀的 skilled 技術高超的	bad 不擅長的 awful 爛的 terrible 糟糕的

- The child prodigy **is excellent at** quantum physics, but **bad at** interacting with others.
  那天才兒童在量子物理學上非常優秀，卻很不會和別人互動。

♪044-02 **2.** Johnny is a pâtissier. He makes **good** macarons and éclairs.

強尼是一位甜點師。他做的馬卡龍和閃電泡芙很好吃。

其他表達美味的形容詞還有「delicious、yummy、terrific、mouth-watering、tasty」等。

♪044-03 **3.** Drinking tea makes me uncomfortable. **Sorry for** your tea.

我喝茶會不舒服。抱歉，沒辦法喝你的茶。

用來表達對他人感到抱歉或遺憾的說法：

be sorry about	I'm sorry about your accident.
be sorry for	I'm sorry for your accident.
be sorry + that 子句	I'm sorry that you got into an accident.
be sorry to +原形動詞	I'm sorry to see you hurt in the accident.

以上四句都是「對於你的意外，我很遺憾。」的意思。

The Secrets of Tea

你知道嗎？茶文化源自亞洲的中國，最早可以追溯回西元前三世紀。一起認識更多「茶文化」！

Follow these steps to drink TEA.
跟隨以下步驟來品茶。

Steep 沏茶		Sip 啜飲		Savor 品味
Observe 觀察	▸▸	Smell 嗅聞	▸▸	Taste 品嚐

More Details…
看看更多關於「茶」的小細節

Explanation 解釋	• Observe 觀察茶湯的顏色與沈澱物。 • Smell 嗅聞茶，感受鼻間縈繞的蒸氣與香味。 • Taste 感受茶在口中蔓延的香氣。
Trades 貿易	• 茶的原產地：China 中國。 • 世界上最大的茶葉進口國：U.K. 英國、Russia 俄羅斯、Pakistan 巴基斯坦、U.S. 美國、Egypt 埃及。 • 茶葉生產國：China 中國、India 印度、Kenya 肯亞、Sri Lanka 斯里蘭卡。 • 小知識：紅茶佔茶葉貿易的 75%。

Review 1

A 填空練習

- Can I make a reservation for ___________ tonight?
  我可以預約今天晚上的晚餐嗎？
  答案請見 P.016
- Do you have any special ___________?
  您有什麼特殊要求嗎？
  答案請見 P.028

B 引導造句

- reserve 預約
  I need to ____.
  我想預約今晚，四人桌。
  答案請見 P.019
- what 什麼
  ____.
  您想要哪種沙拉呢？
  答案請見 P.022
- prefer 偏好
  ____.
  答案請見 P.028

C 引導寫作

標題	My Meals Today 我的今日三餐
介紹早餐	
介紹午餐	
介紹晚餐	
喜歡的東西	

參考短文：我今天早上吃了火腿三明治當早餐。我喝了牛奶。今天中午吃了雞肉沙拉當午餐，搭配沙拉醬。我還喝了一杯果汁。晚上，我和家人吃了泰式料理。泰式料理是我最喜歡的異國料理。

Chapter

02

Daily and Public Transportation
日常與大眾運輸

- UNIT 01 Metro and MRT 地鐵與捷運
- UNIT 02 Train and Express 火車及特快車
- UNIT 03 Uber or Taxi 代步計程車
- UNIT 04 Driving Situations 行車狀況
- UNIT 05 Gas Station and Charging Station 加油站和充電站

UNIT 01

Metro and MRT

地鐵與捷運

♪048-01 **Where can I get a subway ticket?** 我要在哪買地鐵票？

♪048-02 Where is the ticket vending machine?
自動售票機在哪裡？

♪048-03 How much is the fare to New York station?
到紐約站要多少錢？

♪048-04 Don't we need a transfer? 我們不需要換乘嗎？

♪048-05 Where can I recharge my transportation card?
我可以在哪邊加值交通卡？

How to Say

在異國，地鐵系統有著不同的名稱，看看以下的說法，你曾看過幾種呢？

- **metro**：（美式）源於法文，有地鐵的意思，也可泛稱公車等交通系統。
- **subway**：（美式）地下通道、地鐵的意思。
- **underground**：（英式）地鐵，完整說法是 underground railway。
- **tube**：（英式）口語的地鐵。

單字地圖 Vocabulary

Metro System 地鐵系統 ♪049-01

tickets 票 ♪049-02

- transportation card 交通票卡
- recharge 加值
- top up 儲值
- balance 餘額
- single ticket 單程票

補 one-way ticket 單程票

- return ticket 來回票

補 one-way ticket 單程票

directions 方向 ♪049-03

- turn left 左轉
- turn right 右轉
- go straight ahead 直走
- transfer 轉車

stations 車站 ♪049-04

- train 車
- train number 車次號碼
- platform 月台
- gap 間隙
- priority seat 博愛座
- entrance 入口
- front exit 前站出口
- rear exit 後站出口

transport 運輸 ♪049-05

- bus 公車
- train 火車
- railway 鐵路
- traffic 交通

information 資訊 ♪049-06

- peak hour 尖峰時段
- non-peak hour 離峰時段
- timetable 時刻表
- map 地圖

other 其他 ♪049-07

- machine 機器
- elevator 電梯
- escalator 手扶梯
- handrail 扶手

More to Know

你知道這些大眾交通運輸的全名怎麼說嗎？

- **MRT**：臺灣捷運，全名為Mass Rapid Transit，意為大眾快速交通系統。
- **THSR**：臺灣高鐵，Taiwan High Speed Railway，臺灣高速鐵路。

Story

Who ♪050-01
You are a tourist in a foreign city.
你是個旅客，在異國城市遊玩。

Where ♪050-02
You are in the metro station, looking at the signs on the wall.
你在一個地鐵站裡，看著牆上的指示。

When ♪050-03
Your train is coming in 5 minutes. It's noon.
你的車會在五分鐘內抵達。現在是中午。

What ♪050-04
You are looking at the signs to tell the direction.
你正在看指示來分辨方向。

How to Speak

指示牌的關鍵：聽懂關鍵單字，了解關鍵訊息！

- This train is **bound for** ______. 本列車開往 ______ 方向。
- Train No.____ is now **arriving at platform** ____. 車次 ____ 已抵達 ____ 月台。

Dialogue

啊！我搭錯方向了！

♪051-09 對話練習！

♪051-01 Oh, no, I think **I took the wrong line**. I don't know this street.
喔不，我想我搭錯線了。我不知道這條街道是哪。

♪051-02 You'd better get off at the next stop.
你最好下站就下車。

♪051-03 How long will it take me to get to Central Park?
我還有多久能到達中央公園？

♪051-04 Sorry, there is no Central Park on this route.
不好意思，這條路線上沒有中央公園。

我需要轉車嗎？

♪051-05 Should we transfer at the next stop?
我們該在下一站轉車嗎？

♪051-06 That's right.
沒錯。

♪051-07 Why do we need to transfer?
為什麼我們需要轉車？

♪051-08 Because this is not the express bus.
因為這不是直達車。

More to Know

『搭乘交通工具』的英文該怎麼表示呢？

- take the blue line 搭乘藍線
- take the line 3 搭乘 3 號線
- get off at the ____ stop on the blue line 在藍線上的 ____ 站下車
- transfer to the blue line 轉乘藍線

Sentences & Grammar

♪052-01 **1.** Can you tell me **which station I should go to**? Do I have to transfer?

你能告訴我應該去哪一個車站嗎？我必須轉車嗎？

間接問句：用 who 以外疑問詞（what、when、where、which、how、及 why）開頭的問句，若改成間接問法，則詞序需回到直述句的形式。 拆解與重組：

Which station should I go to? 我該去哪個車站呢？	＋	Can you tell me? 你能告訴我嗎？
＝ Can you tell me which station should I go to?		

♪052-02 **2. By the way**, how can I get to the platform 6?

順便問一下，我怎樣才能到達 6 號月臺？

by the way 順便、順道一提。

同樣意義的也有「incidentally」，只是 by the way 更加口語化，通常也放在句首或句尾。

- I had a great weekend with my boyfriend. **By the way**, he proposed.
  我和我男朋友度過了一個愉快的週末。順便說一聲，他求婚了。

♪052-03 **3. Turn right** and you will see the platform 6.

向右轉你就可以看到第六月臺。

轉彎的說法：

make a ... turn	take a ... turn	turn right / left

- The driver **made a left turn** after the stop sign. 司機在停止前進的標誌後左轉。

Ticket Information

♪053-01 搭乘交通工具前往目的地，踏上旅程總是讓人迫不及待！不過，這些車票上都少了資訊，你能幫忙填上正確的資訊嗎？

Single Ticket
Date 2022/ ______ /______
No. 20221230613709

Hsinchu ► Taichung

Train No. 690
Car 9 Seat 9A

____

Date 2023/05/23
No. 20230523841022

Tainan ► Taipei

Train No. 123
Car 6 Seat 13E

Single Ticket
Date 2023/06/30
No. 20230630951013

______________ ► ______________

Train No. ______________
Car ______ Seat ______

解答

1. 2022/12/30
2. Round trip Ticket
3. Hualien ►Taitung, Train No. 228, Car 7 Seat 7B

UNIT 02

Train and Express

火車及特快車

♪054-01 **Hi, is there any express ticket to New York?**
嗨，請問有到紐約的特快車嗎？

♪054-02 Can I get a one-way ticket to Paris?
有去巴黎的單程票嗎？

♪054-03 Could you tell me if there are any seats left on the train?
你能告訴我這趟火車還有座位嗎？

♪054-04 Excuse me, can I change to a sleeper?
不好意思，我能換到臥鋪車廂嗎？

♪054-05 Is this seat taken? 這個座位有人嗎？

How to Say

買票時，你可以要求：

- I prefer a **window** seat. 我更傾向於**靠窗**的座位。
- A **berth** ticket, please. 請給我一張**臥鋪**票。
- I want to book a **first-class** seat. 我想預訂一個**頭等艙**的座位。

Vocabulary

♪055-01
Train Station 火車站

♪055-02
tickets 車票

- regular ticket 成人票
- concession ticket 優待票
- early bird ticket 早鳥票
- student ticket 學生票
- class 等級

補 first class 頭等艙
economy class 經濟艙

♪055-03
buy tickets 買票

- book 預定
- reserve 將……留給；預約
- sold out 售罄
- vacant 空的
- available 可獲得的

♪055-04
seats 座位

- window seat 靠窗的位置
- aisle seat 靠走道的位置
- non-reserved seat 自由座
- reserved seat 對號座
- standing-room-only tickets 站票

♪055-05
berth tickets 臥鋪票

- berth 船或火車上的臥鋪
- upper berth 上臥鋪
- lower berth 下臥鋪
- pullman berth 頭等臥鋪

補 Pullman 豪華火車車廂

♪055-06
cars 車廂

- couchette 硬臥車廂
- sleeping car 臥鋪車廂
- baggage car 行李車廂
- parlor car 豪華車廂
- dining car 用餐車廂

♪055-07
types 種類

- shuttle bus 區間車
- express 直達車
- tourist train 觀光列車
- cargo train 貨運火車

More to Know

此生必搭的 3 台特色火車！世界上最美的火車路線：

- Bernina Express 瑞士貝爾尼納特快車
- Blue Train South Africa 南非藍色列車
- Rocky Mountaineer Railtour 加拿大洛磯山脈景觀列車

情節故事 Story

Who ♪056-01
You are an office worker, stuck in a traffic jam on your way.
你是個辦公室員工，在路上遇到塞車。

Where ♪056-02
You are driving to the train station.
你正開車前往火車站。

When ♪056-03
You don't have the time. Your smartphone shows it's ten to seven.
你沒有帶手錶。你的手機顯示目前六點五十分。

What ♪056-04
You are calling your best friend to ask her to help you.
你打給你最好的朋友，請她幫你。

How to Speak

若要說錯過欲搭乘的火車或班機，要怎麼表達呢？

- I missed my train. 我錯過了我的火車。
- I've missed my flight just now. 我剛剛錯過了我的班機。

Dialogue

沒有趕上火車，下班車是幾點呢？

♪057-08 對話練習！

♪057-01 What's wrong with you? I heard you missed your train.
怎麼回事？我聽説你沒有趕上火車。

♪057-02 I got stuck in traffic. When does the next train leave?
我在路上塞車了。下班火車幾點發車？

♪057-03 At about 7:30. Do you need me to book a ticket online for you?
大約七點半。你需要我在網路上先幫你訂票嗎？

♪057-04 Yes, I think I can be there on time to catch the train.
好，我想我應該可以準時到達、趕上火車。

我要買特快車票

♪057-05 Hi, I need two express tickets to Melbourne tomorrow.
你好，我想要兩張明天去墨爾本的特快車票。

♪057-06 Sorry, express tickets were sold out.
不好意思，特快車票賣完了。

♪057-07 Well, it looks like I can only take the bus.
好吧，看來我只能搭公車了。

More to Know

網路科技發達，如果要在網路上買票，就要看懂這些資訊！

- train number 車次
- time period 時刻
- departure station 出發站
- arrival station 抵達站
- passport number 護照號碼
- regular car 一般車廂
- business car 商務車廂
- bicycle-friendly train 單車友善車廂

Sentences & Grammar

♪058-01 **1. I'd like to buy a ticket to New York tomorrow.**

我想買一張明天到紐約的票。

「purchase」與「buy」同義。

- A down payment of $10 million is required to **purchase** this villa.
  購買這棟別墅需付一千萬頭期款。

其他有購買之意的單字：「shop」，通常指以購買為目的到處找、到處看。

♪058-02 **2. Sorry, there are no seats available.**

不好意思，沒有座位了。

I 和有「擁有、持有」之意的「have」相較，「there be 句型」表達在某時間地點有某人事物、發生了某事物，也常用來指位置。

- Where **there are** winners, **there are** losers.
  有贏家之處就有輸家
- **There used to be** a peach tree in his backyard.
  他家後院以前有棵桃樹。

♪058-03 **3. I prefer a window seat.**

我更傾向於靠窗的座位。

prefer 的用法：

prefer ＋	名詞	prefer something 更喜歡某物
	動名詞	prefer traveling 更喜歡旅遊
	to ＋原形動詞	prefer to travel 更喜歡旅遊
	that 子句	prefer that... 更喜歡⋯⋯

prefer A to B：偏好 A 更勝於 B。

- These young men **prefer** traveling around **to** settling down somewhere.
  這些青年寧願到處旅行，勝於定居某地。

Wich train to take?

忙碌的車站中，旅客來來去去。現在你是一名站務員，協助這些旅客找到自己的火車吧！

Timetable 時刻表

	Train No.	Destination	Time	Platform
North Bound	263	Taipei	9:01	Platform 1A
North Bound	290	Keelung	9:12	Platform 1B
South Bound	160	Tainan	9:05	Platform 2A
South Bound	184	Pingtung	9:23	Platform 3A

I am taking train 263. Which platform should I go to?
我要搭乘 263 列車。我該前往哪個月台呢？

You can take train 263 on platform _________.
你可以在第____月台搭乘 263 號列車。

Excuse me, I want to know which train to take to Keelung. Can you help me?
不好意思，我想知道哪台車可以到基隆。你能幫幫我嗎？

Sure. You can take train ______.
當然可以。你可以搭______。

解答

1. 1A　　2. 290

UNIT 03

Uber or Taxi

代步計程車

♪060-01 **Where are you going, Miss?** 你要去哪裡，女士？

♪060-02 I'd like to go to the Main Station, please. 我要到火車站。

♪060-03 Is the train station far from here? 火車站離這裡遠嗎？

♪060-04 Please drive faster, I am in a hurry.
請開快一點，我在趕時間。

♪060-05 Hurry up, sir. I must catch the train.
請快一點，我必須趕上這列火車。

How to Say

聽懂司機的回答！

- No problem, I will **take a shortcut**. 沒問題，我會抄近路的。
  - take a shortcut 抄捷徑
- We can arrive at the airport **within ten minutes**. 我們在十分鐘之內就能趕到機場。
  - within... 在……（時間）之內
- Don't worry, it is not rush hour now. 不要擔心，現在不是交通高峰期。

單字地圖 Vocabulary

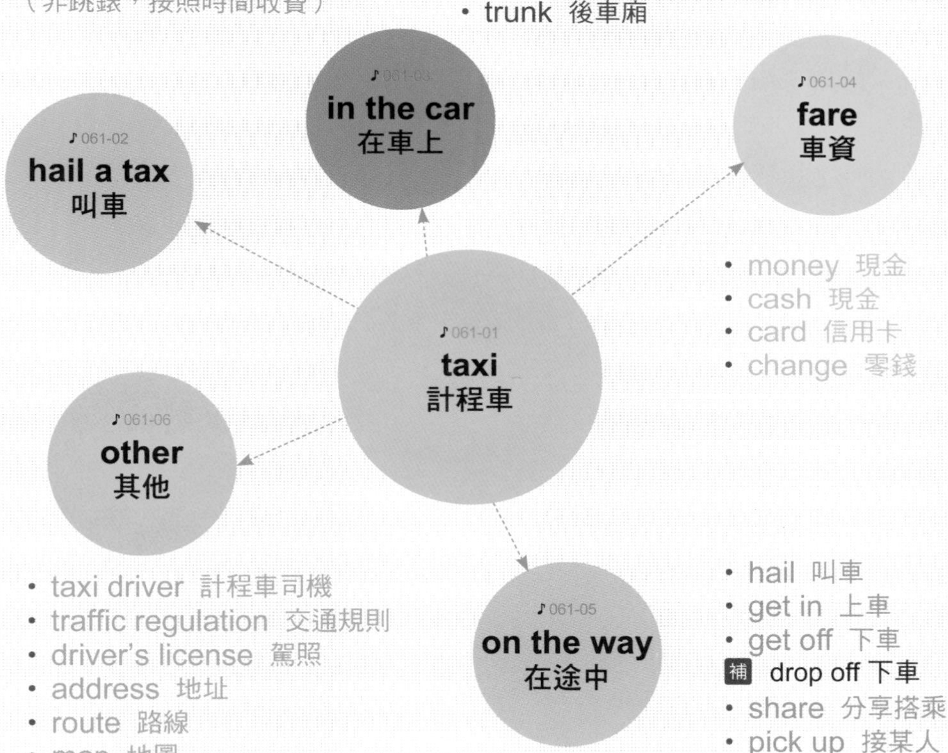

hail a tax 叫車

- cab 計程車
- Uber 計程車（美國）
- charter 包車（非跳錶，按照時間收費）

in the car 在車上

- meter 里程器

補 by meter 跳表

- seat belt 安全帶
- fasten 繫緊
- luggage 行李
- back seat 後座
- trunk 後車廂

fare 車資

- money 現金
- cash 現金
- card 信用卡
- change 零錢

on the way 在途中

- hail 叫車
- get in 上車
- get off 下車

補 drop off 下車

- share 分享搭乘
- pick up 接某人

other 其他

- taxi driver 計程車司機
- traffic regulation 交通規則
- driver's license 駕照
- address 地址
- route 路線
- map 地圖

More to Know

常見說法：學得道地，才能說得道地！

- buckle up = fasten the seat belt 繫緊安全帶
- hail a taxi = catch a cab = grab a taxi 叫計程車（攔車）
- Keep the change. 不用找了。

在美國，有些人會將找的零錢給司機作為小費。若是您用刷卡或是線上支付，也別忘了給司機一筆小費喔！

情節故事 Story

Who You are a taxi driver.
♪062-01 你是一名計程車司機。

Where You are standing by your car.
♪062-02 你正站在你的車旁。

When It's almost nine o'clock. It's rush hour in the morning.
♪062-03 快要九點了。是早上的尖峰時段。

What You are looking for clients to take your drive.
♪062-04 你在找哪邊有顧客攔下你的車。

How to Speak

想像你是計程車司機，掌握兩個和客人溝通的金句！

- It is _______ dollars initially and _______ dollars for each mile.
  起步價是______美元，之後每英里______美元。
- We can get there in _______ minutes.
  我們______分鐘就能到達那裡。

Dialogue

我快遲到了，可以開快一點嗎？

♪063-09 對話練習！

♪063-01 I am going to be late; can you go a little faster?
我要遲到了，你可以開快點嗎？

♪063-02 I'm afraid not, it is rush hour now.
恐怕不行，現在是高峰期。

♪063-03 We can make a detour. And can we get to my company within twenty minutes?
我們可以繞道。可以二十分鐘內到達我的公司嗎？

♪063-04 Well, it's hard to promise you. But I will try my best.
嗯，很難保證一定趕得上。但我會盡力。

請問多少錢？可以刷卡嗎？

♪063-05 **How much does it cost** to get to the airport?
到機場需要多少錢？

♪063-06 Fifty dollars.
五十美元。

♪063-07 Can I use a credit card?
我可以刷卡嗎？

♪063-08 Of course.
當然可以。

More to Know

「How much... ……多少錢？」的句型：

- How much is **it**? ________多少錢？
- How much does **it** cost? ________要多少錢？

此兩句中，「it」可換成想詢問的物品或事情，像本文中詢問的便是「從某處到某處的車資」。

Sentences & Grammar

♪064-01 **1.** The traffic is bad now, are you in a **hurry**?
塞車了，你趕時間嗎？

hurry 的動詞指催促、匆忙、使趕緊。名詞則指倉促、急切、忙亂。常見片語：in a hurry 匆忙地、no hurry 別急。

- I was **hurrying** the kids to get ready for the morning, and we **hurried** to the airport, but the airline staff are **in no hurry** to check in the passengers at all.
  今早我催促孩子們準備好，然後我們匆匆趕到機場，但航空公司員工卻一點都不急地給乘客辦手續。

♪064-02 **2.** We can try **another** road.
我們可以試試另一條路。

another 的用法：

another	＋單數名詞	
	＋數字	＋複數名詞

- The candidate has **another** **ten places** to stop by tonight.
  候選人今晚還要再跑十攤。

♪064-03 **3.** By the way, how **is** the meter **calculated**?
順便問一下，計程表是怎麼計算的？

被動式為「be 動詞＋過去分詞」，適用於要強調被動之人事物，或主動者太過普遍或不清楚時。

主動語態：

- Someone **smacked** me on the head.
  有人打我的頭。
  為主動語態，強調動手者。

被動式：

- I **was smacked** on the head **by** someone.
  我被某人打了頭。
  重點是被打的「我」，且動手者不明，故「by someone」省略也不影響句子的重點。

Check the map

♪065-01 坐上了計程車，發現本該載你一程的司機也對這個社區不熟！？先聽音檔，然後一起來看看，你的目的地該怎麼走呢？

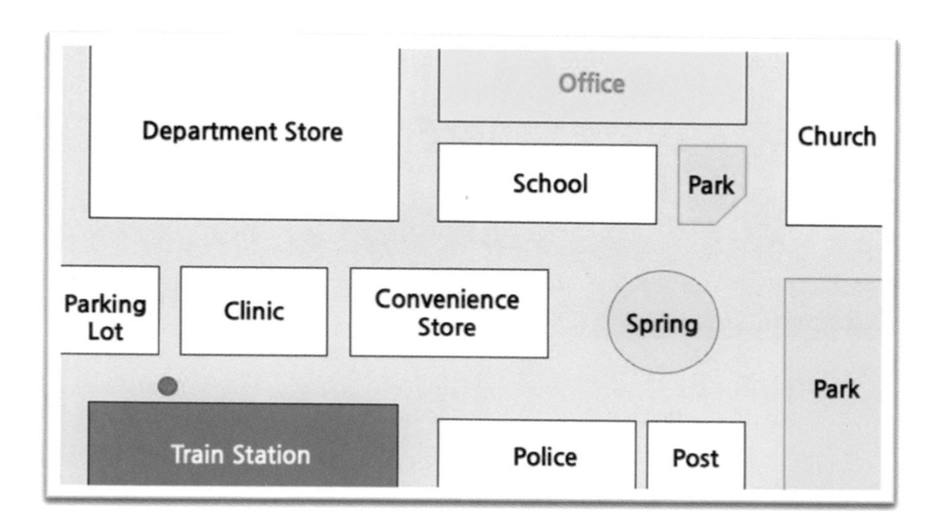

解答

Please go down straight along the road. Take a left turn at the spring. The office is across from the church.

UNIT 04

Driving Situations

開車狀況

♪066-01 **When and where did the accident happen?**
交通事故是何時何地發生的？

♪066-02 It happened on the highway at midnight.
事故是在半夜的高速公路上發生。

♪066-03 I remember the runaway is a man with a red T-shirt.
我記得肇事逃逸者是一名穿紅色 T 恤的男子。

♪066-04 The heavy rain is responsible for the accident.
事故是大雨導致的。

How to Say

事故的發生猝不及防，在緊急情況下，你可以應用的兩個句子：

- Was there anyone hurt? 有人受傷嗎？
- Who is to **blame for** this car accident? 誰該為事故負責？
  - ▪blame for 因……被指責
- Did anyone **witness** the accident? 有人目擊事故現場嗎？
  - ▪witness 目擊；目擊證人（可以是動詞，也可以是名詞）

Vocabulary

common signs 常見標示

- detour 車輛改道
- road construction 道路施工
- one way 單行道
- dead end 死路
- road work ahead 前方道路施工

stop signs 停止標誌

- no temporary parking 禁止臨時停車
- vehicles prohibited 禁止車輛進入
- no pedestrians 禁止行人通行
- no bicycles 禁止腳踏車進入
- no motorcycles 禁止摩托車進入

♪067-04
attention 注意

- slippery when wet 道路濕滑
- right lane reduction 右側車道縮減
- road bump 路面顛簸

limits 限制

- speed limit 最高限速
- height limit 車輛高度限制
- length limit 車輛寬度限制
- no left / right turn 禁止左／右轉
- no U-turn 禁止迴轉
- no overtaking 禁止超車

♪067-05
caution 當心

- caution pedestrians 當心行人
- caution bicycles 當心腳踏車
- signal ahead 注意號誌
- caution children 當心兒童
- fork in the road 注意岔路
- caution deer 鹿出沒注意
- caution horse 馬出沒注意

More to Know

在路上，能看到一些關於建築或地標的告示：

- parking lots 停車場
- gas 加油站
- airport 機場
- hospital 醫院
- tent camping 露營地
- handicapped accessible facility 無障礙空間

情節故事 Story

Who You are an office worker.
♪068-01 你是個辦公室職員。

Where You are sitting in your car, on the way home.
♪068-02 你正在坐在你的車裡，在回家的路上。

When It's quite late. It's already nine-thirty in the night.
♪068-03 很晚了。現在已經是晚上九點半。

What You are driving on your way home.
♪068-04 你正開車回家。

How to Speak

開車上路有許多要留意的號誌或標示，你知道道路相關的英文有什麼嗎？

- highway 高速公路
- freeway 高速公路
- tollway 收費公路
- interstate route 州際公路（美國）
- interchange 交流道
- intersection 交叉路口
- solid double yellow line 雙黃線
- roundabout 圓環
- crosswalk 斑馬線

Dialogue

被員警臨檢

♪069-08 對話練習！

♪069-01 Pull your car over to the side of the road, sir. Now roll down your window.
先生，請靠邊停車。現在，降下車窗。

♪069-02 What's wrong, officer?
怎麼了，警官？

♪069-03 We are going to check if you are drunk driving. Blow into the breathalyzer, please.
我們要檢查一下你是否酒駕。請吹氣。

♪069-04 I never drink.
我從不喝酒。

♪069-05 Please do as I told you, or you'll be **punished**.
請照我說的做，不然你會受到懲罰。

受罰是 punish，罰款則是 fine。

咦？這裡不能右轉？

♪069-06 It's prohibited to take a right turn here, sir. It's said the road is closed for repair.
這個路口禁止右轉，先生。據說是因為修路，所以封閉道路。

♪069-07 Bad luck. We have a long way to go to get to the next crossroad.
真不走運。下一個路口要好遠。

More to Know

到了國外自駕不免會遇到行車狀況，如找停車位、不小心被開單等，這時候如何用英文應對就變得很重要！

找停車位

- **How much** is the parking fee here? 這裡停車怎麼收費？
- **How long** can I park here 我可以在這裡停多久？

Sentences & Grammar

♪070-01 **1.** You will be **fined** $20 for overtime parking.
你超時停車將被罰款二十美金。

fine 當動詞與名詞時，有罰款、罰錢之意。

- The county hall **fines** every infected who doesn't stay in quarantine.
  縣政府對每個不居家隔離的確診者祭出罰款。
- Tax evasion leads to heavy **fines**.
  逃稅會被罰很多錢。

♪070-02 **2.** I got a **ticket** for parking overtime.
我因為停車超時被開單了。

ticket 當名詞時為與違規相關之傳單、罰單，當動詞時指因違規行為而開傳單或罰單，與 fine 類似。

- The sports car owner doesn't care about the $50,000 speeding **ticket**.
  那跑車車主不在乎 $50,000 的超速罰單。
- I got **ticketed** for parking at the tow zone.
  我因在拖吊區停車而被開單。

♪070-03 **3.** **If** you park your car here for a long time, the policeman will give you a ticket.
如果你長時間在這裡停車，交通警察會開單。

「假設……」的用法：未來可能會發生的事。 針對未來假設原因時（非不符常理的事），以現在式表達，則可能造成的結果需用未來式。

If you **park** your car here...	the policeman **will**...
現在式	未來式

- **If** you **don't** start saving now, your life **will** be hard in old age.
  =Life **will** be hard in old age **if** you **don't** start saving now.
  若你現在不開始儲蓄，老年的生活會很辛苦。

圖示辨識 Learn the SIGNs!

道路上總有著許多不同的號誌，看一看，你知道這些號誌的含義嗎？

解答

no entry 禁止通行	no parking 禁止停車	no U-turn 禁止迴轉
road work ahead 前方道路施工	caution deer 鹿出沒注意	slippery when wet 道路濕滑
caution children 當心兒童	fork in the road 注意岔路	caution bicycle 當心腳踏車

UNIT 05

Gas Station and Charging Station

加油站和充電站

♪072-01 **Could you tell me where the self-service tanker is?**
你能告訴我自助加油機在哪嗎？

♪072-02 Please follow the prompt of the self-service tanker to fill your car. 請按照自助加油機的提示來加油。

♪072-03 I don't know how to use the self-service tanker. Could you please show me how to do?
我不會使用自助加油機。請問你能示範一下嗎？

♪072-04 Choose the gas you need first, then pay in cash or by credit card.
首先，選擇你需要的汽油種類，然後用現金或者信用卡支付。

How to Say

來到加油站，該怎麼和加油站的服務生對話呢？

- Would you like **diesel** or **gasoline**? 您加柴油還是汽油？
- Please fuel my car with number 93 gas. 請幫我加 93 號汽油。

單字地圖 Vocabulary

gas stations and charging stations 加油站與充電站 ♪073-01

gas stations 加油站 ♪073-02

- fire extinguisher 滅火器
- pillar 柱子
- gas hose 油槍

補 nozzle 油槍

- self-service pump 自助加油
- gas pipe 油管

gas 汽油 ♪073-03

- diesel 柴油
- gasoline 汽油
- octane number 辛烷值
- lead 鉛
- fuel 燃料

types 種類 ♪073-04

- 87 Regular / Unleaded 87普通無鉛汽油
- 89 Plus / Mid-Grade 89中級汽油
- 91 Supreme / Premier 91高級汽油
- 93 V-Power 93高級汽油

automobiles 汽車 ♪073-05

- compact car 小型車
- mid-size car 中型車
- standard car 標準型車
- full-size car 大型車

other 其他 ♪073-06

- convertible 敞篷車
- truck 貨車

補 trailer 拖板車

- sedan 轎車

charging stations 充電站 ♪073-07

- electric device 電子裝置
- E.V. 電動車（新聞用語）

補 electric vehicle 電動車

- charge 充電
- charger 充電器
- charging network 充電網
- supercharger （特斯拉）快充站
- battery 電池
- battery station 換電站

More to Know

美國沒有「95 加滿」喔！

美國的汽油分類與臺灣不同，加油站分有「自助加油站」或「服務加油站」。一般來説，車子的使用手冊或油箱會註明要加什麼油種，大部分的汽車加「Regular」的就可以，較高級的歐洲車則大多加「Premium」的汽油。

情節故事 Story

Who You are a customer who is waiting in line.
♪074-01 你是一個排隊的顧客。

Where You are in the gas station of Costco.
♪074-02 你在 Costco 的附屬加油站。

When It's Saturday. You come here to buy groceries and to add gas.
♪074-03 今天是星期六。你來這裡買日用品跟加油。

What You are lining up in the Costco gas station.
♪074-04 你在 Costco 加油站排隊等候。

How to Speak

在美國，連鎖賣場如 Sam's Club 和 Costco 的油價相對較便宜，許多人會選擇在賣場附屬加油站加油。但要記得，要先是這些賣場的會員，才能加油喔！以下兩個實用問句，詢問付費金額：

- How much does it cost? 要付多少錢？
- How much is it? 這樣多少？

Dialogue

加滿 50 美金送一張洗車券喔

♪075-09 對話練習！

♪075-01 I'd like to gas up my car with 40 dollars.
我要加 40 美金的汽油。

♪075-02 Sir, with 50 dollars, we'll give you a ticket for washing a car.
先生，加油加到 50 美金會送一張洗車券喔。

♪075-03 Can I use the ticket now?
洗車券可以馬上用嗎？

♪075-04 Sure. We serve you in 24 hours.
當然可以。我們 24 小時為您服務。

♪075-05 Ok, gas up my car with 50 dollars, and please wash the car for me.
那我加 50 美金的汽油，請幫我洗車。

這台自助加油機好像壞了？

♪075-06 The self-service tanker seems to be broken.
那台自助加油機好像壞了。

♪075-07 Let me see. This machine is broken. Which kind of gas do you want?
讓我看看，這台機器確實壞了。您要加哪種汽油？

♪075-08 The number 92 gas.
92 汽油。

More to Know

來到加油站，必須要聽懂的指示句：

- Please open the **tank cover**. 請打開油箱蓋。
- Please **turn off** the car. 請您把汽車熄火。

Sentences & Grammar

♪076-01 **1.** Sorry, sir. This self-service tanker **has no** gas.
抱歉，先生，這台自助加油機沒有油了。

表達「沒有」時，若用 **have** 或 **own** 等「有」的相關動詞，可寫「not have ＋名詞」，或「have no ＋名詞」。

有	沒有
have	don't have
own	have no

- This tanker **has** gas.
  油箱裡有油。
- This tanker **has no** gas (at all). =This tanker **does not have** (any) gas (at all). 油箱裡沒有油了。

「**any**」及「**at all**」用來強調「缺乏」的狀態。

♪076-02 **2.** The **balance** of your fuel card is insufficient, please recharge.
您的加油卡餘額不足，請充值。

balance 結存、結餘（特指金融帳戶及帳簿上的金額）。

- What's the **balance** on my account? I usually have a low **balance** at the end of every month.
  我帳戶餘額有多少？通常每個月底餘額都很低。

♪075-03 **3.** Can I **withdraw** the balance from the fuel card?
我可以提領加油卡裡的餘額嗎？

與存提金錢相關字詞還有「withdraw 提款、提領」及「deposit 存放、存錢」。

- All the red-envelop money is **deposited** in my son's account, and he's allowed to **withdraw** a little twice a year.
  所有的紅包錢都被存在我兒子的帳戶，他一年只能小額提領兩次。

Fill the tank!

這裡有四台不同的交通工具，請為他們添加合適的能源，讓它們能夠被正常啟動吧！

- This is a car. 這是一台車子。
- We need to go to a ________________.
  我們需要到加油站。
- It needs gasoline.
  它需要的是汽油。

- This is a car. 這是一台車子。
- It's an electric car.
  這是一輛電動車。
- We need to go to a ________________.
  我們需要到充電站。

- This is a boat. 這是一艘小船。
- It needs ___________.
  它需要的是汽油。
- We can go to a ________________ by the seashore.
  我們可以到岸邊的加油站。

- This is an excavator.
  這是一台挖土機。
- We need to go to a ________________.
  我們需要到加油站。
- It needs ___________.
  它需要的是柴油。

解答

We need to go to a gas station.	We need to go to a charging station.
It needs gasoline. We can go to a gas station by the seashore.	We need to go to a gas station. It needs diesel.

Review 2

A 填空練習

- Where can I __________ my transportation card?
  我可以在哪邊加值交通卡？
  答案請見 P.048

- Hurry up, sir. I must catch the __________.
  請快一點，我必須趕上這列火車。
  答案請見 P.060

B 引導造句

- **How long... ……要多久？**
  How long ______________________________?
  我還有多久能到達中央公園？
  答案請見 P.051

- **How much... ……多少（錢）？**
  ______________________________?
  到機場需要多少錢？
  答案請見 P.063

- **be punished 被懲罰**
  ______________________________.
  答案請見 P.069

C 引導寫作

標題	Take a Train 搭火車
搭火車	
買車票	
塞車了	
趕火車	

參考短文：我打算搭火車出遊。我買了一張到紐約的單程車票。去車站時，我在路塞車了。但我後來準時抵達，趕上了火車。

Chapter

03

School Life
學校生活

UNIT 01 How to select courses? 要怎麼選課呢？

UNIT 02 How to prepare tests? 要怎麼準備考試？

UNIT 03 Let’s go to the library! 一起去圖書館！

UNIT 04 Where is the International Student Center? 國際學生中心在哪呢？

UNIT 05 Move into the Student Dorm! 搬進學生宿舍！

UNIT 01

How to select courses?

要怎麼選課呢？

♪080-01 **What do you think of the course?** 你覺得這個課程怎麼樣？

♪080-02 Could you tell me which courses are suitable for me?
你能告訴我哪些課程適合我嗎？

♪080-03 I think this course is relatively more practical.
我認為這個課程相對更實用。

♪080-04 I want to take courses on African economics. What do you think? 我想選擇研究非洲經濟的課程，你覺得怎麼樣？

♪080-05 I suggest you should have a basic understanding of all the courses. 我建議你應該要對全部課程有個基礎了解。

♪080-06 Maybe economics will help you a lot.
或許經濟學對你的幫助會很大。

How to Speak

在選課時，最重要的是什麼呢？如果想和朋友或家人討論，那麼你要先學會說這一句：

- What is the most important thing for you, the **future job** or **interest**?

對你來說什麼是最重要的？未來的工作還是興趣？

Vocabulary

♪081-01
courses selection 課程選擇

♪081-03
courses 課程

- take the course 選課
- compulsory course 必修課

補 required course 必修課

- elective course 選修課
- select 選擇
- consider 考慮

♪081-02
credits 學分

- get credits 拿到學分
- attend 出席
- absent 缺席
- consult 諮詢

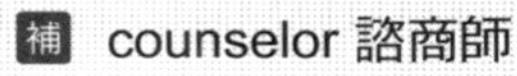
補 counselor 諮商師

♪081-04
exams 考試

- pass the exam 通過考試
- fail the exam 不及格
- test 考試
- quiz 小考
- score 分數

補 grade 分數

♪081-06
practice 練習；實行

- practical 實用的
- useful 有用的
- skill 技巧
- internship 實習
- career 職業
- job 工作

補 skillful 熟練的

♪081-05
study 讀書

- learn 學習
- master 精通
- acquire 習得
- knowledge 知識
- information 資訊
- understanding 理解

More to Know

在美國，「**elementary school 國小**」六年（一到六年級）、「**middle school 國中**」是兩年（七到八年級），「**high school 高中**」則是四年（九到十二年級），且高中和大學一樣採學分制。想申請大學，要採用高中九到十一年級之間三年的 GPA（Grade Point Average 成績平均績點）。

情節故事 Story

Who ♪ 082-01

You are a father. Your daughter is going to university this year.
你是一名父親。你的女兒今年要上大學了。

Where ♪ 082-02

You are sitting in the desk.
你坐在書桌前。

When ♪ 082-03

It's July. It's summer break to the students.
現在是七月，對學生來說是暑假時間。

What ♪ 082-04

You are chatting with your daughter.
你正和女兒在聊天。

How to Speak

兩個簡單的問句，讓你和孩子聊聊選課這個熱門話題！

- What do you take as your required course? 你選了什麼必修課？
- Why did you take this as an elective course?
  你為何選這堂為選修課呢？

Dialogue

有問題的話就與輔導員討論

♪083-08 對話練習！

♪083-01 Discuss with the counselor if you have any questions.
如果妳有問題的話就和輔導員討論。

♪083-02 Ok, I heard he is a warm-hearted man.
好的，我聽說他是一個很熱心的人。

♪083-03 The counselor is a knowledgeable person, so you can talk to him about your problems.
輔導員知識淵博，所以妳可以和他談論妳遇到的問題。

♪083-04 I see. After all, he has a lot of experience.
我明白，畢竟他的經歷很豐富。

妳有幾個必修科目呢？

♪083-05 How many required courses do you have?
妳有幾個必修科目呢？

♪083-06 Let me check it up on our department website. I wish there aren't many.
我來我們的系所網站上查一下。希望不會很多。

♪083-07 Here is the list of the required courses. Let me download it for you
這裡有必修課的清單。我幫妳下載。

More to Know

國外留學選課小常識：選課有什麼要注意的呢？

1. 一定要事先了解學校及科系規定的學分數及修課規定，可以尋求學校的輔導員（**counselor** 或 **advisor**）給予你幫助或建議。
2. 大部分學校都提供「**class shopping**」，可以先上第一堂課看看是否適合，如果發現不適合，可在期限內取消該門學分。
3. 如果即將要去美國求學，可以參考國內外網友常用的選課資訊網站或論壇，上面常有修課學生的回饋，也可作為評斷依據。

Sentences & Grammar

♪084-01 **1. By the way, how are you going to take the course?**
順便問一下，你打算怎麼選課？

be going to 是常見表達未來行動或計畫的說法，類似 will。going to 也能簡化成更口語化的 gonna，改寫例句為下：

- How will you pick courses?
=How are you gonna pick courses?
你要怎麼選課？

♪084-02 **2. I'm still confused about the course selection.**
我仍然對選課很困惑。

confuse 是動詞，意為使困惑，其 ing 形式及過去分詞都是形容詞，但表達的意義不同。

- The author's new novel confuses her readers.
作家的新小說讓她的讀者很困惑。
- This is the author's most confusing novel so far.
這是到目前為止作家最令人困惑的小說。
原有、主動的本身特質，故用 confusing
- Confused readers look for the reason behind it.
困惑的讀者尋找背後的原因。
被其他人事物導致的被動狀態，故用 confused

♪084-03 **3. I suggest you take future career into consideration.**
我建議你把將來的職業規劃考慮進去。

考慮可說「take…into consideration」及「take into consideration＋子句」：

- When choosing a spouse, take into consideration whether you can stand being with the same person for the rest of your life.
選擇配偶時，要考量妳能否在妳餘生都和同一個人長相廝守。

課表 Fill out the course schedule!

♪085-01 這是一份課程的安排計劃表，不過，有些地方似乎還沒決定好。聽聽音檔，究竟這份課表的主人想要選什麼課呢？

Time	Mon	Tue	Wed	Thu	Fri
8-10	X	Math		X	
10-12	Math	X			
13-15	X		X		
15-17			X		
17-19	Tennis	X	Human Geography	X	

解答

Mon – Philosophy

Tue – Green Energy, Physics

Wed – Social Relationship, Environmental Science

Thu – Economics, Environmental Science, Physics

Fri – Lab Day (all day)

UNIT 02

How to prepare tests?

要怎麼準備考試？

♪086-01 **I heard the exam is a comprehensive test.**
我聽說這次的考試沒有範圍。

♪086-02 Do you know what's going to be covered on the test?
你知道考試範圍是什麼嗎？

♪086-03 I don't know how to prepare for the exam.
我不知道如何準備這個考試。

♪086-04 I heard the exam covered a wide range.
我聽說這次考試涉及的範圍很廣。

♪086-05 I think these contents will cover in the test.
我認為這些內容會在考試範圍裡。

How to Say

「考試範圍包括了……」用英文要怎麼說呢？

- You will be examined **on the relationship between economics and ethics**. 考試範圍包括**經濟學與倫理學的關係**。
- The contents covered in the exam are **in the next chapter.** 考試中所涉及的內容**在下一章**。

Vocabulary

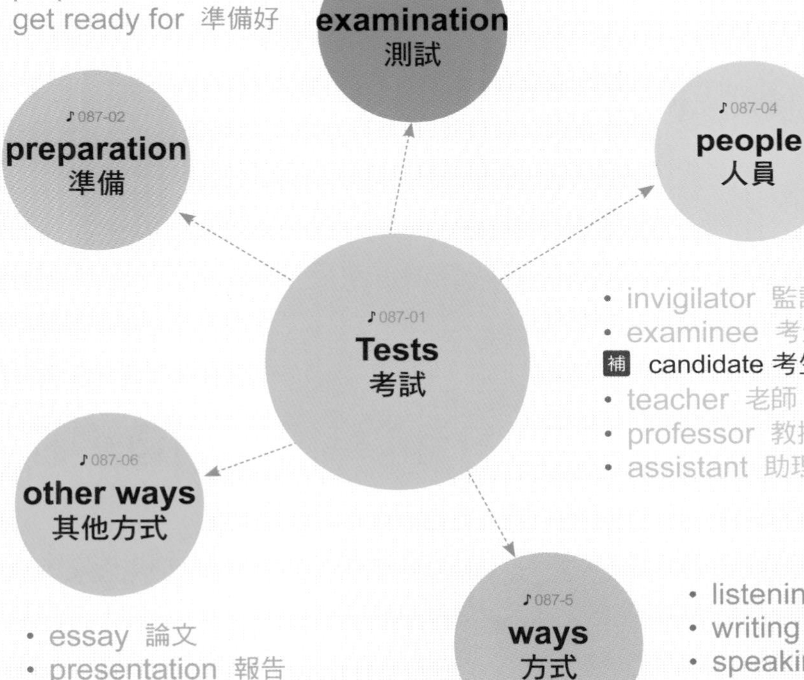

examination 測試
- test paper 考卷
- examination room 考場
- illegible 模糊
- discipline 紀律
- cheat 作弊
- hand in 交卷

preparation 準備
- review 複習
- preview 預習
- stay up 熬夜
- method 方法
- prepare 準備
- get ready for 準備好

people 人員
- invigilator 監試人員
- examinee 考生

補 candidate 考生
- teacher 老師
- professor 教授
- assistant 助理

other ways 其他方式
- essay 論文
- presentation 報告

補 oral presentation 口頭報告
- report 報告

補 written report 書面報告

ways 方式
- listening test 聽力測驗
- writing test 寫作測驗
- speaking test 口說測驗
- reading test 閱讀測驗
- written test 筆試
- oral test 口試

Chapter 03 學校生活

More to Know

美國學期制：原來美國唸書，不只有分上下兩學期！

- 在國內，大部分的大學都是分上下兩學期，上學期從 9 月到隔年 1 月，下學期則是從 2 月到 6 月。不過在美國除了分兩學期外，還有不同的分法。美國有三種校曆制度（**Calendar System**），有學期制（**Semester**）、學季制（**Quarter**）以及三學期制（**Trimester**）。

情節故事 Story

Who You are a university student.
♪088-01 你是一名大學生。

Where You are studying in a conference room in the library.
♪088-02 你在圖書館的討論室中讀書。

When You are studying for the coming exam.
♪088-03 你正為了到來的考試唸書。

What You are studying with your group members of class.
♪088-04 你正和班上的小組成員一起唸書。

How to Speak

成績單上的 A 是幾分？ F 就是被當了嗎？

- 我們在國內，大部分的成績都還是以分數（1-100 分）為主要的評分標準，在國外則不同，大部分的評分等即是以 A ～ F 的評分標準來打分數。美國及大部分國外學院（包含高中及大學），都是用下列評分等級來評審學生的成績：**A+ / A / A- / B+ / B / B- / C+ / C / C- / D+ / D / D- / E / F**。

Dialogue

要不要組個讀書會一起準備？

♪089-08 對話練習！

♪089-01 I'm going to organize a book club for studying for a test. Would you like to join us?
我打算組一個讀書會來準備考試，你要加入我們嗎？

♪089-02 No problem.
沒問題。

♪089-03 You can prepare some questions that you would like to discuss with our partners.
你可以準備一些你想要與夥伴討論的問題。

♪089-04 Sounds great! I've got tons of questions that I would like to ask you guys.
太好了！我有一堆問題想要問你們。

跟同學詢問考試範圍

♪089-05 Mike, do you know what's going to be covered on the test?
麥克，你知道考試範圍是什麼嗎？

♪089-06 Yes, I've asked the counselor about it.
是的，我已經向輔導員詢問過了。

♪089-07 Can you tell me?
你能跟我説嗎？

More to Know

什麼是 GPA ？

如果到美國留學，常常會聽到「**GPA**」，究竟大家常常掛在口中的 GPA 是什麼？上一單元提到 GPA 就是「**Grade Point Average 在校平均成績**」，在美國，學期結束的時候學生都會收到成績單，而成績單上面通常都會有字母分級標示的成績（**0 ～ 4** 分，以 **A ～ F** 分等級）以及平均分數——**GPA**。

Sentences & Grammar

♪090-01 **1.** Candidates are **not allowed to** bring any books or calculators into the examination room.
考生不能攜帶任何書籍和計算器進入考場。

須留意以下用法後接的介係詞及動詞型態：

禁止、不准、阻止	人＋ be 動詞＋ not allowed to ＋原形動詞
	人＋ be 動詞＋ banned ＋ from ＋ Ving
	forbid ＋人＋ to ＋原形動詞
	prohibit ＋人＋ from ＋ Ving

- The ward **forbids** the prisoners **to have** personal items.
  典獄長不許囚犯擁有私人物品。
- That writer **was banned from publishing**.
  這作家以前被禁止出書。
- The principal **prohibits** pupils **from eating** sweets.
  校長禁止學生吃甜食。

♪088-02 **2.** Once you find **cheating**, you will be canceled the exam.
一旦發現作弊則取消考試。

cheat 有詐取、行騙、作弊、哄騙之意。 片語：
- cheat in exams　在考試中作弊。
- cheat on A (with B)　某人對 A 不忠（與 B 出軌）。

♪090-03 **3.** You'**d better** mark the key points in the book.
你最好在書中標出考試重點。

had better / best ＋原形動詞：最好、必須
- They**'d best not bother** Mom now after making such a big mess.
  他們把環境弄得一團亂，他們現在最好別去打擾媽媽。
- Someone's screaming! We **had better call** the police.
  有人在尖叫！我們最好報警。

Take a Note.

這裡有四張照片，請分辨這四張照片是在什麼場所呢？還有其他資訊你能補充的嗎？

- I think they are ________________.
  我想他們正在上課。
- I think this is a ________________.
  我想這裡是教室。

- I think he is an ________________.
  我想他是位監試人員。
- I think they are in a ____________.
  我想他們在教室裡。

- I think she is ________________.
  我想她正在報告。
- I think they are in the __________.
  我想他們正在會議室中。

- I think she is ________________.
  我想她正在讀書。
- Maybe she is ________________.
  也許她正在準備考試。

解答

I think they are in a class.

I think this is a classroom.

I think he is an invigilator.

I think they are in a classroom.

I think she is having a presentation.

I think they are in the conference room.

I think she is studying.

Maybe she is preparing for the test.

Chapter 03 學校生活

UNIT 03

Let's go to the library!

一起去圖書館！

♪092-01 **Excuse me, could you tell me if you have this book in the library?** 不好意思，你能告訴我圖書館有沒有這本書嗎？

♪092-02 I'd like to borrow a book on law. Do you have any suggestions? 我想借一本關於法律的書，你有什麼建議嗎？

♪092-03 Excuse me, this is my library card, and this is the book. 不好意思，這是我的借書證，這是書。

♪092-04 By the way, how long can I keep the book? 順便請教一下，這本書我可以借多長時間？

How to Say

如果你是圖書館員，你可以這樣回答讀者們的疑問：

- **問書在哪邊：**
  Let me check, please. Well, it is on the second shelf. 請讓我查查。嗯，在第二層書架上。
- **某一本書有狀況：**
  I'm afraid the book has been overdue. 這本書恐怕已經過期了。
  This book can only be read in the library. 這本書只能在圖書館裡閱讀。

單字地圖 Vocabulary

Novels and Books 小說與書籍 ♪093-01

literature 文學 ♪093-02

- comedy 喜劇
- drama 戲劇
- literary realism 現實主義文學
- romance 浪漫文學
- satire 諷刺文學
- tragedy 悲劇
- tragicomedy 悲喜劇

classic 經典類 ♪093-03

- crime 犯罪類
- detective 偵探類
- horror 恐怖類
- humor 幽默類
- legends 傳奇類
- suspense 懸疑類
- thrillere 驚悚類

fiction 科幻小說 ♪093-04

- meta fiction 後設小說
- mystery 神秘小說
- mythology 神話
- science fiction 科幻小說

fantasy 奇幻文學 ♪093-05

- mythology 神話
- fairy tale 童話故事
- mystery 神秘小說
- mythology 神話
- folklore 民間故事

non fiction 非科幻小說 ♪093-06

- biography 自傳
- essay 小論文
- journalism 期刊
- lab report 實驗報告
- memoir 傳記
- narrative nonfiction 敘事性非小說
- self-help book 心理自助書

More to Know

其實，圖書館裡也有其他類型的書籍，除了各種面向的小說、傳記、論文等藏書以外，還會有工具書類型的書籍，如以下：

- **dictionary** 字典
- **almanac** 年鑑
- **atlas** 地圖集
- **encyclopedia** 百科全書

情節故事 Story

Who ♪094-01
You are a librarian.
你是一名圖書館員。

Where ♪094-02
You are are in a library. Here is the place you work.
你在你工作的圖書館。

When ♪094-03
It's 4 p.m. It's time to check the books on the shelves.
現在是下午四點。正是去書架確認書籍的時候。

What ♪094-04
You are checking the condition of the books on the shelves.
你正在確認書架上書籍的狀況。

How to Speak

有人打開了圖書館的大門，走到接待的櫃檯……

- **當你是圖書館管理員時，你會說：**
  Your **library card**, please. 請出示您的借書證。
- **若你是想要借書的民眾，你會說：**
  Good day. I want to **apply for** a library card. 您好。我想申請一張借書證。

Dialogue

我找不到這本書，可以幫我嗎？

♪095-08 對話練習！

♪095-01 I can't find this book. Can you help me?
我找不到這本書，可以幫我嗎？

♪095-02 Sure. Over there, on your left.
當然可以了，就在你的左手邊。

♪095-03 Thank you, and this?
謝謝，這本呢？

♪095-04 It's on the second shelf.
就在第二層書架上。

這本書逾期了，要繳納罰金喔！

♪095-05 The book is overdue, and you have to pay a fine. 10 dollars.
這本書逾期了，您需要交罰金。10 元。

♪095-06 Really? How much? I can't believe I forgot to return the book again. Can you send me the notice via e-mail next time?
真的嗎？多少錢？我真不敢相信我又忘記還書了。下次能麻煩您用電子郵件寄通知給我嗎？

♪095-07 Sure! You can register on our website. We will notify you of the due date whenever you borrow a book from here.
當然可以，你可以到我們的網站上註冊。之後你在這借書我們都會通知你書籍的到期日。

More to Know

想要在美國辦理借書證，你需要準備什麼呢？

- 請準備有照片的證件，如國際駕照、護照或美國綠卡。
- 準備在當地居住的證明，如水電費單。

若是你尚未無法證明你在美國居住，有些圖書館也提供「**limited status**」，讓你一次可以借閱一本書。

Sentences & Grammar

♪096-01 **1. Ok, please fill out an application form first.**
好的，請填寫一張申請書。

「fill」有填滿之意，「fill out」特指針對「表格、試卷、問卷」等的填寫。

- The campaign team conducts polls by asking voters to **fill out** online surveys.
  競選團隊透過請有投票權的人填寫網路問卷來做民調。

♪096-02 **2. Could you tell me how to have a library card?**
你能告訴我如何能辦理借書證嗎？

「what、where、when、whom、how」等的問題用間接法問時，若問句主詞普遍或無須描述，且時態不涉及過去時，可用「to＋原形動詞」，如例句。 但若主詞較複雜，則不可省略，並以完整直述句來問，如：

- Could you tell me **how** someone under six has a library card?
  你能告訴我六歲以下如何能辦理借書證嗎？

♪096-03 **3. Please wait a minute, you'll get a library card in five minutes.**
請等一下，五分鐘後給你圖書證。

表達時間很短除了 a minute 外，也可說 a moment 及 a second。

♪096-04 **4. You can have a temporary library card.**
你可以辦理一個臨時借書證。

temporary 臨時性的、暫時性的。

- The farm needs lots of **temporary** labor during the harvest season. 農場在採收季需要大量臨時勞力。

Fill out the Form.

♪097-01 **Emily 是圖書館的管理員，而下面是申請借書證的申請單，聽聽 Emily 和 Peta 的聊天內容，和她們一起檢查看看，這些資料是否正確呢？**

1.

■ ID cards (photo needed)	■ Approved
■ Documents to prove you live here	□ Unapproved

2.

□ ID cards (photo needed)	□ Approved
□ Documents to prove you live here	□ Unapproved

3.

□ ID cards (photo needed) '	□ Approved
□ Documents to prove you live here	□ Unapproved

4.

□ ID cards (photo needed)	□ Approved
□ Documents to prove you live here	□ Unapproved

5.

□ ID cards (photo needed)	□ Approved
□ Documents to prove you live here	□ Unapproved

解答

2.

■ ID cards (photo needed)	□ Approved
□ Documents to prove you live here	■ Unapproved

3.

□ ID cards (photo needed) '	□ Approved
□ Documents to prove you live here	■ Unapproved

4.

□ ID cards (photo needed)	□ Approved
■ Documents to prove you live here	■ Unapproved

5.

■ ID cards (photo needed)	■ Approved
■ Documents to prove you live here	□ Unapproved

UNIT 04

Where is the International Student Center? 國際學生中心在哪呢？

♪098-01 **Excuse me, how can I apply to be a volunteer?**

不好意思，請問我如何能申請成為志工？

♪098-02 How can I login on the school system?

要怎麼登入學校系統？

♪098-03 Could you tell me if there are any forums in our school?

你能告訴我學校有線上論壇嗎？

♪098-04 Excuse me, where can I get a class schedule?

請問哪裡可以領取課程表？

How to Say

聽懂關鍵字，助益差很多！獎學金、歡迎會？這些活動或事情要怎麼用英文表達呢？

- Did you know about the **scholarship** of our school?
  你知道我們學校有獎學金這件事嗎？
- A **welcome party** will be held today. Would you like to go with me?
  今天會舉辦一個歡迎餐會。你要和我一起去嗎？

單字地圖 Vocabulary

♪099-01
school 學校

♪099-02
class 等級

- third-class scholarship 三等獎學金
- second-class scholarship 二等獎學金
- first-class scholarship 一等獎學金

♪099-03
scholarship 獎學金

- apply 申請
- award 頒獎
- waive 放棄
- entitle 授權
- receive 獲得
- donate 捐獻

♪099-04
applications 申請

- eligibility 合格
- qualification （資格）合格
- duration 有效期間
- 補 deadline 期限
- document 文件
- 補 attachment 附件
- contact 聯絡

♪099-05
competitions 競爭

- qualification 資格
- apply for 申請某物
- available 可得到的
- regulation 規則

♪099-06
other 其他

- fellowship 獎學金
- expense 費用
- tuition fee 學費
- per 每個
- semester 學期
- reimbursement 報銷
- enroll 註冊

More to Know

海外留學生不可不知

國外高等學院，大部分都設有**國際學生事務處（International student center）**，主要是幫助海外留學生找尋宿舍、住宿處，生活或學業方面的協助。如果有機會到海外留學，有什麼需要協助幫忙的，不妨可以到國際學生事務處尋求協助。

情節故事 Story

Who ♪ 100-01

You are a worker in the education workshop in the ISU.
你是國際學生處中負責教育工作坊的職員。

Where ♪ 100-02

You are in the office.
你在辦公室裡。

When ♪ 100-03

It's early in the morning.
現在是早上。

What ♪ 100-04

You are helping a foreign student out for the workshop.
你正在幫助一名外國學生報名工作坊。

How to Speak

在國外讀書的莘莘學子也會有遇到挫折的時候，如果是你，你會怎麼安慰或給予建議呢？也許，你可以試試這句：

- Call your family if you feel lonely.
  如果你感到孤獨的話，打電話給家人。

重點對話 Dialogue

我是國際生，可以參與教育工作坊嗎？

♪ 101-07 對話練習！

♪ 101-01 I'm an international student. Can I join the education workshop?
我是國際生，可以參與教育工作坊嗎？

♪ 101-02 Of course. Please fill out this application form.
當然可以。請填寫這份申請表。

♪ 101-03 Do I need to provide relevant materials?
需要提供相關資料嗎？

♪ 101-04 Yes. You need to provide the certification of studying at school.
要，請提供在校證明。

我無法登入學校系統

♪ 101-05 I can't login into the school system. Can you help me?
我無法登入學校系統，可以幫我嗎？

♪ 101-06 No problem. Let me show you.
沒問題，我示範給你看。

More to Know

國際學生事務處 ISC（International student center）業務項目有：

1. **國際學生服務**：關於生活起居、學校課程方面的諮詢。
2. **海外留遊學計畫諮詢**：協助當地學生到海外留學的諮詢。
3. **護照服務**：如果護照、簽證有疑問也可尋求 ISC 協助。
4. **工作諮詢**：若有打工需求，大部分 ISU 可以提供適合的建議。
5. **舉辦茶會**：讓國際學生對於學校能有更進一步認識，適應海外生活。

Sentences & Grammar

♪102-01 **1. Are** you **used to** American foods?

你吃得慣美國的食物嗎？

表示習慣時，可用「be 動詞 / get / become used to」＋名詞／動名詞。 但「used to」＋原形動詞，指「過去經常」（故只會以過去式出現）。

- The foreigner never **gets used to** the humidity in Taiwan.
  那外國人一直無法習慣臺灣的潮濕。
- The family **used to** eat out once a month.
  這家人以前一個月外食一次。

♪102-02 **2. How** do you solve the language problem?

你是怎麼解決語言問題的？

除了用 how 來詢問「如何」外，也能改用 in what way / manner / method。

- **In what way** did the parents calm the screaming kids?
  爸媽是用什麼方法來安撫尖叫的小朋友？

♪102-03 **3.** I **usually** practice speaking and listening with my counselor.

我通常和我的輔導員練習口語和聽力。

頻率：

never 0%	rarely 1~10%	occasionally 10~40%	sometimes 40~70%	often usually frequently 70~99%	always 100%

♪102-04 **4.** Have you **adapted to** the living environment here?

你適應這裡的生活環境嗎？

adapt to ＋名詞／動名詞 使自己適應於……。

- The business staff failed to adapt to the digital age.
  這家公司在趕上數位時代這塊上失敗了。

Information Bulletin

♪103-01 這裡是佈告欄，上面張貼了一些資訊。請聽聽看學生們的對話，找出佈告欄上少的資訊吧！

Bulletin 佈告欄

Tea Party at ISC!!!
See more details on website:
____

Karaoke Contest!
Sign here:
____

____
On Wednesday Night!
At _______

____
____
____

解答

What does it say?
It says, “check out tea party information on website: www.school.abc.isc” !

This poster shows the karaoke contest is on Aug 2nd, at the ISC salon!

September Birthday party! The location is at the J&K Dinner!

What does this poster show?
Beach Cleaning. Clean up together on this Sunday!

Chapter 03 學校生活

UNIT 05

Move into the Student Dorm!

搬進學生宿舍

♪104-01 **Don’t make any noise after turning off the light.**
關燈之後不得大聲喧嘩。

♪104-02 Please be kind to all public goods in the dormitory.
請善待宿舍內的一切公共物品。

♪104-03 Clean the dormitory thoroughly once a month.
每個月要徹底打掃一次宿舍。

♪104-04 The dormitory should be kept clean.
宿舍內應保持乾淨和整潔。

♪104-05 It is best not to place valuables in the dormitory.
宿舍內最好不要放置貴重物品。

How to Say

宿舍生活是一件不簡單的事情，尤其當大家來自不同家庭、不同地區，生活習慣也不相同，這時，可以先和室友約好一起訂下生活公約，讓彼此都能過得舒服一些。關於生活公約，你會需要的範例：

- Smoking **is not allowed** in the dormitory. 請勿在宿舍內抽煙。
- The garbage **must be** put in the garbage can. 垃圾必須放進垃圾桶內。

Vocabulary

♪105-01
dormitory 宿舍

♪105-02
building 建築物

- floor 樓層
- separate 分開
- bathroom 浴室
- shower 淋浴間

♪105-03
apartment 公寓

- residence hall 宿舍
- coed dorm 男女合宿
- single-sex dorm 單一性別宿舍（女宿／男宿）

♪105-04
rule 規定

- policy 條款
- bulletin board 公佈欄
- lifestyle 生活方式
- non-smoker 非吸菸者
- prerequisite 必備條件
- announcement 公告

♪105-05
necessity 必需品

- bed set 床具組
- towel 毛巾
- water fountain 飲水機
- washing machine 洗衣機
- dryer 烘乾機

♪105-06
facility 設備

- wardrobe 衣櫃
- sink 洗手台
- toilet 馬桶
- lamp 檯燈
- light switch 燈開關
- bunk bed 上下舖的床
- stairs 梯子

♪105-07
other 其他

- roommate 室友
- room type 房間類型
- neat 乾淨
  補 cleanliness 清潔度
- routine 例行公事
- on-campus 校內的
- off-campus 校外的

More to Know

宿舍生活中，有些事情你也許會需要請教或是得到室友的允許。有禮貌地提出要求或詢問，會讓事情更加順利地進行。介紹兩個禮貌的請求問句：

- **May I** use the desk by the window? 我能用靠窗的書桌嗎？
- **Do you mind if** we use this table together? 你介意我們一起用這張桌子嗎？

情節故事 Story

Who You are a foreign student in the campus.
♪106-01 你是校園中的外國學生。

Where You are in the dorm. In your room.
♪106-02 你在宿舍的房間裡。

When It's nine in the night.
♪106-03 現在是晚上九點。

What You are meeting your roommates.
♪106-04 你正和室友們見面。

How to Speak

參考以下的自我介紹短文，適當修改，練習自我介紹吧！

Hello, please allow me to introduce myself. I'm glad to meet you, I am **Mike**. I hope we can get along very well in the future. May I have your phone numbers or other contact information?

大家好，請讓我自我介紹。認識大家很高興，我是**麥可**。希望我們以後能相處得很好。我可以跟你們要電話號碼或其他聯絡資訊嗎？

Dialogue

你住的是幾人房呢？

♪107-08 對話練習！

♪107-01 Tina, where do you live?
緹娜，你住在哪邊？

♪107-02 I live in apartment 9.
我住在 9 號公寓。

♪107-03 How many people do you live with?
你住的是幾人房？

♪107-04 I live in a four-people room. What about you?
我住的是四人房。你呢？

♪107-05 I live in a three-people room with a bathroom.
我住的是 3 人房，房間裡有一間浴室。

國際生住在哪一棟宿舍呢？

♪107-06 Excuse me. Which dormitory is for international students? How do I get here?
不好意思，請問國際生住在哪一棟宿舍？從這裡要怎麼走呢？

♪107-07 The south of the campus. Follow me. I'll take you there.
在校園的南邊。跟我走，我帶你去。

More to Know

聽懂宿舍管理員的要求或指令！初來乍到，都會先向宿舍的管理處或是學校報到，請記住下面標示的單字，這也許會幫助你更快完成報到。

- Please **register** your name here. 請在這裡登記你的名字。
- Here is the **key** to your dormitory. 這是你宿舍的鑰匙。
- Never forget to **turn off** the lights and air-conditioner before going out.
外出前不要忘了關燈和空調。

Sentences & Grammar

♪108-01 **1.** My hobbies are listening to music and reading books. **How about you**?
我的愛好是聽音樂和讀書，你們呢？

「How / What about...?」是常見的追問與反問方式，想更簡單，甚至能說「and...?」。

- I saw the "Free Coffee" sign. **What about** tea?
  我看到「免費咖啡」的招牌，那茶呢？
- She likes it here. **And** him, the boyfriend?
  她喜歡這裡，那他呢？她的男朋友。

♪108-02 **2.** I can **help** you if you have any questions.
你們有任何問題都可以找我。

表達協助時，可說 help (sb) ＋原形動詞。

- The boy **helps** the elders cook. He also helps walk the dog.
  小男孩幫長輩煮飯，也協助遛狗。

♪108-03 **3.** **Let's** do the cleaning by turns after. But first, we had better put the shoes outside.
我們之後可以輪流打掃。但首先，我們最好把鞋子放到外面。'

let's 是 let us 的縮寫，但 let us 多用於正式場合。兩者後接原形動詞。

- In this day of sorrow, **let us** pray for all the victims.
  在這悲傷的一天，讓我們為所有受害者祈禱。

♪108-04 **4.** Who is **on duty** today?
今天誰值日？

on duty 意指值班，反義為 off duty。

Self-Introduction!

不論是在學校或是職場，與他人相見，第一印象很重要！跟著下面的表格，一起準備好一段簡單易懂的自我介紹！

Hi!	問候
I am Lynn Lin. I come from Taiwan. You can call me Lynn.	名字、國家
I major in Mathematics. / I am a photographer.	科系／職業
There are four members in my family. My husband, me, and two cats.	家庭成員
I love to take pictures and travel around in my free time.	興趣 1
I enjoy go to cinemas alone.	興趣 2
I love dramas, I can watch dramas every day.	興趣 3
Nice to meet you all!	結尾
嗨！ 我是林琳。我來自臺灣。你可以叫我琳。 我主修數學系。／我是個攝影師。 我家有四個成員。我的丈夫，我，以及兩隻貓。 休閒時，我喜歡拍照和四處旅遊。 我喜歡自己去看電影。 我喜歡影集，我可以每天都看影集。 很高興認識大家！	
It's Your Turn! 試試看，模仿上面的文章，寫出自己的自我介紹：	

知識補充站

聊天禁忌！外國人超討厭別人問這幾件事：
大多數歐美國家的人並不喜歡一見面就問年紀，和亞洲地方恰恰相反；還有比較隱私的問題，像是薪資等，也是不熟的時候千萬別問的事情喔！
下次和外國人聊天，記得別踩到別人的地雷喔！

Review 3

A 填空練習

- I think this course is relatively more ___________.
  我認為這個課程相對更實用。 答案請見 P.080

- I don't know how to ___________ for the ___________.
  我不知道如何準備這個考試。 答案請見 P.086

B 引導造句

- **second 第二（的）**
  It's ____.
  就在第二層書架上。 答案請見 P.095

- **international 國際的**
  ____?
  我是國際生，可以參與教育工作坊嗎？ 答案請見 P.101

- **dormitory 宿舍**
  ____.
  答案請見 P.107

C 引導寫作

標題	Prepare for a Presentation
考試將近	
組讀書會	
準備內容	
考試範圍	

參考短文：考試將近。我和朋友打算組讀書會來準備考試。我們會準備一些想要討論的問題。聽說這次考試範圍很廣，但我認為我們準備的內容會在考試範圍裡。

Chapter 04

Workplace 職場

UNIT 01 How to prepare your resume? 如何準備履歷？
UNIT 02 How to prepare for an interview? 如何準備面試？
UNIT 03 Company Policies 公司規定
UNIT 04 In the Office... 在辦公室裡
UNIT 05 Documents and Procedures 文件與流程
UNIT 06 Talking on the Phone 電話應對
UNIT 07 Hold a Meeting 舉行會議
UNIT 08 Let’s talk about laying off and quitting. 我們來聊聊資遣與離職。

UNIT 01

How to prepare your resume?

如何準備履歷？

♪112-01 **You'd better prepare a resume in advance.**
最好提前準備一份履歷。

♪112-02 Do you have any questions about the resume?
你對這份履歷有任何的意見嗎？

♪112-03 Your resume will be very impressive.
你的履歷會讓人印象深刻。

♪112-04 May I have a look at your resume? 我能看看你的履歷嗎？

How to Speak

Guide to Resume Formats 履歷架構懶人包！

- Prepare your **personal information** with name, phone number, e-mail, and your address. 準備你的個人資訊，包括姓名、電話、電子信箱，還有地址。
- Put these on your resume as well: **education**, **work experience**, **skills**, and **achievements**, and **autobiography**. 這些資訊也要放上履歷：學歷、工作經歷、技能、成就、自傳。

單字地圖 Vocabulary

♪ 113-01 **resume 履歷**

♪ 113-02 **introduction 介紹**

- photo 照片
- basic information 基本資料
- personality 個人特質
- strengths 優點
- weaknesses 缺點

♪ 113-03 **skill 技能**

- design 設計
- edit 編輯
- copywriter 文案手
- advertising 廣告
- analysis 分析
- evaluate 評估
- audit 審核

♪ 113-04 **background 背景**

- education 學歷
- university 大學
- college 院校
- family 家人
- birthplace 出生地
- city 城市
- country 國家

♪ 113-06 **ability 能力**

- advance 進步
- assign 指派
- boost 提升
- enhance 強化
- fulfilled 達到的
- skilled 熟練的
- simplify 簡化

♪ 113-05 **work experience 經歷**

- management 管理
- manager 經理
- team 團隊
- teamwork 團隊合作
- part-time job 兼職
- full-time job 全職

More to Know

What should be listed on the resume? 履歷上應該要有什麼資訊呢？

- personal information 個人資訊
- objectives 應徵職位
- education 學歷
- work experience 工作經歷
- activities 參與活動
- skills 技能
- achievements 成就
- interests 興趣

跟著上方的指示依序列點排出、填入資訊，就能擬出一份你的履歷囉！

情節故事 Story

Who ♪114-01
You are are a senior in the workplace.
你是這個職場上的前輩。

Where ♪114-02
You are at a café.
你在一間咖啡廳裡。

When ♪114-03
It's a leisure Thursday night.
悠閒的週四晚上。

What ♪114-04
You are on a date with a friend. He is asking you for some advice.
你和一個朋友正在約會。他要向你請教一些建議。

How to Speak

給新鮮人的建議！想要給在職場新鮮人一些建議，你可以嘗試下列兩句：

- Detailed **personal skills** are better. 詳細的個人技能更好一些。
- Make sure your resume clearly reflects **your qualifications for the job**. 請確保履歷能明確告訴面試者你的能力可以勝任這份工作。

重點對話 Dialogue

履歷需要修改嗎？

♪115-09 對話練習！

♪115-01 Is there anything else I need to change in my resume?
我的履歷還有需要修改的嗎？

♪115-02 **Generally speaking,** it's perfect.
總體來說很完美。

♪115-03 Then, do you have any suggestions for this resume?
你對這份履歷有什麼建議嗎？

♪115-04 Not really. Maybe you can put a few photos in the attachment.
其實沒有。也許你可以在附件中放幾張照片。

可以幫我看看自傳嗎？

♪115-05 Can you help me check my autobiography?
你能幫我檢查我的自傳嗎？

♪115-06 Sure. Let me see.
當然。我看一下喔。

♪115-07 Is there anything wrong with my autobiography?
我的自傳有什麼問題嗎？

♪115-08 Well, you are supposed to write it objectively.
嗯，你應該客觀地撰寫。

More to Know

在英文常用的用法中，常會用一些片語放在開頭來強調本句話的語氣：

- Generally speaking, ... 一般來說
- Apparently, ... 顯然的
- Honestly, ... 其實
- Frankly speaking, ... 誠實地說
- Likewise, ... 同樣的
- Unfortunately, ... 不幸的是

這些片語都是美國人日常對話中常見用法，其中，「Honestly 其實……」在口語中有著較強烈的負面語氣，多半是會接著不認同的話語。

Sentences & Grammar

♪116-01 **1. You do have to focus on your practical experience.**

最好集中於你的工作經歷上。

肯定句通常不會出現助動詞，但要強調時就能寫出，後方接原形動詞。

- The food **does** taste weird.
  食物的確嚐起來怪怪的。
- Women in ancient China **did** have their feet bound.
  古代中國的女性真的有裹小腳。

do 當「動詞」時：

I 我	you 你、你們	he / she / it 他、她、它、牠	we 我們	they 他們	過去式（所有主詞）	過去分詞（所有主詞）
do	do	does	do	do	did	done

do 當「現在式與過去式的助動詞」時：

	I 我	you 你、你們	he / she / it 他、她、它、牠	we 我們	they 他們	過去式（所有主詞）
肯定	do	do	does	do	do	did
否定	do not don't	do not don't	does not doesn't	do not don't	do not don't	did not didn't

♪116-02 **2. Please perfect your job intentions.**

請將工作意向填寫完整。

「肯定祈使句」使用原形動詞，若要強調，可在動詞前加 do，如上面例句也能改寫成：

- Please do complete your job intentions.
  「否定」情境為「do not / don't ＋原形動詞」，若要強調，則可寫「don't you ＋原形動詞」，因為祈使句對象為你或你們。
- **Do not** talk to me ever again!
  =**Don't** talk to me ever again!
  =**Don't** you talk to me ever again!
  永遠別再跟我說話了！

Autobiography!

Name: Merlot Ellen Sun

First Name + *Middle Name* + *Family Name*

Gender: Male

Female or *Male* or *don't want to tell*

Birth Date: 02/07/1985

Date / *Month* / *Year*

Good day. My name is Merlot Sun. I was born in Taipei, Taiwan.
嗨。我的名字是孫梅洛。我出生在臺灣的臺北市。

自我簡介

I graduated from University ABC. I majored in Physics. I was a salesperson and I had worked in DEF company for four years.
我畢業於 ABC 大學。我主修物理系。我之前是一名業務員，我曾在 DEF 公司上班四年。

學經歷簡介

I am good at communicating. I can complete my tasks perfectly. I enjoy working in a team.
我很擅長溝通。我能將份內工作都做好。我喜歡和團隊合作。

能力簡介

I believe that my traits well fit the requirements of this position. Thank you, and hope to hear from you soon.
我相信我的特質十分吻合貴職位的需求。謝謝您，希望能早日得到您的消息。

未來期許

UNIT 02

How to prepare for an interview?

如何準備面試？

♪118-01 **It's my great honor to have this opportunity to introduce myself.** 很榮幸能有機會自我介紹。

♪118-02 I graduated from Birmingham University and my major is business administration.
我畢業於伯明罕大學，主修商業管理系。

♪118-03 I hope I can have the opportunity to give full play to my professional abilities.
我希望我能有充分發揮我的專業能力的機會。

♪118-04 In addition to the above mentioned, I like reading books on management in my spare time.
除了上述提到的，私下我還喜歡看管理相關書籍。

How to Say

結束語：

- That's all about myself, thank you very much.
  這就是關於我的介紹，非常感謝。

單字地圖 Vocabulary

♪119-01
interview 面試

♪119-02
attire 著裝

- suit 套裝
- casual 休閒的
- formal 正式的
- pants 長褲

補 shorts 短褲

- shirt 襯衫
- blouse 女性襯衫

♪119-03
questions 問題

- problem 問題
- situation 狀況
- curious 好奇的
- solve 解決
- deal with 處理

補 handle 處理；掌控

♪119-04
answers 答案

- reaction 反應
- behavior 行為
- feeling 感覺
- action 行為
- result 結果
- direct 直接的
- polite 有禮貌的
- manner 禮儀

♪119-05
positions 職位

- rank 職位
- level 等級
- competition 競爭
- society 社會
- job 職務
- firm 公司
- temporary 暫時的
- permanent 固定的

♪119-06
experience 經驗

- process 過程
- knowledge 知識
- skill 能力
- happen 發生
- affect 影響
- influence 影響
- change 改變

More to Know

『opportunity V.S. chance』：「機會」用英文怎麼說？

Question：

I really cherish this ________. 我很珍惜這次的機會。

- opportunity – 可遇不可求的機會；可能性
- chance – 機會；時機

Answer：opportunity

情節故事 Story

Who You are an interviewer in the online interview.
♪120-01 你是線上面試的面試者。

Where You are sitting at the desk in the living room.
♪120-02 你正坐在客廳的書桌前。

When It's three in the afternoon. Today is Monday.
♪120-03 現在是下午三點。今天是週一。

What You are having an online interview with a company manager.
♪120-04 你正和公司主管線上面試。

How to Speak

面試得分關鍵！這裡有三個面試常見問題，想一想，你會怎麼回答？

- **Why** do you want to do this work? 為什麼你想做這個工作呢？
- **What's the reason** for you choosing this job?
  你選這個工作的原因是什麼？
- **Do you know** about our company? 你了解我們公司嗎？

Dialogue

網路視訊面試

♪121-08 對話練習！

♪121-01 When can I know your decision?
什麼時候能知道面試結果？

♪121-02 We will give you our final decision in two days.
我們會在兩天內給你我們的最終決定。

♪121-03 Thank you. I expect to hear from you as soon as possible.
謝謝你，期待能儘快得到你的消息。

為什麼你適合這份工作呢？

♪121-04 Why are you qualified for this job?
為什麼你適合這個工作？

♪121-05 I believe this work will exert my talents, and I worked as an intern here last summer.
我相信這個工作能施展我的才能，且去年夏天我曾在此實習。

♪121-06 What's the reason for choosing this job? Do you know about our company?
你選這個工作的原因是什麼？你了解我們公司嗎？

♪121-07 Yes, I've got similar experiences of this job before.
是，我之前曾做過類似的工作。

More to Know

這樣回答更加分！

- My **ideal profession** is to be a manager.
  我理想的職業就是當一名管理者。
- I want to do what I like. 我想要從事喜歡的工作。
- I know this job is with **prospects of promotion**. 這個工作有晉升空間。

Sentences & Grammar

♪122-01 **1.** I **heard** there is a chance for regular training in this job.
我聽說這個工作有定期培訓的機會。

表達聽說時常用 heard，因常是之前聽到的。若聽到的消息是現在正在進行的事，或普遍性原則，則後接的子句則為現在式。

♪122-02 **2.** I **have** more challenges with this job.
這個工作對我來說更具有挑戰性。

have 當動詞時：

I 我	you 你、你們	he / she / it 他、她、它、牠	we 我們	they 他們	過去式 / 過去分詞（所有主詞）
have	have	has	have	have	had

have 當現在完成式與過去完成式的助動詞時：

	I 我	you 你、你們	he / she / it 他、她、它、牠	we 我們	they 他們	過去完成式（所有主詞）
肯定	have	have	has	have	have	had
否定	have not haven't	have not haven't	has not hasn't	have not haven't	have not haven't	had not hadn't

♪122-03 **3.** I can be qualified to this job **as** I have specialized skills.
因為我具備專業技能，所以能勝任這個工作。

as 當連接詞，也有因為之意，後接完整句子，如例句也可寫成：

- I can be qualified for this job **because** I have specialized skills.

其他例句：

- People are sick **as** they have been stressed for months.
  人們生病了，因為幾個月來壓力很大。

Experience an Interview!

想像你正在面試，試著用你的經歷回答以下問題吧！

Please introduce yourself. 請介紹一下自己。

It's my great honor to have this opportunity to introduce myself. I graduated from ______________________ and my major is ______________________. I hope I can have the opportunity to give full play to my professional abilities.

很榮幸能有機會自我介紹。我畢業於__________，主修__________。我希望我能有充分發揮我的專業能力的機會。

- introduce 介紹
- present 介紹
- self-introduction 自我介紹
- major in 主修
- minor in 副修

What do you do in your leisure time? 你悠閒時都做什麼呢？

I like ______________________________ in my spare time.

空閒時，我喜歡__________________。

- spare time = free time = leisure time 空閑時間
- spare 多出來的
- leisure 空閑

Why are you qualified for this job? 為什麼你適合這個工作？

____.
And I believe this work will exert my talents.

____。
而且，我相信這個工作能施展我的才能。

- qualify 使合格
- qualification 合格
- equip 具備
- equipment 裝備
- talent 才能
- gift 天賦

Chapter 04 職場

UNIT 03

Company Policies

公司規定

♪124-01 **Excuse me. Please tell me where the human resources department is.** 不好意思，請告訴我人力資源部在哪裡。

♪124-02 Could you tell me which the supervisor's office is?
請問你能告訴我哪間是主管的辦公室嗎？

♪124-03 Is there anything I need to know about the rules?
請問有什麼必須知道的規章制度嗎？

♪124-04 This is my first day at work, what should I know?
這是我上班的第一天，我應該注意什麼呢？

♪124-05 By the way, what are my duties?
順便請問一下，我的工作職責是什麼？

How to Say

職場上最重要的——「Welfare 福利」！

- How about the **welfare** of our company? 請問公司的福利制度？
- Could you tell me some **special benefits**?
  請問你能告訴我特殊的福利規定嗎？

單字地圖 Vocabulary

♪125-01
Rule 規定

♪125-02
regulation 規定

- official 正式的
- procedure 步驟
- usual 一般的
- discipline 紀律
- control 控制
- obey 遵守
- follow 聽從

♪125-03
welfare 福利

- bonus 獎金
- award 獎金
- punish 懲罰
- 補 punishment 懲罰
- blame 指責

♪125-04
duty 職責

- responsibility 責任
- authority 權力
- ensure 確保
- certain 肯定的
- on time 準時
- claim 聲稱
- resign 辭職

♪125-05
colleague 同事

- team 團隊
- group 小組
- co-worker 同事
- cooperate 合作
- 補 operate 操作
- collaborate 合作

♪125-06
office 辦公室

- room 空間
- space 空間
- organization 組織
- unit 單位
- department 部門
- agency 辦事處

♪125-07
other 其他

- purpose 目的
- reason 理由
- determination 意志
- need 需求
- requirement 規定
- demand 要求

More to Know

簡單的自我介紹三步驟——打招呼、介紹部門、結束語！

1. Hello, I am Jason. This is my first day at work.
   大家好，我是傑森，今天是我上班的第一天。
2. I worked in the business department before. Now I am a newer in the financial department.
   我以前在業務部工作，現在我是財務部的新員工。
3. I'm glad to be part of the team! 很高興成為團隊的一員！

情節故事 Story

Who You are new to the workplace.
♪ 126-01 你是辦公室新人。

Where You are in the office.
♪ 126-02 你在辦公室裡。

When It's the first day for you to work here.
♪ 126-03 這是你在這裡上班的第一天。

What You reading the office rules on the wall, waiting for the manager to take you around.
♪ 126-04 你正在讀牆上的辦公室規定，一邊等主管帶你看看環境。

How to Speak

Office Rules 辦公室規定：

- **Harmony:** Discriminatory behaviors or harassments are not allowed in the workplace. **和平：**禁止同仁間出現歧視行為或騷擾行為。
- **Clean:** No strict dress rules but please mind your own personal appearance. **乾淨：**沒有嚴格服裝規定，請注意個人儀容。

重點對話 Dialogue

請多指教！

♪127-06 對話練習！

♪127-01 Hello. This is my first day at work. Let me introduce myself. I am Jack.
大家好，今天是我上班的第一天。請允許我介紹一下我自己，我是傑克。

♪127-02 Welcome aboard. You are supposed to report to the personnel.
歡迎加入我們。你應該先到人事部報到。

♪127-03 Thanks. I've already been there.
謝謝，我已經去過了。

服裝規定

♪127-04 Is there any dress rule for our company?
請問公司有服裝規定嗎？

♪127-05 Our company requires everyone to wear formal clothes on meeting days. You can wear casually except on meeting days.
公司規定所有人在會議日都要穿正裝。會議日以外的時候都可以穿便服。

More to Know

Office Regulations 辦公室準則：

- **Duty:** Fulfill job duties. Be polite to colleagues, customers, and clients.
  職責：完成工作職責。對同事、顧客、客戶有禮貌。
- **Protection:** Treat properties (including office supplies and appliances... etc.) properly.
  保護：善待物品（包括辦公室日用品與電器等）。

Sentences & Grammar

♪128-01 **1.** Welcome **aboard**. Just ask if you need anything.
歡迎加入我們的行列。如果你有什麼需要儘管開口。

aboard 和 abroad 都是副詞，拼法相似，但 aboard 指在某交通工具上、並排、進入，而 abroad 有在國外、外面之意。

- All passengers **aboard** this plane are students going to study **abroad**.
  這飛機上的所有乘客都是要去出國念書的學生。

♪128-02 **2.** **Didn't** you punch in yesterday? That's a regulation of the company.
你昨天沒有打卡嗎？這是公司規定。

碰到否定問句時，若同意問句內容，要回答「No」。若不同意，要回答「Yes.」。以下是針對例句的回答。

- No, I didn't. I needed to rush home and just forgot.
  是啊，我沒打卡。我得趕回家，所以就忘了。
- Yes, I punched in! The security actually reminded me to.
  不是，我有打！其實，保全有提醒我。

♪128-03 **3.** You are supposed to punch in before 8:30 and punch out after 5:30 every work day **according to** our company rule.
根據公司的規定你應該在工作日八點半之前打卡，五點半之後打卡下班。

除了「according to」外，「in accordance with」與「based on」都有根據之意。3 種用法都後接名詞。

- **In accordance with** company policy, age discrimination isn't tolerated.
  根據公司規定，年齡歧視不被見容。
- The actress had a tough childhood **based on** her autobiography.
  依女演員的自傳來看，她的童年很辛苦。

What's Important?

♪129-01 **羅斯曼是辦公室中初來乍到的菜鳥，他決定要聽從其他同事的建議，整理出一張表格，請你幫助羅斯曼，將下面的辦公室筆記一起寫完吧！**

Rothman's Notes in the Office: 羅斯曼的辦公室筆記：	
1. Solutions 解決問題	Try to find solutions first. Find someone to ask if you cannot solve the problem. 遇到問題時，先嘗試解決。真的不行，要適時尋求同事的幫助。 _______________(1) would be the solution in the end. 團隊合作常會是最終解答。
2. Discipline 紀律	_________________(2): Suits. No shorts!! 服裝規定：正裝。不能穿短褲！！ Clean up your seat on Monday mornings. 每週一早上打掃自己的座位。
3. Punctuality 準時	Notice never be late for meetings!! 注意，會議千萬不能遲到！！
Who can help? Dial: 誰能幫忙？撥打： #______(3) to Sandy, she can tell you everyone's duty. #______ 給珊迪，她會告訴你大家的職責劃分。 #456 to _______(4), she knows everything about the printing machine. #456 給__________，她知道影印機的大小事。 #789 to Hank, he can help you with the ________________________(5). #789 給漢克，他能幫你__________________ 。	

解答

(1) Teamwork　(2) Dress Rule　(3) 123
(4) Jessica　(5) document files

職場

UNIT 04

In the Office...

在辦公室裡

♪130-01 **I'd like to order two printers and ten calculators.**
我要訂購兩台印表機和十個計算機。

♪130-02 I need ten staplers and two boxes of paper clips.
我需要十個釘書機和兩盒迴紋針。

♪130-03 Could you deliver it this afternoon? 今天下午能送到嗎？

♪130-04 We need to order stationery every month.
我們每個月都需要訂購辦公用品。

♪130-05 By the way, you'd better apply to the manager for the quantity of office supplies.
順便說一下，你最好跟經理申請購買辦公用品的數量。

How to Say

請求別人協助時，你可以善用以下兩個問句：

- **Please check the quantity of** stationery again.
  請重新核對辦公用品的數量。
- **Please order** twenty notepads as soon as possible.
  請儘快訂購二十本記事本。

單字地圖 Vocabulary

♪131-01 What's in the office? 辦公室常見物品

♪131-02 stationery 文具

- calculator 計算機
- stapler 釘書機
- paper clip 迴紋針
- correction tape 修正帶
- tape 膠帶
- scissors 剪刀
- cutter 美工刀
- envelope 信封

♪131-03 computer 電腦

- monitor 螢幕
- printer 列表機
- keyboard 鍵盤
- mouse 滑鼠
- laptop 筆記型電腦

♪131-04 computer-related 電腦相關

- speaker 喇叭
- database 資料庫
- disk 磁碟
- application (app) 應用程式
- software 軟體
- browser 瀏覽器
- webpage 網頁
- search engine 搜尋引擎

♪131-05 in the office 在辦公室裡

- printer 列表機
- scanner 掃描器
- fax machine 傳真機
- air conditioner 空調
- cubicle 隔間
- locker 儲物櫃

♪131-06 boss 老闆

- chairman 總裁
- vice chairman 副總裁
- president 董事長
- vice president 副董事長

♪131-07 company positions 工作職位

- consultant 顧問
- assistant 助理
- accountant 會計
- procurement 採購
- marketing 行銷
- sales 業務員
- engineer 工程師

More to Know

常見縮寫「C.E.O」指的到底是什麼職位？

- **C.E.O** – chief executive officer 執行長
- **C.F.O** – chief financial officer 財務長
- **C.I.O** – chief information officer 資訊長
- **C.O.O** – chief operating officer 營運長
- **C.T.O** – chief technology officer 技術長

Chapter 04 職場

情節故事 Story

Who ♪ 132-01
You are a worker in the company and have worked here for five years.
你是公司的職員，而且已經在這裡工作五年了。

Where ♪ 132-02
You are in the office with your colleagues.
你和同事在辦公室裡。

When ♪ 132-03
It's 12:00. It's time for lunch.
現在中午十二點。該吃午餐了。

What ♪ 132-04
You are waiting for your colleague to go to the restaurant.
你在等同事一起去餐廳。

How to Speak

想要推薦新來的同事員工餐廳有什麼好吃的，你可以這樣說！

- Our restaurant has more dishes than any other **staff restaurant**.
  我們公司餐廳的菜色比其它員工餐廳來得多。
- I suggest you have spaghetti, which is a specialty of the **staff canteen**. 我建議你吃義大利麵，這是員工餐廳的招牌料理。

Dialogue

影印機怎麼使用呢？

♪133-08 對話練習！

♪133-01 Excuse me. How can I use that copier?
不好意思。請問那台影印機該怎麼使用呢？

♪133-02 Please follow me. I will show you.
請跟我來，我會展示給你看。

♪133-03 How can I reproduce color photographs?
我怎麼才能複印彩色照片？

♪133-04 You need to buy some special paper first.
你需要先買一些特殊紙張。

中午一起吃飯

♪133-05 Do you want to go to lunch together?
中午要一起吃飯嗎？

♪133-06 Sure, I am in the mood for Mexican food.
當然好。我想吃墨西哥料理。

♪133-07 Ok. Please wait for me for ten minutes.
好，請等我十分鐘。

More to Know

工作日中午用餐的時段是一個令人興奮或放鬆的時刻，該怎麼詢問別人關於吃飯的問句呢？

- What's good today? 今天有什麼好吃的？
- What time do we have lunch? 我們幾點吃午餐？
- Are there any Korean foods in the staff restaurant?
員工餐廳裡有韓國料理嗎？

Sentences & Grammar

♪134-01 **1.** You can have a **rest** in the pantry.
你可以在茶水間休息一下。

暫停某事或某活動來休息：

take / have	＋ a / some	＋ rest	＋ from	＋名詞／動名詞

- The programmer **took some rest from** coding all night.
程式設計師從整晚寫程式抽身休息一下。

♪134-02 **2.** I'd really **appreciate** it if you could tell me where the pantry is.
若你能告訴我茶水間在哪，我會很感激。

appreciate 可表達感謝、感激，常被用來委婉問問題或請人幫忙。

- Parents would really **appreciate** it if childcare were subsidized by the government.
若政府補貼托育費用，父母會很感激。

♪134-03 **3.** **Go straight ahead** and turn right. It's in the corner.
一直走然後向右轉，就在角落裡。

go straight ahead 指往前直走，但 go ahead 則除了實體移動的意義外，也間接表達鼓勵人做某事。

- The firm urges its employees to **go ahead** with their own innovative ideas.
企業鼓勵員工放手發揮其創新點子。

♪134-04 **4.** If you **want to** chat, you'd better go to the tearoom in front.
如果你想聊天的話最好到前面的茶水間裡。

want to 更口語的寫法為 **wanna**，一樣後接原形動詞，不管主詞為何都不用變化，如例句改為「If you **wanna** chat…」，意義不變。在問句中則依主詞使用助動詞。限制是僅能用於現在式，「A want B to」句型也不能改用 wanna。

Order stationery together!

♪135-01 傑克要幫大家訂購文具，和傑克一起看看大家需要什麼吧？

Name	Item	Quantity
Jack	ruler blue pen	1 3
Sandra	tape envelope	2 30
Alan		
Wendy		
Carol		
Vicky		
Rebecca		
John		

解答

Alan	stapler scissors	1 1
Wendy	mouse keyboard	1 1
Carol	cutter tape	1 2
Vicky	correction tape	3
Rebecca	disk	2
John	locker	5

UNIT 05

Documents and Procedures

文件與流程

♪136-01 **Shall we sign the contract now?** 我們現在可以簽合約了嗎？

♪136-02 Let's make a new contract. 讓我們制定新的合約吧。

♪136-03 Are you satisfied with the proposed contract?
您對這個擬好的合約滿意嗎？

♪136-04 You are supposed to consult with the manager before making the contract.
在制定合約前，你應該先和經理商量一下。

♪136-05 We'll sign the contract tomorrow afternoon.
我們約定明天下午簽合約。

How to Say

對合約有疑慮時，不需要急著簽約，你可以先表達你的意見：

- **I'm not satisfied with** this clause in the contract.
  我對合約中的這項條款不滿意。
- Could you **make some concessions** on this clause?
  你能對這項條款做些讓步嗎？

單字地圖 Vocabulary

♪ 137-01
What about the documents? 跟文件有關的

♪ 137-02
document 文件

- official document 公文
- confidential document 機密文件
- legal document 法律文件
- forged document 偽造文件
- private document 私人文件

♪ 137-03
printer 印表機

- print 列印
- copy 複印
- letter 字體
- symbol 符號
- ink 墨水
- machine 機器
- laser printer 雷射印表機

♪ 137-04
text 文字

- title 標題
- context 上下文
- bold 粗體字
- newspaper 報紙
- book 書籍
- magazine 雜誌
- journal 期刊
- report 報導
- the press 新聞界

♪ 137-05
related 相關

- reporter 記者
- photographer 攝影師
- local press 地方報導
- freedom of the press 新聞自由

♪ 137-06
sign 簽名

- signature 簽名
- autograph （名人的）親筆簽名
- written 書面的

♪ 137-07
other 其他

- procedure 步驟
- step 步驟
- measure 步驟，措施
- conventional 常規的
- traditional 傳統的
- ordinary 普通的

More to Know

上面提及的偽造，專有名詞是「**forgery 偽造文書**」，意旨造假文件或刪改文件以達到特定目的或藉此獲得利益。相關的還有「**piracy 盜版**」和「**illegal copy 盜印**」等。

情節故事 Story

Who You are an office worker in the department.
♪138-01 你是這個部門的職員。

Where You are at the secretary's desk.
♪138-02 你站在祕書的桌子前。

When It's three in the afternoon. Still early.
♪138-03 現在是下午三點。還很早。

What You are waiting for the boss to sign on your document.
♪138-04 你在等老闆幫你的文件簽名

How to Speak

有禮貌的說明「文件需要簽名」的說法：

- Could you please **sign here**? 您能在這裡簽名嗎？
- These documents need **your signature**. 這幾份文件都需要您簽名。
- This document **needs to be signed** on the last page.
  這份文件需要在最後一頁簽名。

請給老闆簽名

♪139-08 對話練習！

♪139-01 The document needs to be signed by the boss.
這份文件需要老闆簽名。

♪139-02 Alright, I'll send it to the boss's office right away.
好的，我馬上送到老闆辦公室。

♪139-03 Where's our boss? The document is in urgent.
老闆去哪了？這份文件有點緊急。

♪139-04 He has just gone out. You can call him.
他剛剛出去。你可以打電話給他。

請副本給我

♪139-05 Please give me a copy of this email when you received it.
這封電子郵件回信時請副本給我。

♪139-06 Ok, I've sent you a copy of the e-mail. Please receive it.
好，我已經將電子郵件的副本寄給你了。請查收。

♪139-07 OK, I've seen it already.
好，我已經看到了。

More to Know

想要寫 e-mail 卻沒有頭緒嗎？寫 e-mail 之前，請掌握住三個重點！

1. **Greetings 招呼語**：「Hi」比「Dear」更普遍！
2. **Closing lines 結尾語**：Looking forward to hearing from you.
期待您的消息。
3. **Sign-offs 結尾語**：非正式的有「Best, / Warmly, / Regards, / Cheers, /Take care,」等，正式則有「Sincerely, / Warm wishes, / Respectfully yours」等。

Sentences & Grammar

♪140-01 **1.** Send the document to the supervisor's office for signature **at once**.
趕緊將這份文件送到主管辦公室簽核。

at once 有立刻、馬上之意，與 immediately 及 right away 一樣。

- The shoppers ran to the sales section **at once**.
  血拚者立即殺到打折區。

其他表示次數的說法：

once	twice	數字＋ times
一次	二次	三次以上

- The school team lost once and won twice this year.
  今年校隊一敗兩勝。

♪140-02 **2.** We would like to inform you **that** your report has passed.
我們想要通知你，你寫的報告通過了。

以 that 開頭的名詞子句，被當成主句的受詞或補語時，可將 that 省略。如例句中的 that 名詞子句就是補語，故可寫成：

- We would like to inform you your report has passed.

♪140-03 **3.** We would **be grateful if** you could resend the attachment.
如果你重新發送附件，我會很感激。

表達感謝也可用「be grateful for...」：

- The patient **is** extremely **grateful for** the liver from an anonymous donor.
  病人萬分感謝匿名捐獻者捐出的肝。

此外，例句假設未來的事：

- We **will** be grateful if you can resend the attachment.

其中，will 及 can 改為 would 及 could，聽起來更委婉、更有禮貌。

File the documents!

粗心的貝琪將下面的信封弄亂了，你可以幫助貝琪，將這些信封送到正確的位置嗎？

A: I am waiting for a document. There are contracts inside.
我在等一份文件。文件是合約。

B: I am waiting for a sealed document with a "confidential" sign on it.
我在等一份密封起來的文件，上面有著「機密」的標示。

C: I am waiting for a document. My mom sent it to me.
我在等一份文件。我媽之前寄給我的。

D: I am waiting for a document. There are official documents inside.
我在等一份文件。裡面有公文。

1. Official Document To __________
2. Confidential Document To __________
3. Private Document To __________
4. Private Document To __________

解答

1. To D　2. To B　3. To C　4. To A

UNIT 06

Talking on the Phone

電話應對

♪ 142-01 **Hello, who's calling, please?** 您好，請問哪位？

♪ 142-02 This is John. Can I speak to Lucy?
我是約翰，我能跟露西說話嗎？

♪ 142-03 I want to make sure of her operation time.
我想要確定一下她的手術時間。

♪ 142-04 Hello, I'm Lucy's colleague, David.
你好，我是露西的同事，大衛。

♪ 142-05 May I ask who's on the line? 請問是哪位？

How to Say

如果是緊急電話，需要幫對方留言，你可以這樣說：

- Would you like to **leave a message**? 請問您要留言嗎？
- For what matters are you calling him? Is it **urgent**?
  請問有什麼事？很緊急嗎？
- May I have your **contact information**? 請問可以留下您的聯繫方式嗎？

單字地圖 Vocabulary

♪143-01 phone 電話

♪143-02 action 動作
- dial 撥號
- call 打電話
- press 按下
- ring 電話鈴響
- get 找某人（電話中詢問）
- reach 找某人（電話中詢問）
- repeat 重複
- hear 聽見

♪143-03 device 裝置
- cellphone 手機
- telephone 電話
- smartphone 智慧型手機
- phone call 來電
- number 號碼

♪143-04 operator 接線生，總機
- wrong 錯誤的
- message 訊息
- connection 連線
- signal 訊號
- pardon 不好意思（請原諒我）

♪143-05 phrases 片語
- hang on 稍等
- hold on 稍等
- speak up 大聲一點

補 loud 大聲的
louder 更大聲

- leave a message 留下訊息
- speak to 跟某人說話

補 talk to 跟某人講話

- call back 回電
- call collect 打給對方的付費電話

♪143-06 free 有空的
- available 有空的
- unavailable 抽不開身的
- occupied 沒空的
- busy 忙碌的

♪143-07 chat 聊天
- discuss 討論
- text 文字聊天
- send 傳送（訊息）
- app 應用程式（縮寫）

Chapter 04 職場

More to Know

你知道「打給我」要用哪個動詞嗎？「打電話」又是用哪個動詞呢？

- call me 打給我
- **make** a phone call 打電話
- call me **at** work 打到我辦公室
- call me **at** this number 打這支電話給我

情節故事 Story

Who You are an operator in the office.
♪144-01 你是公司的接線生。

Where You are in the office.
♪144-02 你在辦公室裡。

When It's two p.m. It's meeting time for the managers.
♪144-03 現在是下午兩點。是主管們開會的時間。

What You are answering the phone for the manager.
♪144-04 你幫主管接了電話。

How to Speak

Oops! 對方好像打錯電話了！你可以這樣回答他：

- We have no Jack; **you have the wrong number**
  這裡沒有傑克，您打錯了。
- Sorry, there's no Mike here. 不好意思，這裡沒有麥可這個人。

Dialogue

要幫您留言嗎？

♪145-08 對話練習！

♪145-01 Hello, this is Carol.
您好，我是卡蘿。

♪145-02 Hi, is your supervisor there?
嗨，你的主管在嗎？

♪145-03 Sorry, the supervisor is on a business trip. Would you like to leave a message?
不好意思，主管正在出差。要幫您留言嗎？

♪145-04 Thank you. This is Emmett. Please tell him that I have been waiting for him.
謝謝。我是艾密特。請告訴他我有重要的事找他。

這裡是客服部

♪145-05 This is the customer service department. Who do you want to speak to?
這裡是客服部，請問找誰？

♪145-06 Could you put me through to Mike?
請問能幫我轉接麥可嗎？

♪145-07 I am sorry, Mike is in a meeting.
很抱歉，麥可正在會議中。

More to Know

- **不需要代為留言的回答：**

  No, thanks. I'll call him again tomorrow.
  不用了，謝謝，我明天再打給他。

- **轉告同事不在的資訊：**

  Sorry, he has gone home. You can call him on the phone.
  不好意思，他已經回家了，你可以打他的手機。

Sentences & Grammar

♪146-01 **1.** I am sorry, his line is **busy** now.
不好意思，他現在忙線中。

busy 的用法：

busy ＋ Ving	忙著做某動作
busy with...	忙著某事

- My classmates are either busy networking or busy with job hunting.
  我同學不是忙著建立人脈，就是忙著找工作。

♪146-02 **2.** I'**m afraid** you dial the wrong number.
您恐怕打錯電話了。

表達恐怕、遺憾時，要用「be afraid that 子句」，例句就是如此。若想說懼怕某人事物，則可說「be afraid (of...)」。

- We're afraid nothing more can be done with the cancer patient.
  針對那癌症病人，我們很遺憾無法再為他做更多了。
- Ken was afraid of clowns when he was little.
  肯小時候很怕小丑。

♪146-03 **3.** Literature department. This is Natalie speaking. May I ask who's calling?
這裡是文學系，我是娜塔麗。請問您是？

各種機構單位企業等接到電話時，通常會先報名稱。而電話兩端的人自報姓名時，不能用「I am…」或「My name is…」，而是用「This is ＋人名＋ speaking…」，或是「This is ＋人名」。若要詢問對方是誰，需用 this 代替 you。

- This is the Chen's. Mary speaking. Who's this?
  這裡是陳家公館，您好。我是瑪麗。您是？
- Hey, Mary! This is Uncle Ian. May I speak to your dad? 嘿，瑪麗！我是伊恩舅舅。請幫我轉給妳爸，好嗎？

Voice Messages

♪147-01 仔細聽電話訊息，幫忙在下面的欄位中填入正確的資訊。

1.

Who called? ____________

Her / his phone number: ____________

Why is she or he calling?

____

2.

Who called? ____________

Her / his phone number: ____________

Why is she or he calling?

____

3.

Who called? ____________

Her / his phone number: ____________

Why is she or he calling?

____

單字補充站

1. Mr. Chen 0912-345-678 Please call back. He wants to know if the contract is signed.	陳先生 0912-345-678 請回電。他想知道合約是否簽名了
2. Cathy 02-2333-2333 She called for the shipping problems.	凱西。 02-2333-2333 她打來確認運送的問題。
3. Morris He didn't leave his number. He wants to confirm the meeting time.	莫瑞斯。 他沒有留下電話。 他想確認會議時間。

UNIT 07

Hold a Meeting

舉行會議

♪148-01 **Are the theme and time of the meeting determined?**
會議的主題和時間確定了嗎？

♪148-02 Don't forget to confirm the topic and time of the meeting.
不要忘記確認會議的主題和時間。

♪148-03 I've been working on the conference process recently, and the theme and time of the meeting have not been determined.
我最近一直在製作會議流程，會議主題和時間還沒有確定。

♪148-04 Please let me briefly introduce the theme and time of today's meeting. 請讓我簡單介紹下今天會議的主題和時間。

How to Say

當被問及會議相關的問題，如果都已經安排好了，你可以這樣回答：

- It's almost **determined**. 基本上確定了。
- I think everything is **in order**. 我想一切都安排好了。

單字地圖 Vocabulary

Meeting 會議 ♪149-01

greet 打招呼 ♪149-02

- welcome 歡迎
- begin 開始
- end 結束
- attend 出席
- attendee 出席者
- staff 職員
- figure 人物
- location 位置

agenda 議程 ♪149-03

- purpose 目的
- item 項目
- list 清單
- copy 文件
- topic 主題
- issue 議題
- badge 名牌
- minutes 會議記錄

meetings 會議 ♪149-04

- conference 會議
- seminar 研討會
- reception 報到處
- banquet 宴會（商業）
- ceremony 典禮

decision 決定 ♪149-05

- agreement 同意
- disagreement 反對
- choice 選擇

補 choose 選擇

- possibility 可能性
- opinion 意見
- approve 贊同
- accept 接受
- argument 爭執

other 其他 ♪149-06

- solution 解決方法
- go over 回顧
- break 休息
- inform 通知

More to Know

會議中常見的片語：

- A.O.B 臨時動議（= any other business）
- to sum up 總結

情節故事 Story

Who You are an officer heading to the meeting room.
♪150-01 你是一名前往會議室的職員。

Where You are standing on the hallway.
♪150-02 你站在走廊上。

When It's 11 a.m. The meeting should be started in 10 minutes.
♪150-03 現在早上十一點。會議會在十分鐘內開始。

What You are chatting with your colleagues.
♪150-04 你正在和同事聊天。

How to Speak

和同事討論今天開會會討論什麼問題，你可以這樣說：

- What will we discuss at the meeting?
  這次會議我們要討論什麼問題？
- We will talk about the **personnel transfers** within the company.
  我們要討論公司內部的人事調動。

重點對話 Dialogue

今天會議延遲

♪151-09 對話練習！

♪151-01 Do you know the meeting was postponed to 2 o'clock in the afternoon?
你知道今天的會議延遲到下午兩點了嗎？

♪151-02 Really? **What's the reason?**
真的嗎？有什麼原因嗎？

♪151-03 I am not clear. But I heard the manager had an argument with the supervisor.
我不太清楚，但是我聽說經理和主管起爭執了。

♪151-04 Is that the reason why the meeting was delayed?
那是會議延遲的理由嗎？

♪151-05 I think so.
我覺得是。

會議主題

♪151-06 Excuse me. Do you know what the topic of our tomorrow's meeting is?
打擾一下，你知道我們明天的會議主題是什麼嗎？

♪151-07 Production figure.
生產資料。

♪151-08 Thanks! I need to prepare documents.
謝謝！我要來準備文件。

More to Know

- **the reason why** ……的理由

It's **the reason why** we don't talk anymore.
這就是為什麼我們不再交談的原因。

I want to know **the reason why** you give up. 我想知道你放棄的理由。

Sentences & Grammar

♪152-01 **1.** I will send you the report of the meeting **as soon as possible**.
我會儘快把會議的報告寄給你。

as... as... 的用法：

as... as	＋ it is（it is 可省略）	＋形容詞
as... as	＋ that 子句（that 可省略）	

- The factory produces **as quickly as** the products are sold.
  工廠生產的速度就像產品銷售的速度一樣快。
- Players ate **as much as** they could in the eating contest.
  大胃王選手盡其所能地吃。

♪152-02 **2.** Then I will give out **copies** of the report to you, and I hope you will be more impressed with the data.
然後我會把報告的副本寄給大家，希望大家對這些資料有個更深刻的印象。

copy 當名詞時指副本、影本；當動詞時指有影印、抄寫、抄襲之意。

♪152-03 **3.** In general, our company still has **a lot of** problems in finance.
總體上講，我們公司在財務方面還有很多的問題。

表達多數、大量時：

a lot of	＋可數名詞及不可數名詞
lots of	

很多：

many large number of	＋可數名詞
much large amount of	＋不可數名詞

- Tourists had **much** fun seeing a large number of dolphins swimming around the boat.
  遊客看到數量龐大的鯨豚圍著船游來游去，開心極了。

Make a Meeting Minutes.

♪153-01 **一起參與會議，完整這份會議資料吧！**

Topic: Details of Project ____(1) 標題：計畫______的細節討論	
Member 與會成員	Ella (Manager), Cathy, Brandon, Debby, Alex 經理艾拉，凱西，布蘭登，黛比，艾力克斯
Location 地點	Conference Room 會議室
Date 日期	_________________(2) , 2022 2022 年______月______日
Time 時間	__________________(3)
Discussion 討論	______________(4) of Project H Deadline and the production period 計畫 H 的______ 完成期限與製作期
Conclusion: 1. Double check the budget. Turn it in before next Wednesday. (Cathy) 2. Postpone the deadline to February 3rd. 結論： 1. 請凱西在下個週三之前重複確認預算。 2. 將完成期限延至二月三號。	

解答

1. H　　2. December 1st 12 月 1 日　　3. 10:00-11:00　　4. Budget 預算

UNIT 08

Let's talk about laying off and quitting. 我們來聊聊資遣與離職。

♪154-01 **I'm not happy here. I want to quit.**
我在這裡上班不愉快，我想辭職了。

♪154-02 I'm not willing to do this endless work.
我不願意做沒完沒了的工作。

♪154-03 I plan to quit next week and then move abroad.
我打算下週辭職，之後移居國外。

♪154-04 I want to quit and find a better job in a big company.
我想要辭職，然後去大公司找一份更好的工作。

How to Say

關心同事離職的原因，你可以這樣詢問：

- **What** are you going to do after you leave? 離職後你打算做什麼？
- **Why** are you leaving? 為什麼你要離職？
- I heard you had the idea of quitting. 我聽說你有了辭職的想法。

單字地圖 Vocabulary

♪155-01
Resign and Lay off 辭職與解雇

♪155-02
resign 辭職

- resignation 辭職
- quit 辭職，放棄
- leave 離開
- position 職位
- payment 薪水

♪155-03
employ 雇用

- employment 就業
- employer 雇主
- employee 員工
- unemployed 失業的
- between jobs 待業中
- unpaid leave 留職停薪

♪155-04
lay off 解僱

- fire 開除
- discharge 解僱
- strike 罷工
- severance pay 資遣費
- terminate 解僱

♪155-05
retire 退休

- retirement 退休
- step down 下台，離職，退位
- age 年紀
- ill 生病的
- pass 過世

♪155-06
duty 責任

- responsible 負責任的
- control 控制
- undertake 執行，從事
- engage in 從事

♪155-07
other 其他

- priority 優先考量

補 priority seats 博愛座

- important 重要的
- transition 轉變

補 transit 運輸

- turn into 變成
- change 轉變
- process 過程

More to Know

與責任相關的片語：

- **priority 首要任務**
- **make a transition with 工作交接**
- **be responsible for 負起……責任**

情節故事 Story

Who You are a worker. You want to quit your job.
♪ 156-01 你是一名職員。你想要離職。

Where You are in the pantry, having a cup of hot tea with a colleague.
♪ 156-02 你在茶水間裡，和同事一起喝一杯熱茶。

When It's June. It's summer.
♪ 156-03 現在是六月，夏天到了。

What You tell the colleague that you are leaving.
♪ 156-04 你告訴同事你要離開了。

How to Speak

向同事執行「交接」指令，你可以這樣說：

- Please **hand over** the documents **to** Peter. 請和彼得交接這些檔案。
- Please **hand over** your work **within** a week.
  請在一個星期內交接完你的工作。

Dialogue

資遣公告

♪157-07 對話練習！

♪157-01 Did you see the announcement from the personnel department? Mike was fired.
你看到人事部的公告了嗎？麥可被解雇了。

♪157-02 Really? Was it because he lost the company's biggest client?
真的嗎？是因為他丟了最大客戶的事嗎？

♪157-03 I am not clear.
我不清楚。

♪157-04 I saw the announcement of the personnel, which reads him was fired.
我看到人事的公告了，上面寫著他被辭退了。

離職

♪157-05 I think I'm not qualified for the job and want to leave.
我想我不能勝任這個工作，想離開這裡。

♪157-06 I thought you were working well. This job fits you well.
我原本以為你工作的很順利。這個工作很適合你呢。

More to Know

不論做什麼工作、做了多久，將手邊的文件隨時整理好是工作上最重要的事情。那麼，「整理文件」要怎麼說呢？如果想要「按照順序整理」，用英文要怎麼表達呢？請見以下：

- First, **sort** these files **according to importance**.
  首先，將這些文件按照重要性排序。
- Let's start with the **file classification**. 我們先從文件分類開始吧。

Sentences & Grammar

♪158-01 **1.** I was **dismissed**, what should I do now?
我被解雇了，現在該怎麼辦？

解雇的說法除了 dismiss 外，也有 fire 和 lay off。be made redundant 指被變得多餘，套用在職場就代表被解雇。

- Manual laborers **were made redundant** after machines were introduced.
體力勞動性質勞工在機器被引進後就被炒了。

♪158-02 **2.** You are supposed to **communicate** with the manager.
你應該和經理溝通一下。

communicate 溝通、交流、傳達。

- Management in Asian companies isn't used to **communicating** with employees.
亞洲企業的管理層不習慣與員工溝通。

♪158-03 **3.** You'd better find out **why** you were dismissed.
你最好找出被辭退的原因。

此例句中是將「疑問詞 why 開頭的名詞子句」當「find out」的受詞。另一方式可換成「the reason」，後接 that 子句，即：

- You'd better find out **the reason (that)** you were dismissed.

♪158-04 **4.** I'd be happy to hear your **advice**.
我很高興能聽到你的建議。

advice 與 suggestion 同義，用法如下：

可數名詞：	a	suggestion
	suggestions	
不可數名詞：	a piece of some lots of	+ advice

Gossip Time!

和朋友一起聊聊公司近況吧！回想本單元學過的單字，你都學會了嗎？一起挑戰寫寫看下面空格該填入的單字吧！

Did you see the announcement from the personnel department? Sam was _________.
你看到人事部的公告了嗎？山姆被解雇了。

I saw it. He is a good colleague to me.
He was ___________________. It surprised me.
我有看到。他對我來說是個很好的同事。 他被資遣，我很驚訝。

Why did you _________? 你 什麼要辭職？

I'm not happy here. So I ________.
我在這裡上班不愉快，我就辭職了。

Who will take your _______________ after you quit? Kent?
那你離職之後誰接你的責任？肯特嗎？

Yes. I _________________ to Kent this week.
對，我這禮拜交接給肯特了。

Oh, I see. And did you tell your colleagues that you are _________________?
喔，了解。那你有跟其他同事說你要離開了嗎？

解答

fired / laid off / quit / quit / responsibility / handed over / leaving

Review 4

A 填空練習

- It's my great honor to have this _______introduce myself.
  很榮幸能有機會自我介紹。 答案請見 P.118

- I'd like to order two ___________ and ten ___________.
  我要訂購兩台印表機和十個計算機 。 答案請見 P.130

B 引導造句

- **This is... 我是⋯⋯**

  This is ___________ . Can I ___________ ?.
  我是 ______ （請填入你的名字），我能跟露西說話嗎？ 答案請見 P.142

- **introduce 介紹**

  ____?
  請讓我簡單介紹下今天會議的主題和時間。 答案請見 P.148

- **quit 辭職**

  ____.
  答案請見 P.154

C 引導寫作

標題	A day in the office 辦公室的一天
上班第一天	
訂購辦公用品	
打電話給客戶	
確認會議時間	

參考短文：今天是我上班的第一天。我和同事訂購了三隻筆和一支尺。下午，我打了通電話給客戶。我和客戶確認了下週二的會議時間。

Chapter

05

Go Shopping
去逛街

UNIT 01

Shopping at the Supermarket

超市購物

♪ 162-01 **Your total is 512 dollars.** 您的帳單是 512 美元。

♪ 162-02 The bill comes to 125 dollars. 帳單總計是 125 美元。

♪ 162-03 How would you like to pay? 您怎麼付款？

♪ 162-04 Will you pay by cash or by card?
現金結帳還是銀行卡結帳？

♪ 162-05 Please enter the password and sign here.
請在這裡輸入密碼並簽字。

♪ 162-06 This is your change. 這是找您的零錢。

How to Speak

想要用信用卡結帳，你可以這樣問：

- Can I **pay by** credit card? 我能用信用卡結帳嗎？
- Do you **accept** credit card? 你們接受信用卡結帳嗎？

單字地圖 Vocabulary

♪163-01 **foods 食物**

♪163-02 **fast food 速食**

- deli 即時食品（熱食沙拉等）
- canned food 罐頭食品
- boxed meal 盒裝微波食物
- lunch meat 午餐肉

補 spam 午餐肉

♪163-03 **staples 主食**

- rice 米
- grains 穀物
- pasta 義大利麵
- breakfast cereal 早餐穀片
- noodles 麵條

♪163-04 **condiments 醬料**

- ketchup 番茄醬
- mustard 黃芥末醬
- hot sauce 辣醬

♪163-05 **drinks 飲料**

- milk 牛奶
- yougurt 優酪乳
- vinegar 醋
- juice 果汁
- cider 蘋果或洋梨汁發酵而成的含酒精飲料
- soda 汽水
- sparkling water 氣泡水
- distilled water 蒸餾水

♪163-06 **snacks 零食**

- chip 薯片
- cookie 餅乾
- candy 糖果
- gum 口香糖

♪163-07 **other 其他**

- vegetables 蔬菜
- fruits 水果
- meat 肉類
- seafood 海鮮
- beverage 飲料
- dairy products 奶製品
- alcohol 酒類

More to Know

- **超市商品分類：**國外的超市規模大，可以想像是臺灣的大賣場。商品種類多、數量也多，如果想要找尋商品的話，可以依據商品分類來尋找比較容易喔！
- **看懂特價訊息：**Today we have a **clearance sale**. 我們今天清倉出售。

情節故事 Story

Who ♪ 164-01
You are a customer in the supermarket.
你是超市裡的顧客。

Where ♪ 164-02
You are buying groceries in the supermarket.
你在超市裡買日用品。

When ♪ 164-03
Today is Aug 25th. The payday is Sep 5th.
今天是八月二十五號。發薪日是九月五號。

What ♪ 164-04
You are wondering what's on sale.
你正在想有什麼是正在特價的呢。

How to Speak

想要知道哪些商品在打折，這樣開口問：

- Is there anything **on sale** today? 今天有特價嗎？
- Does the cup have a **special offer**? 這個杯子在打折嗎？

重點對話 Dialogue

今天商品大優惠

♪165-08 對話練習！

♪165-01 I would like to **check out**.
我要結帳。

♪165-02 Do you have a membership card?
您有會員卡嗎？

♪165-03 Yes, I do. Is there a discount today?
我有。今天有優惠嗎？

♪165-04 All goods are thirty percent off, and ten percent off again on closing.
今天商品全部 7 折，會員結帳再 9 折。

♪165-05 That's awesome!
太棒了！

♪165-06 Would you like to get 1 more chocolate chip cookie? It's now buy 2 get one free.
您要再多拿一份巧克力脆片餅乾嗎？現在買二送一喔。

♪165-07 Sure!
好啊！

More to Know

錢的不同表示法：

- fortune 財富
- cash 現金
- bill 鈔票
- coin 硬幣
- change 找零
- credit card 信用卡
- debit card 金融卡
- withdraw 提款
- save 存錢

Sentences & Grammar

♪166-01 **1.** Excuse me, where is the **toothbrush**?
不好意思，請問牙刷在哪裡？

> **tooth** 為單顆牙齒，複數就變成 **teeth**。
>
> toothbrush 外，由 tooth 衍生的字或片語有「tooth whitening 牙齒美白、tooth fairy 牙仙、toothache 牙痛」等。
>
> 然而，「**dent**」為牙齒的拉丁詞根，由此也衍生出相關字詞，如「dental 牙齒的、dentist 牙醫、denture 假牙」等。

♪166-02 **2.** Could you let me know the man clothes are on **the first floor** or on **the second floor**?
你能告訴我男裝是在一樓還是在二樓嗎？

> 指定樓層時要用序數，但在英國、前英國殖民地國家、日本、部分歐洲國家等地，一樓是 ground floor，二樓則為 first floor，依此類推。
>
> - This apartment has **ten floors** with a pool on the **tenth floor**.
>   這棟公寓有十層樓，十樓有泳池。
>
> 其他樓層包含「basement 地下室」與「top floor 頂層」。

♪166-03 **3.** Today only kitchen utensils are ten **percent off**.
今天只有廚房用具打九折。

> 英語表達打折折數的方式與中文相反，10% off 指價格的十分之一被去掉了，就是打九折之意。
>
> - We offer **buy one, get one free** for large de-caf coffee, and there's an additional **twenty percent off** for the purchase of four large at once, so that's **sixty percent off** each.
>   大杯低咖啡因咖啡買一送一，一次買四杯再打八折，這樣是每杯四折。

Let's make dinner!

你打算為了今天的晚餐大展身手，所以到超市購買食材，但就是有幾樣東西找不到在哪裡……試著詢問店員看看吧！

- ~~pasta 義大利麵~~
- ~~ketchup 番茄醬~~
- tomato 番茄
- ~~pork 豬肉~~
- ~~onion 洋蔥~~
- ~~garlic 大蒜~~
- salt 鹽巴
- pepper 胡椒
- ~~rosemary 迷迭香~~
- ~~basil 羅勒~~

Excuse me, where can I get ____________________?
不好意思，請問番茄在哪裡？

It is on the first shelf.
在第一個貨架上。

I see. I'm also wondering where's the _______ and _______.
我了解了。我也想知道鹽巴跟胡椒在哪裡。

They are on the third shelf on the second floor.
在二樓的第三個貨架上。

Thank you.
謝謝。

單字補充站

- pork 豬肉
- chicken 雞肉
- beef 牛肉
- mutton 羊肉
- tomato 番茄
- onion 洋蔥
- garlic 大蒜
- scallion 青蔥

UNIT 02

Clothing Shopping

購買服飾

♪168-01 **Can I try this shirt on?** 這件襯衫可以試穿嗎？

♪168-02 What is your size? 您穿什麼尺寸呢？

♪168-03 Sorry, this white coat is not allowed to try on.
抱歉，這件白色的外套沒辦法試穿。

♪168-04 I'll get you a new one to try on. 我拿一件新的來給您試穿。

♪168-05 Which one would you like to try on? 您想要試穿哪件？

♪168-06 I'd like to try on the red dress. 我想試穿那件紅色的連衣裙。

♪168-07 Maybe you can try on a large one.
也許您可以穿大一號的試試看。

How to Say

問店員的更衣室在哪邊：

- Where is the changing room? 更衣室在哪裡？
- Sorry, the changing room is full. 抱歉，更衣室已經滿了。
- The changing rooms are on your right. 更衣室在你的右手邊。

Vocabulary

♪169-01 **clothes 衣服**

♪169-02 **outfits 著裝**

- blouse 女用襯衫
- shirt 男用襯衫（現代美式英語也可衍伸為上衣）
- uniform 制服
- one-piece suit 一件式套裝
- dress 洋裝

♪169-03 **tops 上衣**

- T-shirt T 恤
- polo shirt Polo 衫
- jumper 套頭衫
- turtleneck 高領毛衣
- hoodie 連帽 T 恤
- cardigan 開襟毛衣
- jacket 夾克
- sweatshirt 運動衫
- sweater 毛衣
- pullover 套頭毛衣

♪169-04 **coats 外套**

- leather jacket 皮外套
- trench coat 風衣
- baseball jacket 棒球外套
- cloak 斗篷
- hosiery 針織衫

♪169-05 **bottoms 下身**

- pants 褲子
- trousers 褲子
- jeans 牛仔褲
- sport pants 運動褲
- leggings 內搭褲
- skirt 裙子
- mini skirt 迷你裙
- long skirt 長裙
- shorts 短褲

♪169-06 **underwears 內衣褲**

- boxer 男生四角褲
- panties 女生內褲
- bikini 比基尼
- bra 內衣
- sports bra 運動內衣
- lingerie 內衣
- underpants 內褲
- tank top 無袖背心

♪169-07 **socks 襪子**

- stockings 絲襪
- ankle socks 踝襪
- low cut socks 船型襪
- flat socks 隱形襪
- pantyhose 絲襪
- tights 褲襪
- fishnets 網襪

More to Know

衣服的材質：

- wool 羊毛
- velvet 絲絨
- silk 絲
- cotton 棉
- fleece 羊毛
- leather 皮革
- chiffon 雪紡
- linen 亞麻
- cashmere 克什米爾羊毛

Chapter 05 去逛街

情節故事 Story

Who ♪170-01
You are a customer in a shopping mall.
你是購物中心裡的消費者。

Where ♪170-02
You are in a clothing store.
你在一間服飾店。

When ♪170-03
It's fall.
現在是秋天。

What ♪170-04
You are trying a sweater on.
你在試穿一件毛衣。

How to Speak

想要要求衣服的款式或顏色，你可以這樣說：

- I want to change to a **light** sweater. 我想換一件淺色的毛衣。
- I'd like a pair of jeans in **latest** style. 我想要一條最新款的牛仔褲。
- Do you have any other **colors** about this shirt?
  這件襯衫有別的顏色嗎？

Dialogue

有其他顏色或尺寸嗎？

♪171-08 對話練習！

♪171-01 I am looking for a sweater.
我想買一件毛衣。

♪171-02 How about this one? It's the most popular style this year.
這件怎麼樣，這是今年最流行的款式。

♪171-03 Can I try it on?
我能試穿嗎？

♪171-04 Yes, the fitting room is over there.
可以，更衣室在那裡。

♪171-05 I like this style very much, but do you have a larger size?
我很喜歡這個款式，但是有大一號的嗎？

♪171-06 I'm sorry, madam. The larger size of this sweater is out of stock.
抱歉，女士。這件毛衣大一號已經沒有庫存了。

♪171-07 Oh, alright. What a pity!
喔，好吧。真可惜！

More to Know

想要找什麼風格的衣服呢？

- casual 休閒的
- formal 正式的
- elegant 高雅的
- comfy 舒服的
- vintage 復古的
- formal casual 正式休閒裝
- denim 單寧
- plain 素色
- bohemian 波西米亞風

Sentences & Grammar

♪172-01 **1.** This dress doesn't **suit** me very well.
這件衣服不太適合我。

suit 與……相配、適合。

- This stylish haircut will **suit** Jane, who's the lead singer of a rock band.
  這個時髦的髮型將很適合身為搖滾樂團主唱的簡。

♪172-02 **2.** I like the style of this dress very much, but it doesn't **fit** me.
我很喜歡這件裙子的款式，但是大小不適合。

fit 當動詞和名詞，都能用來表達合身。

- The boots are a comfortable **fit**.
  這靴子很舒適合腳。

♪172-03 **3.** I think the collar of this shirt is **too** loose.
我覺得這件襯衫的領子太鬆了。

too 通常在語氣上比「so、very、really」強烈，更強調太、過分地。「too ＋形容詞＋ for 人＋ to ＋動詞」：表達太過如何而不能做某事。

- The street is **too** narrow for me **to** drive through.
  街道窄到我無法開車穿過。

♪172-04 **4.** This dress is a little tight. Do you have a **bigger** one?
這件衣服有點緊，有大一點的嗎？

母音為短母音的單音節形容詞，比較級要重複字尾加 er，最高級要重複字尾加 est，如：

形容詞	比較級	最高級
big	bigger	biggest
thin	thinner	thinnest

Which one is the best?

艾咪的生日快到了，而你想要買一件衣服當作生日禮物給她；請透過提示，看看哪一件最適合艾咪吧！

About Amy
艾咪大小事

- I She doesn't like red.
  她不喜歡紅色。
- I She prefers dress to pants.
  比起褲子，她更喜歡洋裝。

- I She likes cotton clothes.
  她喜歡棉質的衣服。
- I She doesn't think leather jacket suits her very well.
  她認為皮外套不太適合她。

- A blouse
- Black
- Chiffon I

A

- A dress
- Pink
- Cotton

B

- A jacket
- Brown
- Leather

C

解答

The answer is B. 答案為 B。

A	B	C
▪襯衫（女用）	▪洋裝	▪皮外套
▪黑色	▪粉紅色	▪棕色
▪雪紡	▪棉質	▪皮革

UNIT 03

Shopping for Shoes

購買鞋子

♪174-01 **Do you have these shoes in my size?**
請問這雙鞋有我的尺寸嗎？

♪174-02 This style of shoes is on my pants; do you have my size?
這雙鞋的款式很搭我的褲子，請問有我的尺寸嗎？

♪174-03 The black leather shoes have been short in size.
那款黑色的皮鞋只剩下零碼了。

♪174-04 This pair of sports shoes looks great. Do you have size 23?
這雙運動鞋看著真不錯，有 23 號嗎？

♪174-05 Sorry, there is no bigger size. 抱歉，已經沒有更大號了。

♪174-06 We need your size to transfer from the head office.
您的尺寸我們要從總部調貨。

How to Say

想買鞋，要先確認腳的尺寸：

- What size do you wear? 您穿幾號？
- I wear size 23. 我穿 23 號。

單字地圖 **Vocabulary**

♪175-01 **shoes** 鞋子

♪175-02 **casual** 休閒鞋
- flats 平底鞋
- slip-ons 平底休閒鞋
- oxford 牛津鞋
- loafers 樂福鞋

♪175-03 **heels** 高跟鞋
- Mary Janes 瑪莉珍鞋
- high heels 高跟鞋
- platform shoes 厚底高跟鞋
- wedges 楔型鞋
- kitten heels 短跟鞋

♪175-04 **boots** 靴子
- thigh high boots 高筒靴
- knee high boots 及膝靴
- cowboy boots 牛仔靴

♪175-05 **sneakers** 球鞋
- trainers 運動鞋（英國）
- runners 運動鞋（澳洲）
- canvas shoes 帆布鞋

♪175-06 **slippers** 拖鞋
- flip-flops 夾腳拖鞋
- rain boots 雨鞋
- sandals 涼鞋

♪175-07 **other** 其他
- clogs 木屐
- ballet flats 平底芭蕾舞鞋
- open toe 露趾鞋
- peep-toe 魚口鞋

More to Know

Size List 各國尺寸一覽：

	女			男			
cm	23	24	25	26	27	28	29
UK	4	5	6	7	8	9	10.5
US	6	7	8	8	9	10	11.5
EUR	37	38	39.5	41.5	42.5	44	46

情節故事 Story

Who ♪176-01
You work in a shoe shop.
你在鞋店工作。

Where ♪176-02
You are in the shoe shop you work.
你在你工作的鞋店裡。

When ♪176-03
It's a happy night.
這是一個開心的晚上。

What ♪176-04
You are chatting with a customer.
你正在跟顧客聊天。

How to Speak

想要別的款式，那就問問看吧！

- Do you have any other shoes in this color?
  你們有沒有這個顏色、其它款式的鞋子？
- We also have dozens of different styles of high heels.
  我們還有十幾種不同款式的高跟鞋。

重點對話 Dialogue

我想找平底鞋

♪177-09 對話練習！

♪177-01 Would you like to try on these white high heels, madam?
女士，您想試試這雙白色的高跟鞋嗎？

♪177-02 No, I'd like to buy a pair of flat shoes.
不了，我想買一雙平底鞋。

♪177-03 This way, please. There may be your style.
這邊請，這裡可能有您想要的款式。

♪177-04 I'd like to try on that pair with patterns.
我想試穿那雙上面有花紋的鞋子。

有大一號嗎？

♪177-05 Sir, does this pair fit your feet?
先生，這雙鞋合腳嗎？

♪177-06 They are too tight; do you have a bigger pair?
太緊了，有大一號的嗎？

♪177-07 I'm sorry; this is the last pair of this style.
抱歉，這是這個款式的最後一雙了。

♪177-08 Please get me a pair of other styles.
請幫我拿一雙其它款式的吧。

More to Know

確認尺寸，才能拿到適合的鞋子！

- Would you please tell me your **American size**?
請您說一下您的美國尺寸？
- I only know my **Britain size** is 4.5.　我只知道我的英國尺寸是 4.5。

Sentences & Grammar

♪178-01 **1.** Do you have any sports **shoes**?
請問你們有運動鞋嗎？

shoe 是鞋子統稱，運動鞋類說法有「sports shoes / sneakers 運動鞋」。

♪178-02 **2.** If you are not **satisfied with** this shoe, we have other styles.
如果您對這個鞋子不滿意，我們還有其它款式。

satisfy 為動詞，代表使滿足、符合。
形容詞「satisfying」意指「事物令人感到滿意的」。
形容詞「satisfied」，則指「某人感到滿意的」。

- The product quality **satisfies** our standard, so we're quite **satisfied** with your performance. Hopefully our future interactions will be as **satisfying** as this one.
  產品品質達到我們的標準，所以我們挺高興的。期待未來我們之間的互動會像這次如此令人滿意。

♪178-03 **3.** **Apart from** sports shoes, we also have the latest styles of boots.
除了運動鞋，我們還有最新款的靴子。

apart from 除了……之外。也可用「other than、besides」代替。

- The hotel provides late-night snacks **other than** standard breakfast.
  飯店在標準早餐外還提供消夜。

♪178-04 **4.** I don't want **a pair of** high heels; do you have any flat shoes?
我不想買高跟鞋，你們有平底鞋嗎？

意指一雙的 pair 本身為複數性質，故即使只有一雙，在動詞變化上也要以複數對待。

- **A pair of** limited Air Jordan is gonna cost you a fortune.
  一雙限量版 Air Jordan 喬丹鞋得花你很多錢。

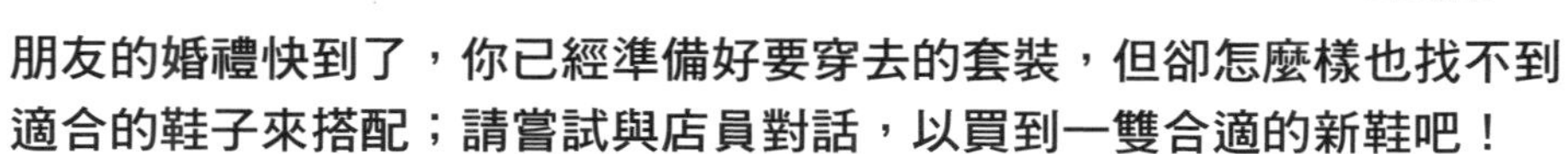

朋友的婚禮快到了，你已經準備好要穿去的套裝，但卻怎麼樣也找不到適合的鞋子來搭配；請嘗試與店員對話，以買到一雙合適的新鞋吧！

I'd like to buy a pair of ________. 我想買一雙牛津鞋。

牛津鞋是以下哪個呢？

☐ Oxford ☐ flip-flops ☐ cowboy boots

This way, please. There may be your style.
這邊請，這裡可能有您想要的款式。

I'd like to ________ that pair with patterns.
我想試穿那雙上面有花紋的鞋子。

試穿該怎麼說呢？

☐ try on ☐ try in ☐ try outots

Does this pair fit your feet? 這雙鞋合腳嗎？

They are too tight; do you have a ________ pair?
太緊了，有大一號的嗎？

大一點該怎麼說呢？

☐ same ☐ smaller ☐ bigger

解答

- 牛津鞋／夾腳拖鞋／牛仔靴
- try on
- 相同的／小一點的／大一點的

UNIT 04

Shopping for Accessories

購買首飾

♪180-01 Excuse me, do you provide packaging?
打擾了，你們店有包裝嗎？

♪180-02 Yes. But you have to pay extra money.
是的，但是你得另外付錢。

♪180-03 You can choose the packaging for the jewelry, and we will pack it for you. 你可以為珠寶選擇包裝，我們會替你包裝好。

♪180-04 It is a free service in our shop. 這是我們店裡的免費服務。

♪180-05 I want to give it to my mother as a birthday present.
我想把它作為生日禮物送給我媽媽。

How to Say

買好了想要的東西，如果要送人，就可以請店員順手包裝起來。那麼，「請幫我包裝」的英文要怎麼說呢？

- Can I get the brooch gift-wrapped? 可以幫我把胸針包裝成禮物嗎？
- I'd like to get it gift-wrapped. 我想把它包裝成禮品。

單字地圖 Vocabulary

♪181-01 Shopping for accessories 購買首飾

♪181-02 metal 金屬

- bronze 銅
- silver 銀
- gold 金
- platinum 白金（鉑）
- stainless steel 不鏽鋼

♪181-03 accessories I 配件（一）

- earrings 耳環
- ring 戒指
- necklace 項鍊
- bangle 手環
- watch 手錶

♪181-04 accessories II 配件（二）

- bracelet 手鍊
- jewelry 珠寶
- choker 頸鍊
- anklet 踝鍊
- sunglasses 太陽眼鏡
- pocket watch 懷錶
- bow tie 領結
- necktie 領帶
- scarf 圍巾
- belt 皮帶
- tie pin 領帶夾
- pendant 吊墜

♪181-05 semi-precious stones 半寶石

- jade 玉
- pearl 珍珠
- amber 琥珀
- ivory 象牙
- moonstone 月長石
- crystal 水晶
- turquoise 土耳其石

♪181-06 precious stones 寶石

- diamond 鑽石
- emerald 綠寶石
- ruby 紅寶石
- sapphire 藍寶石

More to Know

有時候肉眼看不出飾品的材質，你可以試試問對方：

- Is it **pure gold** or **karat**? 這是純金的還是 K 金的？

情節故事 Story

Who You are a young man who is searching for a gift.
♪182-01 你是一個在找禮物的年輕人。

Where You are in a shopping mall.
♪182-02 你在一間購物中心裡。

When It's June. Your partner's birthday is coming.
♪182-03 現在是六月。你伴侶的生日就快到了。

What You are buying some lovely accessories in a shop.
♪182-04 你正在店裡買一些可愛的首飾。

How to Speak

「可以請你幫我包起來嗎？」這一句用英文怎麼說呢？

- Would you please **gift-wrap** the necklace for me?
  你能幫我把項鍊包裝起來嗎？
- May I have it in a brocade casket or something?
  請問可以幫我放進首飾盒或是其他包裝嗎？

重點對話 Dialogue

有推薦的嗎？

♪183-08 對話練習！

♪183-01 What can I do for you, sir?
你需要點什麼，先生？

♪183-02 I am looking for a necklace for my partner since her birthday is coming. Can you recommend some for me?
我女朋友生日就要到了，我想給她買個項鍊作禮物。能為我推薦幾個嗎？

♪183-03 What about the necklace? It's popular with young girls.
這款項鍊怎麼樣，年輕女孩通常會喜歡。

♪183-04 Ok, I will take it. Please wrap it for me.
好的，我要了，請幫我包起來。

有純銀的嗎？

♪183-05 The gold earrings suit your complexion well. You look pretty with them.
這個金耳環很適合你的膚色。你戴上很漂亮。

♪183-06 But I am allergic to metal, do you have pure silver ones?
但是我對金屬過敏。你們有純銀的嗎？

♪183-07 Yes, we do.
有的。

More to Know

「材質＋產品」的說法：

- I'm sorry there aren't any **brass products** in our shop.
很抱歉，我們店裡沒有任何銅製的商品。
- Do you have rings **made of pure silver**? 你們有純銀製的戒指嗎？

Sentences & Grammar

♪184-01 **1.** The beads of the bracelet **are made of** crystal.
手鐲上的珠子是水晶做的。

用某東西製造出來是 be made，後接不同介係詞有不同意義。

- Fish sauce is literally **made from** fish.
  就如字面所講，魚露是用魚做的。
  ▶▶成品看不出原料
- The furniture is **made of** Chinese cypress.
  家具是用檜木造的。
  ▶▶成品看得出原料為何
- Pancake is **made with** milk, flour, and eggs.
  鬆餅是由牛奶、麵粉、與蛋做成。
  ▶▶成品由各種原材料製成，通常用來形容食物

♪184-02 **2.** The **platinum** rings are more expensive than the golden ones.
白金戒指比黃金的貴。

在「platinum 白金」外，「gold 金」與「silver 銀」也是常用於首飾的金屬。

另外，金是以上三種金屬中名詞與形容詞不同的金屬（名詞 gold，形容詞 golden），而 golden 也指似金的，故 gold ring 指純金戒指，golden ring 則就不一定是純金，有可能是鍍銅、外觀金色的戒指，

♪184-03 **3.** There isn't any farmed pearl in our shop. Only natural ones are **available**.
我們店裡沒有販賣人工養殖的珍珠。只賣天然珍珠。

以物品來說，available 指可買到的、可得到的。針對時間的話，則指有空的。

- Foreign beer is only **available** in high-end supermarkets.
  外國啤酒只有在高級超市才買得到。
- Dr. Wang isn't **available** until 13:00 on Friday.
  王醫生週五到下午一點才有空。

最佳店員 Best-seller!

你身為一個在飾品店打滾多年的店員，總是能挑選出符合顧客需求的商品；今天來店裡的客人一樣源源不絕，讓我們來為他們選出最好的飾品吧！

A. A ring with a big diamond that comes with an appraisal
B. A necklace with shiny emerald
C. A pair of flower-shaped earrings, which is made of pure silver

I am looking for a necklace for my mom since her birthday is coming. She loves emeralds but doesn't like sapphire.
我媽媽生日就要到了，我想給她買個項鍊作禮物。她喜歡綠寶石但不喜歡藍寶石。

Which one should you recommend? 你該推薦哪個飾品呢？ ________

❷ I am looking for earrings, but I am allergic to metal. Do you have pure silver ones? Oh, and I like lovely ones.
我想要買耳環。但是我對金屬過敏，你們有純銀的嗎？哦，然後我喜歡可愛款式的。

Which one should you recommend? 你該推薦哪個飾品呢？ ________

❸ I am looking for a proposal ring. I like this style, but I wonder if the diamond comes with an appraisal.
我想要找求婚用的戒指。我喜歡這個款式，但我想知道這塊鑽石是否有鑑定書。

Which one should you recommend? 你該推薦哪個飾品呢？ ________

解答

- B. 一條鑲有閃亮綠寶石的項鍊
- C. 一對純銀的花形耳環
- A. 一枚有鑑定書的大鑽石戒指

UNIT 05

Makeup and Skin Care

化妝品和保養品

♪186-01 **Do you have perfume in the shop?** 你們店裡有香水嗎？

♪186-02 What's the smell of this perfume? 這種香水是什麼味道？

♪186-03 May I have a look at your lipstick? 我能看看你們的口紅嗎？

♪186-04 Can you recommend a moisturizer for me?
能給我推薦一種化妝水嗎？

♪186-05 What's the effect of this sunscreen?
這種防曬乳的效果怎麼樣？

♪186-06 How should I use this facial mask? 這種面膜應該怎麼使用？

How to Say

- **說明想要的產品：**

  I want to buy a bottle of remover.　我想買一瓶卸妝水。

- **說明自己的狀況：**

  My skin is neutral; what kind of lotion is for me?
  我是中性皮膚，哪種潤膚乳適合我？

單字地圖 Vocabulary

Makeup and Hairstyle 化妝與髮型
♪187-01

cosmetics 化妝品
♪187-02

- concealer 遮瑕膏
- foundation 粉底
- liquid foundation 粉底液
- brow pencil 眉筆
- eyeliner 眼線筆
- eye shadow palette 眼影盤
- mascara 睫毛膏
- lipstick 口紅
- blush 腮紅

cosmetic applicators 彩妝工具
♪187-03

- brush 粉刷
- powder puff 粉撲
- fake eyelashes 假睫毛
- oil-absorbing sheet 吸油面紙
- cotton pad 化妝棉
- mirror 鏡子

skin care products 護膚產品
♪187-04

- makeup remover 卸妝乳
- facial cleanser 洗面乳
- toner 化妝水
- facial mask 面膜
- lip balm 護唇膏
- water spray 保濕噴霧

body care products 身體保養品
♪187-05

- body wash 沐浴乳
- body lotion 身體乳
- hand lotion 護手霜
- hand cleanser 洗手乳
- hand cream 護手霜
- perfume 香水

skin care 肌膚保養
♪187-06

- combination skin 混合性肌膚
- sensitive skin 敏感性肌膚
- normal skin 中性肌膚
- dry skin 乾性肌膚
- oily skin 油性肌膚
- acne 青春痘
- facial 臉部用
- gentle 溫和的

hair care 頭髮保養
♪187-07

- shampoo 洗髮精
- conditioner 潤髮乳
- hair treatment 護髮精華
- hair spray 髮膠
- hair dryer 吹風機
- hair curler 電棒捲
- comb 梳子

More to Know

「hairstyle 髮型」的說法：

- perm 燙髮
- dye 染髮
- bangs 瀏海
- straight hair 直髮
- curly hair 捲髮
- haircut 理髮

情節故事 Story

Who ♪ 188-01
You are a customer in the cosmetics shop.
你是美妝店的顧客。

Where ♪ 188-02
You are standing in front of the shelf of skin products.
你站在肌膚商品區的層架前。

When ♪ 188-03
You are suffering from the skin problems for few days.
你的皮膚有點狀況，已經好幾天了。

What ♪ 188-04
You are searching for something to improve the situation.
你正在看有什麼東西可以紓緩症狀。

How to Speak

向店員說明你的狀況：

- What products can **improve** my skin condition?
  有什麼產品可以改善我的皮膚狀況？
- My face is dry, and my T-zone has oil easily.
  我的臉很乾燥，但是 T 區很容易出油。

Dialogue

敏感肌適合哪種乳液呢？

♪ 189-09 對話練習！

♪ 189-01 Do you have any lotion in your shop?
你們有乳液嗎？

♪ 189-02 We have lotion for all skin types. What kind of skin do you have?
我們有適合各種肌膚的乳液，你是什麼膚質？

♪ 189-03 I am sensitive, and which kind of lotion is suitable for me?
我是敏感肌膚，哪種乳液適合我呢？

♪ 189-04 This one is very gentle and is just right for sensitive skin.
這款很溫和，適合敏感的肌膚。

防曬怎麼挑？

♪ 189-05 May I have a look at your sunscreen products?
我能看看防曬產品嗎？

♪ 189-06 These are the best-selling sunscreens this year.
這些是今年最暢銷的防曬乳。

♪ 189-07 Wow, it's so many; which one should I take?
哇，這麼多，我應該買哪一個呢？

♪ 189-08 If you are often outdoors, choose this one.
如果你經常在戶外活動，就選這款。

More to Know

- I have ______ type. 我是________肌膚。
  - combination skin 中性肌
  - dry skin 乾性肌
  - mixed skin 混合肌
  - sensitive skin 敏感肌

Sentences & Grammar

♪190-01 **1.** The basic **ingredient** of this cream is plant essence.
這款面霜的基本成分是植物精粹。

ingredient 和 material 很像，都指原料，但 ingredient 更指混合物的組成部分，所以多用於食品、化妝品、或化學性質產品方面。

- **Ingredients** of vegan foods do not include natural eggs or milk.
純素食品的原料不含天然蛋奶。
- The **material** of this jewel is mainly platinum.
這件飾品的原料主要是白金。

♪190-02 **2.** These facial cleansers can remove **acnes** from your skin.
這幾種洗面乳可去除你皮膚上的痘痘。

acne 和 pimple 是痤瘡、粉刺、青春痘之類的痘痘，其他皮膚狀況：

skin aging 膚質老化	wrinkle 皺紋
oily skin 油性皮膚	enlarged pores 毛孔粗大

♪190-03 **3.** I want to know what the side **effects** of these cosmetics have.
我想知道這些化妝品有什麼副作用。

effect 是影響、作用的名詞，片語「side effect」為副作用。動詞則是 affect。

♪190-04 **4.** Our **conditioner** will never hurt your hair.
我們的護髮乳絕對不會傷害頭髮。

其他常用洗浴及保養品：

body gel 沐浴乳	hair gel 髮膠	shampoo 洗髮精
moisturizer 潤膚乳	toner 化妝水	essential oil 精油

購買時間 What to buy?

化妝品與保養品等等的日用品，總是生活中不可或缺的一部份；請你試著透過提示猜猜他們需要買什麼東西，再從框格裡選出適合他們的商品並填入吧！

body lotion 身體乳	hair dryer 吹風機	perfume 香水	sunscreen 防曬乳

I need to buy some ______ to moisturize my skin.
我需要買些 ______ 來滋潤我的皮膚。

I'm going to do some outdoor activities next week, so I think I need to buy __________.
下禮拜我要從事一些戶外活動，所以我想我需要買 __________。

My _____ is broken, so I can only let my hair dry naturally now. I need to buy a new one.
我的 ______ 壞了，所以我現在只能讓頭髮自然乾。我需要買一個新的。

Wow! It smells so good. What's the smell of this ________? I'd like to take one. 哇！它聞起來真香。這款 _______ 是什麼味道？我想買一個。

解答

- body lotion 身體乳
- sunscreen 防曬乳
- hair dryer 吹風機
- perfume 香水

Review 5

A 填空練習

- Your total is 512 ___________ .
  您的帳單的是 512 美元。
  答案請見 P.162

- Do you have these ___________ in my size?
  請問這雙鞋有我的尺寸嗎？
  答案請見 P.168

B 引導造句

- **try on 試穿**
  I'd like to ____.
  我想試穿那雙上面有花紋的鞋子。
  答案請見 P.177

- **wrap 包裝**
  ____?
  請幫我包起來。
  答案請見 P.183

- **suitable 適合**
  ____.
  答案請見 P.189

C 引導寫作

標題	Shopping Day! 購物去！
要買毛衣	
試穿看看	
還要買鞋子	
詢問尺寸	

參考短文：我想要買一件粉紅色的毛衣。我拿了一件來試穿，我很喜歡。我還想買一雙皮鞋。但皮鞋沒有我的尺寸。

Chapter

06

Health & Medication
健康與醫療

UNIT 01

Feel uncomfortable…

感到不舒服

♪ 194-01 **What's wrong with you?** ---------- 你怎麼了？

♪ 194-02 What's the matter with you? ---------- 你哪裡不舒服？

♪ 194-03 Tell me what you are feeling. ---------- 告訴我你的感覺。

♪ 194-04 How are you feeling now? ---------- 你現在感覺怎麼樣？

♪ 194-05 You look very pale. ---------- 你的臉色很蒼白。

♪ 194-06 Does your throat hurt? ---------- 你的喉嚨會痛嗎？

♪ 194-07 When did this happen? ---------- 這種情況是從什麼時候開始的？

How to Speak

- **thermometer 體溫計：**

  Keep the **thermometer** in your mouth for 5 minutes.
  把體溫計含在口中 5 分鐘。

- **take medicine 吃藥：**

  Take medicine on time. 請準時吃藥。

單字地圖 Vocabulary

♪195-01
sickness 生病

- sick 生病的
- ill 不舒服的
- illness 生病
- symptom 症狀
- mental disease 心理疾病
- cancer 癌症

♪195-02
have a cold 感冒

- headache 頭痛
- cough 咳嗽
- sore throat 喉嚨痛
- runny nose 流鼻水
- dizzy 頭暈的
- sneeze 打噴嚏
- fever 發燒
- flu 流行性感冒

♪195-03
feel bad 難受

- nausea 噁心
- food poisoning 食物中毒
- stomach flu 腸胃炎
- diarrhea 腹瀉
- stomachache 肚子痛

♪195-04
disease I 疾病（一）

- heart disease 心臟病
- asthma 氣喘
- hay fever 花粉症

♪195-05
disease II 疾病（二）

- insomnia 失眠症
- nearsightedness 近視
- chicken pox 水痘

♪195-06
disease III 疾病（三）

♪195-07
chronic disease 慢性病

- hypertension 高血壓
- stroke 中風
- diabetes 糖尿病

More to Know

Go to the right place 找對地方

- 看**心理醫生**這樣說：see a shrink（美式口語）、go to a psychiatrist、have a psychological counseling
- 做**物理治療**這樣說：physiotherapy
- 做**復健**這樣說：rehabilitation

情節故事 Story

Who ♪196-01
You are a doctor. Many patients come to your clinic every day.
你是個醫師。你的診所每天都有很多患者。

Where ♪196-02
You are working in your clinic.
你正在你的診所上班。

When ♪196-03
It's noon. You just finished your lunch.
現在是中午，你剛吃完午餐。

What ♪196-04
You are preparing to see the clients in the afternoon.
你正在準備下午的看診。

How to Speak

說明失眠狀況：

- I **can't fall into sleep** at night. 我晚上無法入眠。
- I don't **sleep well** at night. 我晚上睡不好。
- I think I've got **insomnia**. 我想我失眠了。

重點對話 Dialogue

去看醫生吧

♪197-07 對話練習！

♪197-01 Why don't you go to see a doctor?
你為什麼不去看醫生？

♪197-02 I just have a cold. I don't have to see a doctor.
我只是感冒了。不必去看醫生。

♪197-03 I'm worried about you. If you continue having a headache, you should go to see a doctor.
我很擔心你。如果你還是一直頭痛，就要去看醫生。

看牙醫

♪197-04 I think you need to see a dentist for your toothache.
我想你牙痛需要看一下牙醫。

♪197-05 I know. I will make an appointment with a dentist someday.
我知道。我之後有一天會預約牙醫。

♪197-06 Don't postpone. I've made an appointment for you to the dentist. You always say that you don't have time.
別拖了。我已經為你預約了看醫生的時間。你總是說沒時間去看醫生。

More to Know

國外沒有健保，所以更要能清楚描述自己的身體狀況！

在臺灣，**健保（NHI, National Health Insurance）**是個方便且體貼的制度，生病不用花大錢也能去**醫院（hospital）**看診。若是人在異地、沒有健保給付，看醫生變成一件很花錢的事情。如果身體**不舒服（uncomfortable）**，不管是到**藥局（pharmacy）**自行買藥或到醫院看醫生，該如何向**藥劑師（pharmacist）**或**醫師（doctor）**表達身體狀況是很重要的。

Sentences & Grammar

♪198-01 1. I have a terrible toothache. I **went to a dentist** yesterday, but it doesn't help.
我牙齒很痛。我昨天去看牙醫，但還是沒有好轉。

看醫生可說「go to the doctor / dentist」或「see a doctor / dentist」。

- Owen **saw a pediatrician** to seek help for his kid's allergy.
歐文去看小兒科醫生，為他孩子的過敏尋求幫助。

♪198-02 2. I **feel like** I have a fever. I have been coughing today.
我覺得我在發燒。而且今天我一直在咳嗽。

feel	＋形容詞
feel like	＋名詞／＋動名詞／＋ that 子句

- The young lady **felt** very insecure. She **felt like** a failure.
這位小姐感到很沒自信。她覺得自己是個失敗者。

♪198-03 3. I always feel dizzy **when** I'm working, and I haven't had any appetite for the past week.
我在工作的時候總是感覺頭暈，而且這個星期我一直沒有食欲。

當背景動作進行時發生另一件事或動作，可混用「when」和「while」，如例句可寫：

- I always feel dizzy **while** I'm working.
不過，「while」更常用在兩個子句的動作同時進行並會延續一段時間，而「when」使用範圍更廣，如兩個子句的動作較短暫或能瞬間完成的，或稍有先後順序，或表示在一段時期發生的事。

- The father **was snoring away** **while** the kids **were screaming and crying**.
小孩在尖叫大哭，而父親卻睡到打呼。

- **When** the couple **just got married**, they **were struggling financially**.
當那對夫妻剛結婚時，經濟很拮据。

What's wrong with you?

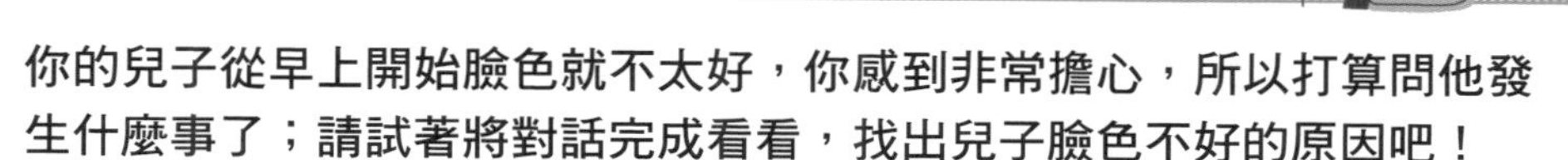

你的兒子從早上開始臉色就不太好，你感到非常擔心，所以打算問他發生什麼事了；請試著將對話完成看看，找出兒子臉色不好的原因吧！

What's wrong with you? You look very ______ .
你怎麼了？你的臉色很蒼白。

臉色蒼白該怎麼說呢？

☐ white ☐ pale ☐ fair

I've been having a _______ since last night.
我從昨晚開始就一直在頭痛。

頭痛該怎麼說呢？

☐ headache ☐ fever ☐ stomachache

I think you need to __________. 我想你需要看一下醫生。

看醫生該怎麼說呢？

☐ see a doctor ☐ watch a doctor ☐ look a doctor

OK, I will make an appointment later. 好，我等等會預約。

預約該怎麼說呢？

☐ take an appointment ☐ do an appointment ☐ make an appointment

解答

- 白色的／皮膚蒼白的／皮膚白皙的
- 頭痛／發燒／肚子痛
- see a doctor
- make an appointment

UNIT 02

At the Doctor's

看醫生

♪200-01 **Where is the registration office, please?**
請問，掛號處在哪裡？

♪200-02 Which department are you going to register with?
你要掛什麼科？

♪200-03 How much is the registration fee? 掛號費是多少？

♪200-04 The registration fee was paid at that window.
掛號費請到那邊窗口繳納。

♪200-05 I don't know which department to register with.
我不知道該掛哪個科的號。

♪200-06 Which doctor do you want to register with?
你想掛哪位醫生的號？

How to Say

Conversation at Doctor's Office 在醫生診間……

- Hello. What seems to be the problem? 你好，怎麼了呢？
- I have a terrible fever and a sore throat. 我發高燒，而且喉嚨痛。

單字地圖 Vocabulary

♪201-01
hospital service 醫院服務

♪201-02
service 服務

- ambulance 救護車
- patient 病人
- rehabilitation 復健
- register 掛號
- health insurance 健康保險
- X-ray X 光
- diagnosis 診斷

♪201-03
room 空間

- operating room 手術室
- patient ward 病房
- hospitalization 住院
- emergency room 急診室
- delivery room 產房
- waiting room 候診室
- nurse station 護理站
- ICU (intensive care unit) 加護病房

♪201-04
item 物品

- band-aid ok 繃
- bandage 繃帶
- mask 口罩
- gauze 紗布
- alcohol swab 酒精棉片
- cotton ball 棉球

♪201-05
tool 工具

- wheelchair 輪椅
- crutch 拐杖
- walker 步行器
- hospital bed 病床
- drip bag 點滴袋
- drip rack 點滴架

♪201-06
equipment 醫療器材

- stethoscope 聽診器
- thermometer 體溫計
- blood pressure cuff 血壓計
- ear thermometer 耳溫槍
- syringe 針筒
- stretcher 擔架
- sling 三角巾
- oxygen mask 氧氣罩

♪201-07
hospital personnel 醫院人員

- EMT (emergency medical technician) 救護人員
- doctor 醫生
- nurse 護理師
- surgeon 外科醫生
- dentist 牙醫師

More to Know

其他科別的醫生，英文這樣說：

- family physician 家庭醫師
- Ent doctor 耳鼻喉科醫師
- psychologist 心理醫師
- ophthalmologist 眼科醫師
- obstetrician 產科醫師
- pediatrician 小兒科醫師

Story

Who ♪202-01
You are a family physician.
你是一名家庭醫生。

Where ♪202-02
You are in the clinic with a patient.
你和看診的病患正在診間。

When ♪202-03
It's Friday afternoon.
現在是週五下午

What ♪202-04
You are talking to the patient.
你正在和患者說話。

How to Speak

身為醫師，說出口的話都會讓看診的病患吊起一顆心或鬆了一口氣，若是要向病患說明狀況，會這樣說：

- Don't worry. You just got ____________. You will be recovered soon.
  別擔心，你只是得了____________。你很快就會復原了。
  - flu 流行性感冒　▪ stomach flu 腸胃炎

Dialogue

我感冒了

♪203-09 對話練習！

♪203-01 What's your trouble?
你哪裡不舒服？

♪203-02 I caught a cold and coughed for two days.
我感冒了，咳嗽了兩天。

♪203-03 Open your mouth. Let me see your throat.
張開嘴，我看看你的喉嚨。

♪203-04 My throat hurts too.
喉嚨也很痛。

要打針嗎？

♪203-05 Do I need an injection?
我需要打針嗎？

♪203-06 You can also choose to **take medicine**.
你也可以選擇吃藥。

♪203-07 Which has a quicker effect?
哪一種效果更快？

♪203-08 You will get eased after an injection.
打針後就會緩解。

More to Know

「吃藥」的英文是「**take medicine**」！

- pill 藥丸
- drug 藥劑；毒品
- caplet 藥錠
- capsule 膠囊
- painkiller 止痛藥
- vitamin 維他命

Sentences & Grammar

♪204-01 **1.** Am I **suffering from** a serious illness?
我是不是得了很嚴重的病。

suffer +接名詞，指經歷、遭受、忍受。 而片語「suffer from」則表示受苦、患病、變糟。

- The poor woman **suffers from** life-long leukemia and has had to **suffer** painful chemotherapies for years.
這可憐的女人終生患有血癌，多年來得忍受痛苦的化療。

♪204-02 **2.** You have a tumor in your brain. You **need** to take several checkups.
你的腦子裡有一個瘤。你需要做幾個檢查。

need to、have to、must 這些單字都是指需要、必須做某種動作時。 故例句可寫成：

- You have to / must have several checkups.

♪204-03 **3.** You have a **slight** nervous breakdown, and your blood pressure is below average.
你有輕微的神經衰弱，且血壓低於平均值。

輕微的 V.S. 嚴重的：

slight =minor 輕微的	⟷	severe =major 嚴重的

- Laura would have died from **major** allergic reaction if there hadn't been a doctor onsite.
要不是有位醫生在場，蘿拉會死於嚴重的過敏反應。

♪204-04 **4.** You have a high fever of 39 **degrees**. Let me see… you have an inflammation in throat.
你發高燒 39 度。讓我看看……你的喉嚨發炎了。

全球有兩種溫度系統，一是攝氏 Celsius，另一是華氏 Fahrenheit。

對話 The best response!

♪205-01 看醫生的時候，醫生總是會詢問一些事，以了解你目前遇到的問題；掃 **QR Code** 聽聽看，醫生問了什麼，而你又該回答什麼呢？

1.

A. I feel hungry.
B. I coughed for days.
C. It's Friday afternoon.

2.

A. Since last weekend.
B. You have a tumor in your brain.
C. Which has a quicker effect?

3.

A. Let me see.
B. My throat hurts, too.
C. I'm relieved to hear that.

解答

1. What's your trouble? 你哪裡不舒服？		
A. 我餓了。	B. 我咳嗽了好幾天。	C. 現在是週五下午。
2. When did this happen? 這種情況是從什麼時候開始的？		
A. 從上個週末開始。	B. 你的腦中有個瘤。	C. 哪一種效果更快？
3. You' ve just got a cold. Don't worry.		
A. 讓我看看。	B. 我喉嚨也很痛。	C. 這樣我就放心了。

UNIT 03

Get Hurt

受傷了

♪206-01 **Does it hurt here at the waist?** 腰這裡痛嗎？

♪206-02 I hurt so much that I couldn't say a word. 我好痛，痛到說不出話了。

♪206-03 You're bleeding! It must hurt. 你流血了！一定很痛。

♪206-04 I don't advise you to use morphine to relieve pain. 我不建議你用嗎啡來止痛。

♪206-05 The painkillers haven't worked yet. 止痛藥還沒有發揮作用。

♪206-06 I can't stand up because of the pain. 我痛得站不起來。

How to Say

表示部位疼痛的說法：

- My back **hurts**. 我的背好痛。
- My head **aches**. 我的頭好痛。

Vocabulary

body parts 身體部位
♪207-01

head 頭部
♪207-02

- brain 腦部
- eyebrow 眉毛
- eyes 眼睛
- nose 鼻子
- ear 耳朵
- chin 下巴
- mouth 嘴巴
- neck 脖子

torso 軀幹
♪207-03

- waist 腰
- skin 皮膚
- breasts 胸部
- chest 胸部
- belly 肚子
- abdomen 腹部
- back 背部
- hips 臀部
- spine 脊椎

limbs 四肢
♪207-04

- hand 手
- knee 膝蓋
- arm 手臂
- thigh 大腿
- armpit 腋下

details 細節
♪207-05

- finger 手指
- palm 手掌
- wrist 手腕
- fingernail 指甲
- calf 小腿
- foot 腳
- toe 腳趾
- ankle 腳踝

organs 內臟
♪207-06

- heart 心臟
- liver 肝臟
- lung 肺臟
- stomach 胃
- kidney 腎臟

other 其他
♪207-07

- muscle 肌肉
- skull 骨頭
- fingerprint 指紋
- hair 頭髮
- Adam's apple 喉結
- jaw 下顎
- throat 喉嚨

How to Say

流動在全身之內，卻不常見——「blood 血液」：

▪ red blood cell 紅血球 ▪ white blood cell 白血球

▪ plasma 血漿 ▪ blood vessel 血管

另外，血型則是「blood type」！

Story

Who ♪208-01 You are a nurse, helping a patient with his wounds on the leg.
你是一名護理師，幫助一位腳受傷的病患。

Where ♪208-02 You are in the clinic, standing by the patient.
你在診所裡，站在病患的身邊。

When ♪208-03 It's late in the night.
現在是晚上了。

What ♪208-04 He also twisted his ankle. He seems painful.
他還扭到了腳踝。看起來很痛。

How to Speak

- The **wound** is so small that it is not serious. 傷口很小，不嚴重。

▪wound 傷口 ▪injure 受傷 ▪hurt 受傷 damage 傷害

重點對話 Dialogue

跌倒扭傷

♪209-08 對話練習！

♪209-01 What's wrong with you?
你怎麼了？

♪209-02 I twisted my ankle.
我扭傷了腳踝。

♪209-03 It's not a big problem. Just apply some ointment.
不嚴重，抹一些消炎藥膏就好。

發炎了

♪209-04 Doctor, why does my throat hurt more?
醫生，為什麼我的喉嚨更痛了？

♪209-05 Let me see. Oh, you have an inflammation in tonsil.
我看看。哦，你的扁桃體發炎了。

♪209-06 What should I do?
我應該怎麼辦？

♪209-07 I'll get you some medicine, and you shouldn't eat spicy food.
我開些藥給你，請注意不要食用辛辣的食物。

More to Know

受傷了！傷到哪了？

要怎麼說明自己哪個部位疼痛呢？

- My ________ hurt. 我________（身體部位）痛。
  - My left arm hurts. 我的左臂疼痛。
- I have ______ pain. 我________（身體部位）痛。
  - I have elbow pain. 我手肘痛。

Sentences & Grammar

♪210-01 **1.** You have to **stop** bleeding in your cut. Be careful of wound infection.
你的傷口必須要止血。小心傷口感染。

stop 的用法：

stop ＋ Ving	停止做某事
stop to ＋原形動詞	指停下手邊正在做的事 轉而去做某事
stop ＋某人事物＋ from ＋ Ving	使某人事物停止做某事

- They **stop talking** to each other.
  他們不再互相對話。
- The director **stopped to talk** to her secretary.
  主任停下來和她秘書說話。

♪210-02 **2.** I need a lot of gauze to bandage the wound. How did you get **hurt** so badly?
我需要很多紗布來包紮傷口。你是怎麼受這麼重的傷的？

片語「be動詞 / get hurt」指受傷；「A hurt B」則代表A讓B受傷。

- The football player got **hurt** in the game. Now his left knee **hurts** a lot.
  足球員在比賽中受傷，現在左膝很痛。
- My ex's lack of care for me deeply **hurt** me.
  我前任對我的不在乎傷我很深。

♪210-03 **3.** I made my head hit **against** the glass door.
我的頭撞到玻璃門。

介係詞 against 有「反對、逆、靠、對著、預防」等意思。

- The addict is fighting **against** the temptation of drugs.
  成癮者正對抗著毒品的誘惑。

Body parts

本章我們學了各種身體部位的說法，也學到了該如何說自己哪裡疼痛；請試著看圖造句，幫助圖片裡的人物說出自己哪裡不舒服吧！

My ________ hurts. 我________痛。	I have ______ pain. 我________痛。
I have ______ pain. 我________痛。	My ________ hurts. 我________痛。

解答

back 背部	knee 膝蓋
wrist 手腕	throat 喉嚨

UNIT 04

Go to the Pharmacy

去藥局

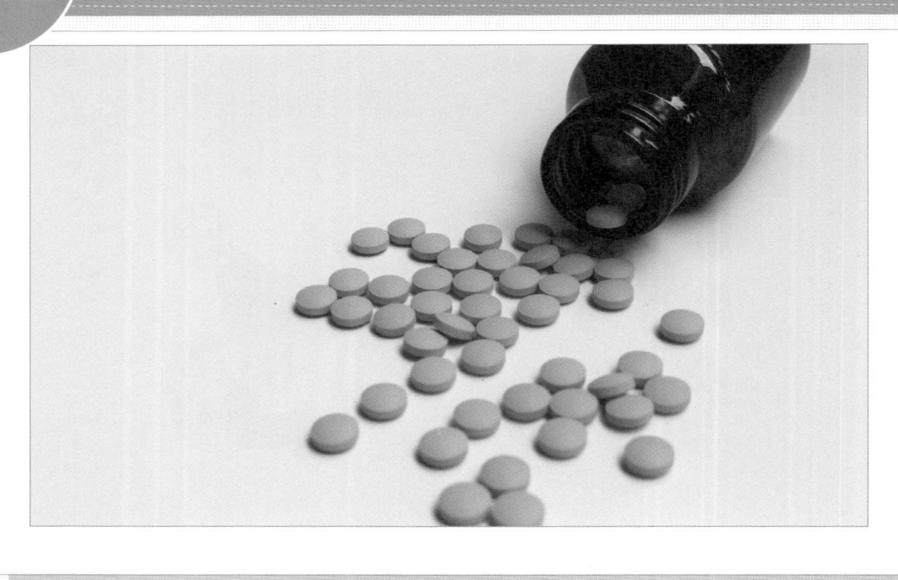

♪212-01 **How many pills should I take each time?**

我每次應該吃幾粒藥？

♪212-02 Take the medicine two times a day after meals.

一天兩次，飯後服藥。

♪212-03 It took three hours for the medicine to come into effect.

這種藥在三個小時後才見效。

♪212-04 This medicine will ease your nerves quickly.

這藥會快速緩解你的神經緊張。

♪212-05 This medicine is very effective for treating the cold.

這種藥對治療感冒很有效。

How to Say

「繼續吃藥，直到……」的說法：

- You shouldn't stop taking the pills **until** you feel better.
  你必須繼續吃藥，直到你感覺好點為止。
- You are not yet well enough to **dispense** with the pills.
  你尚未痊癒，還要繼續吃藥。

單字地圖 Vocabulary

In a pharmacy 在藥局中 ♪213-01

form 形狀 ♪213-02
- tablet 藥片
- ointment 藥膏
- powder 藥粉
- cough syrup 咳嗽糖漿

medicine 藥 ♪213-03
- painkiller 止痛藥
- sleeping pill 安眠藥
- aspirin 阿斯匹靈
- antibiotic 抗生素
- cold medicine 感冒藥
- prescription 處方藥

type 種類 ♪213-04
- eye drop 眼藥水
- fever patch 退燒貼布
- oral 口服（內服）
- external use 外用

cure 治療 ♪213-05
- treatment 治療
- remedy 療法
- heal 癒合；療癒
- reduce 減輕
- relieve 減緩

illness 生病 ♪213-06
- cut 傷口
- trauma 創傷
- condition 狀況
- injury 受傷

other 其他 ♪213-07
- operation 手術
- monitor 監控
- unstable 不穩定的
- danger 危險
- effective 有效的
- pulse 脈搏
- forbidden 禁止的

More to Know

SOS ！情況緊急：聽懂關鍵字，了解情況的嚴重性！

- The patient is in **critical condition.** 病人的情況很危急。
- The patient is **in danger of** losing her life. 病人有生命危險。

情節故事 Story

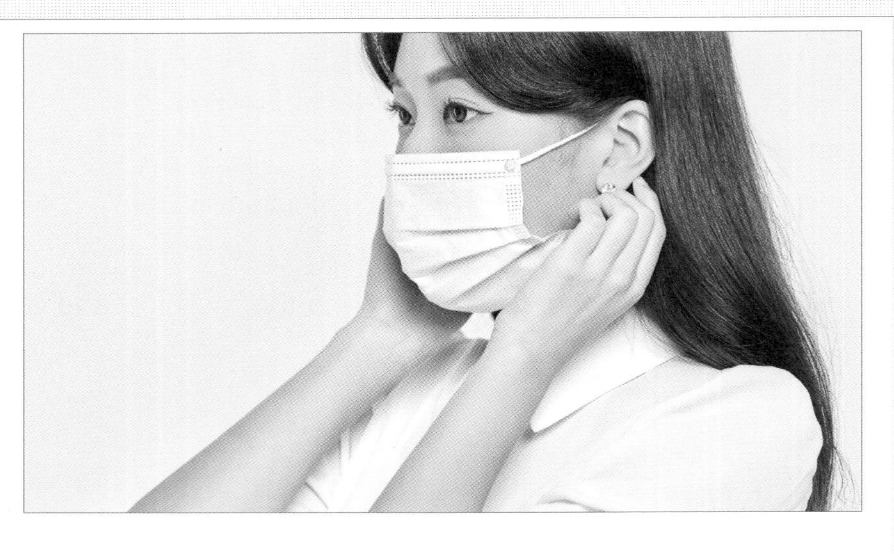

Who You are a patient in the hospital.
♪214-01 你是醫院裡的患者。

Where You are sitting in the waiting area.
♪214-02 你正坐在等候區。

When It's your turn for you to take your prescription.
♪214-03 現在換你去拿處方籤。

What You are asking about problems of side effects.
♪214-04 你問了關於副作用的問題。

How to Speak

藥的副作用是什麼呢？

- Is there any **side effect**? 這種藥有副作用嗎？
- The medicine has some side effects. 藥物多多少少都有點副作用。
- The side effect of this medicine is that you will feel sleepy.
這種藥的副作用就是你會想睡覺。

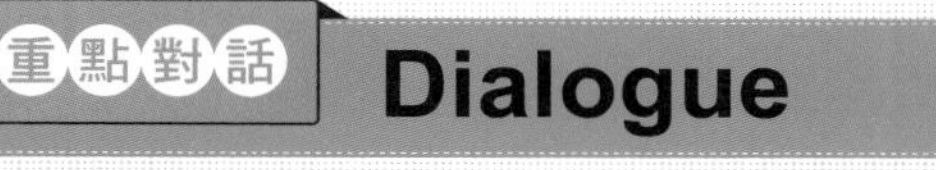

重點對話 Dialogue

記得按時吃藥

♪215-09 對話練習！

♪215-01 Just take these pills, and it's effective on the cough.
服用這種藥丸，它對咳嗽很有效。

♪215-02 How should I take them?
我該怎麼用藥呢？

♪215-03 Take the pills for two days: one in the morning and one at night.
請連續吃三天，一天兩次、早晚各一粒。

♪215-04 I see.
我明白了。

我有藥物過敏

♪215-05 Do I need an injection?
要給我打針嗎？

♪215-06 Yes. The nurse will **inject you with penicillin**.
是的，醫生會幫你注射盤林西林。

♪215-07 But I have an allergy to penicillin.
但是我對盤林西林過敏。

♪215-08 Well, you can take medicine instead. But it isn't as effective as the injection.
嗯，你也可以吃藥。不過吃藥的效果沒有打針來得快。

More to Know

- 注射藥品：inject sb with sth
- 接種疫苗：get a shot、get an injection、get vaccinated
- 疫苗：vaccine

Sentences & Grammar

♪216-01 **1. Remember** to rest. Do more outdoor activities.
記得多休息。多做戶外運動。

remember 與 forget 的用法：

remember	＋動名詞	記得做過某事
	＋ to ＋原形動詞	記得要去做某事
forget	＋動名詞	忘記做過某事
	＋ to ＋原形動詞	忘記要去做某事

- I don't **remember having** said those words, but I'll **remember to write** down what I'm going to say.
  我不記得講過這些話，但以後會記得把要講的話寫下來。

♪216-02 **2.** Don't eat expired food, never. Don't **overdo** exercise.
不要吃過期的食物。不要運動過度。

有些動詞把有著「太過、過度之意」的「over」加在動詞前，代表過度進行此動作。

- My roommates partied well past midnight and all **overslept** the next morning.
  我室友開派對超過半夜，隔天早上都睡過頭了。

♪216-03 **3.** You'd better not take sleeping pills. You shouldn't sleep less than seven hours **every** day.
你最好不要服用安眠藥。你應該每天睡多於 7 個小時。

every 和 each 都有「每一」之意。不過 each 強調個別性，而在至少有三個成員的群體中，every 用來指所有成員。 另外 every 只能當形容詞用，也只能搭配單數名詞；而 each 在形容詞外，也能當代名詞和副詞，並單獨使用。

- **Every** kid in the family is talented. **Each** of us plays different instruments.
  我們家裡的每個孩子都很有天分，每個人都會不同樂器。

Take the right medicine.

你身體不舒服，所以去看了醫生，而醫生也依照你的症狀為了開了藥；哪個藥包才是你的呢？請找出正確的藥包吧！

This medicine is effective for treating the cold and the cough. Please take the pills for three days: take three times a day after each meal. Remember to rest.

這種藥對治療感冒和咳嗽很有效。 請服用三天份：一天三次，飯後服用。記得多休息。

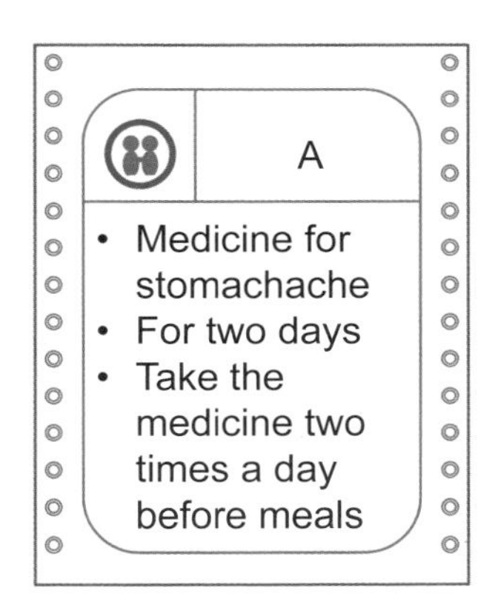

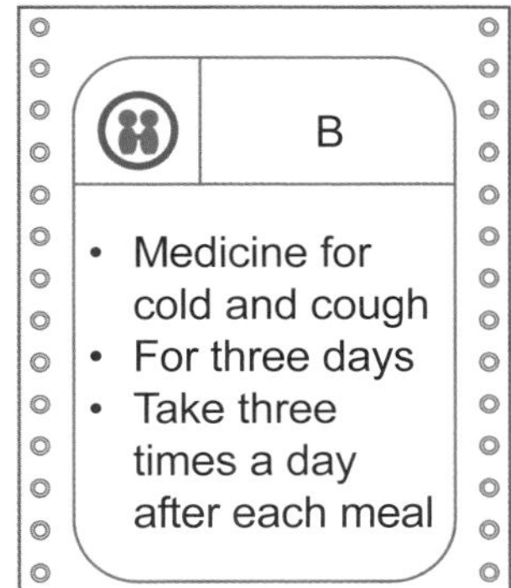

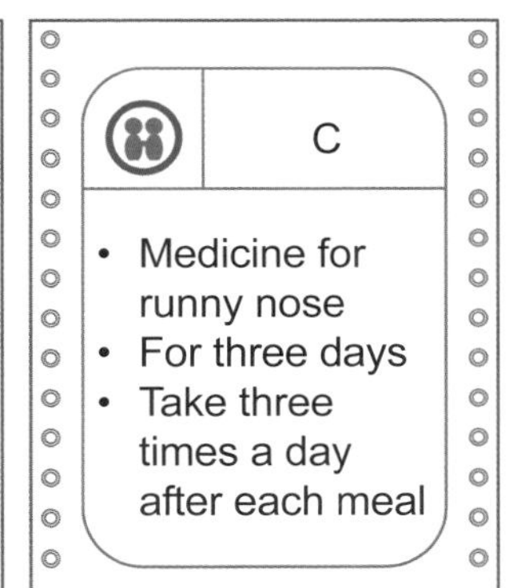

解答

答案為 B。

A 胃痛藥／兩天份／一天兩次，飯前服用

B 感冒咳嗽藥／三天份／一天三次，飯後服用

C 鼻水藥／三天份／一天三次，飯後服用

寫作練習

Review 6

A 填空練習

- What's ___________ with you?
  你怎麼了？ 答案請見 P.194
- You're ___________! It must ___________.
  你流血了！一定很痛。 答案請見 P.206

B 引導造句

- **catch a cold 感冒**
  I _______________________ and coughed for two days.
  我感冒了，咳嗽了兩天。 答案請見 P.203
- **twist 扭傷**
  ____?
  我扭傷了腳踝。 答案請見 P.209
- **cough 咳嗽**
  ____.
  答案請見 P.215

C 引導寫作

標題	Shopping Day! 購物去！
我不舒服	
去看醫生	
頭痛、流鼻水	
吃藥	

參考短文：我生病了，我感到很不舒服。我去看了醫生。我的症狀有頭痛、流鼻水。醫生說我感冒了。我吃了藥，現在我好多了。

Chapter

07

Daily Situation 生活情境

UNIT 01 Go to a Bank 去銀行

UNIT 02 Going to the Post office 去郵局

UNIT 03 Going to the Movie Theater 去電影院

UNIT 04 Customer Service 客服

UNIT 01

Go to a Bank

去銀行

♪220-01 **What kind of account would you like to have?**
您想開哪種帳戶？

♪220-02 You have to finish a form, please. 您需要先填寫一份表格。

♪220-03 I opened a fixed deposit account last year.
我去年開了一個定期存款帳戶。

♪220-04 My father wants to open a current account.
我爸爸想開個活期存款帳戶。

♪220-05 Can you tell me how to open an account?
開戶要辦什麼手續？

How to Speak

想要詢問開戶的最低存款額，就這樣問：

- What's **the minimum deposit** for opening a fixed deposit account?
  開一個定期帳戶的最低存款額是多少？
- Ten thousand dollars. 一萬美元。

Vocabulary

♪ 221-01
financial 金融

♪ 221-02
people 人

- analyst 市場分析師
- banker 銀行家
- broker 證券商
- clerk 行員
- creditor 債權人
- teller 銀行出納員

♪ 221-03
about money 跟錢有關

- ATM card 金融卡
- counterfeit money 假鈔
- cash 兌換
- withdraw 提款
- insufficient funds 透支
- invoice 發票
- identification 身份證明

♪ 221-04
assets 資產

- balance 餘額
- capital 資本
- check 支票
- deposit 存款
- currency 貨幣
- time deposit 定期存款

♪ 221-05
earnings & bonds 盈餘和債券

- dividend 紅利，股息
- credit 信用
- capital loss 資本損失
- deficit 赤字
- loan 借貸

♪ 221-06
holdings 持股

- fund 基金
- security 證券
- share 股票
- stock 股票

♪ 221-07
investments 投資

- current account 活期帳戶
- foreign xchange 外匯
- futures market 期貨市場
- quarter 季度
- quota 配額
- rate 利率

More to Know

負面的相關字：

- bounce a check 跳票
- devaluation 貶值
- downtrend 行情看跌
- inflationary 通貨膨脹的
- mortgage 抵押
- weigh down 下跌

情節故事 Story

Who You are a client of the bank.
♪222-01 你是銀行客戶。

Where You are waiting in a line to the bank counter.
♪222-02 你正在銀行櫃檯的排隊隊伍中。

When It's noon, your lunch break.
♪222-03 現在是午休。

What You want to remit money to someone.
♪222-04 你想要匯款給某人。

How to Speak

每間銀行的規定不太相同，要確認匯款上限，就用這一句：

- Is there an **upper limit** on the amount of remittance?
  請問匯款金額有上限嗎？
- No upper limit. How much do you want to remit?
  沒有上限。你要匯多少錢？

重點對話 Dialogue

信用卡遺失

♪223-10 對話練習！

♪223-01 Can you help me? I lost my credit card yesterday.
可以幫我嗎？我的信用卡昨天丟了。

♪223-02 Don't worry. You should report this loss to your credit company.
不用擔心，你現在應該申請信用卡掛失。

♪223-03 I will report the loss of my credit card later.
我馬上會掛失信用卡。

♪223-04 Then, what do you want to do, replace it or cancel it?
然後，您是想補辦一張還是註銷這張卡？

♪223-05 I want to replace it.
我想補辦一張。

ATM 沒有把卡片退出來

♪223-06 ATM didn't return my card!
ATM 沒有把我的卡片退出來！

♪223-07 Which ATM withdrew your card?
是哪一台 ATM 吞了你的卡？

♪223-08 The number three.
3 號 ATM。

♪223-09 Fill in your name and telephone number on this form. We'll contact you when we find the card.
請在這張表格上填上你的名字、電話。我們找到卡以後會聯繫你。

More to Know

想匯款到某處或給某個人，就這樣表達：

- I'd like to **remit** some money **to England**. 我想匯款到英國。
- I'd like to **remit** some money **to my mother**. 我想匯款給我媽媽。

Sentences & Grammar

♪224-01 **1.** She wonders about the annual **interest** rate of this kind of account.

她想知道這種帳戶的年利率。

interest 當名詞時除了有「愛好、興趣」之意，在金融領域上最常見的意義為「利息」，片語「interest rate」為利率的意思，並搭配「high / low」來形容利率高低。

♪224-02 **2.** Do you **suggest** I open a high-yield savings account?

你建議我開高利息儲蓄帳戶嗎？

suggest、recommend 建議、推薦。不論時態為何，後接子句的主詞都搭配原形動詞。

- The influencer used to **suggest** her followers go on a low-carb diet, and now she **recommends** people eat apples only.
  這網紅以前建議訂閱者進行低碳水飲食，現在推薦大家只吃蘋果。

♪224-03 **3.** What is the **minimum** account balance in order to avoid service fee?

帳戶要求的最低餘額是多少，才能免扣手續費？

minimum 可當形容詞及名詞，反義是 maximum。

- The **maximum** entry of the restaurant is 10 people at once, and customers have to spend a **minimum** of $500 per person.
  餐廳同一時間最多只能有 10 人，每個客人最低消費 $500。

♪224-04 **4.** **In short**, it is convenient for you to withdraw money by this account.

簡而言之，這是一個取款時比較方便的帳戶。

in short、in brief、in sum 總之、簡而言之。

- The new bill is too complicated to explain. **In brief**, more tax.
  新法案太複雜，很難解釋。總之，稅更高了。

I lost my credit card.

你發現你的信用卡不見了！你非常急忙地趕到銀行，想要申請掛失；請試著選出正確答案，並完成對話吧！

What kind of _________ would you like to have?
您想開哪種帳戶？

帳戶該怎麼說呢？

☐ account ☐ counter ☐ fund

No, I don't need to open a new account. I came here for reporting the loss of my ________.
不，我不需要開新帳戶。我來這裡是為了申請信用卡掛失。

信用卡該怎麼說呢？

☐ ATM card ☐ credit card ☐ invoice

I see. What do you want to do, replace it or cancel it?
我了解了，您是想補辦一張還是註銷這張卡？

I want to replace it. 我想補辦一張。

Then, you have to ____________ first.
那麼，您必須先填寫完成這份表格。

填寫完成這份表格該怎麼說呢？

☐ finish this form ☐ do this form ☐ have this form

解答

- 帳戶／櫃台／基金
- 金融卡／信用卡／發票
- finish this form

UNIT 02

Going to the Post office

去郵局

♪226-01 **What's in your parcel?** 你的包裹裡裝的是什麼？

♪226-02 How heavy is the parcel, please? 請問這個包裹有多重？

♪226-03 I received a parcel from America yesterday.
昨天我收到了一個從美國寄來的包裹。

♪226-04 We can't send your parcel. These articles are flammable.
我們不能幫您寄，這些是易燃物。

♪226-05 I'd like to send this parcel to Paris.
我要把這個包裹寄到巴黎。

♪226-06 How long will this parcel be in Japan?
請問寄到日本要多少天呢？

How to Say

包裹寄送前要先秤重，這樣總共需要多少錢呢？

- How much will it cost to send this parcel? 請問寄這個包裹要多少錢？
- Your parcel is over one kilo, and you'll have to pay 10 dollars more. 你的包裹超過了 1 公斤，你要再付 10 美金。

Vocabulary

♪227-01 **postal vocabulary 郵政單字**

♪227-02 **envelope 信封**

- letter paper 信紙
- postcard 明信片
- box 紙箱
- letterhead 印在信紙的信頭
- bulk mail 大宗函件
- postmark 郵戳
- commemorative stamp 紀念郵票
- stamp 郵票

♪227-03 **mail 郵件**

- mail carrier 郵差
- mailbox 郵筒，信箱
- postbox 郵箱
- postage 郵資

♪227-04 **parcel 包裹**

- express 快遞
- package 包裹
- International Parcels 國際包裹
- deliver 投遞

♪227-05 **letter 信件**

- EMS (Express Mail Service) 快捷郵件
- prompt delivery mail 限時郵件
- value-declared mail 報值郵件
- personal mail 私人信件
- air mail 航空郵件
- ocean freight 海運

♪227-06 **information 資訊**

- address 地址
- zip code 郵遞區號
- return address 寄件人地址
- recipient's address 收件人地址
- zone 區域

♪227-07 **postal 郵政的**

- postal clerk 郵政辦事員
- post office box 郵政專用信箱
- postal money order 郵匯票
- postal savings 郵政儲金
- remittances 匯兌

More to Know

隨著紋路、用紙、印刷、浮雕、設計、代表意象的不同，限量郵票在各國間都各自形成一股收集的風潮。而收集郵票的英文，就是「stamps collecting」！

情節故事 Story

Who ♪228-01
You are Sasha. Your best friend is Momo.
妳是紗夏，妳最要好的朋友是桃桃。

Where ♪228-02
You are heading to the post office.
妳正在前往郵局的路上。

When ♪228-03
It's a lovely afternoon.
這是一個風光明媚的下午。

What ♪228-04
You are going to send Momo a letter to share your life.
妳要寄信給桃桃，跟她分享最近的生活。

How to Speak

由於妳想寄到國外，於是妳到郵政櫃檯詢問……

- Where would you like to send this letter to? 你要將這封信寄到哪？
- My best friend lives in Japan. I would like to send it to Japan.
  我最好的朋友住在日本。我要寄到日本。

Dialogue

請問寄到美國要多久呢？

♪229-08 對話練習！

♪229-01 I'd like to send a parcel.
我要寄包裹。

♪229-02 Where would you like to send it?
請問你要寄到哪裡？

♪229-03 America. How long will it take to send to America?
美國，寄到美國要多長時間？

♪229-04 In general, it's ten days.
一般來說，是十天。

我想買紀念明信片

♪229-05 I would like to buy a commemorative postcard.
我想買一張紀念明信片。

♪229-06 There are all kinds of commemorative postcards. Which one do you want?
我們這裡有各種各樣的明信片。你想要哪一種？

♪229-07 I want a commemorative postcard with a view of Paris.
我想要一張帶有巴黎風景的明信片。

More to Know

在國外總會思念家鄉，可以善用當地郵寄寄送明信片、包裹等。也可以到當地的郵局購買紀念性的郵票收藏。

- This stamp is of great **significance**. 這張郵票具有紀念意義。
- I'd like to buy two **airmail stamps**. 我想買兩張航空信郵票。

Sentences & Grammar

♪230-01 **1.** I want to send a letter to my **pen pal** in England.
我要寄信給我英國的筆友。

pal 指好友、伙伴，比「friend」更口語化。英國及前英國殖民地國家更常用「mate」。

- Hank is my best friend. We've been pals since babies.
漢克是我最好的朋友，我們從嬰兒時就是朋友了。

♪230-02 **2.** You should **write down** the name, address and telephone number of the addressee on the envelope.
你要在信封上寫清楚收信人的姓名、住址和電話。

除了「write down 寫下」外，write 的其他片語有「write off 註銷、取消」、「write out 全部寫出」、「write up 詳細描寫」、「write of 把……當作寫作題材」等。

♪230-03 **3.** If we can't **find** the addressee, the letter will be returned to the sender.
如果我們找不到收信人，這封信會退還給寄信人。

find 和「look for」都有尋找之意，但 look for 強調尋找的動作。

- They wished to find the treasure and were looking for clues for years. Unfortunately, they ended up finding dead bodies.
他們希望找到寶藏，多年來一直尋找線索。不幸的是他們最後找到的是屍體。

♪230-04 **4.** This letter is opened only by the **addressee**.
這封信只有收件人才能打開。

addressee 和 receiver 都指收件人，其他郵政相關字詞包含：

sender 寄件人	mail 信件總稱	letter 信
postal code 郵遞區號	stamp 郵票	postmark 郵戳

Our foreign friends!

交朋友不分國界，在現今寄東西給自己的外國朋友也是件容易的事；請幫以下的人物填入正確的國家名稱，讓他們能順利寄出要給朋友的東西！

I'd like to send this parcel to ______ . I think my French friend will love this set of teacups.
我要把這個包裹寄到巴黎。我想我的法國朋友一定會喜歡這組茶杯。

I want to send a letter to my pen pal in _________. How long will it take?
我要寄信給我英國的筆友。這封信寄到目的地要多少時間？

I bought some clothes for my friend who is studying in the ____________. How much will it cost to send this parcel?
我買了一些衣服要給我在美國讀書的朋友。請問寄這個包裹要多少錢？

I would like to buy some commemorative postcards for my friends in __________.
我想買幾張紀念明信片給我在泰國的朋友們。

單字補充站

- Japan 日本
- South Korea 南韓
- China 中國
- Thailand 泰國
- France 法國
- Germany 德國
- Canada 加拿大
- United States 美國

UNIT 03

Going to the Movie Theater

去電影院

♪232-01 **Let's go to the cinema this weekend!**
這週末我們去看電影吧！

♪232-02 Please queue in the lobby for tickets. 請到大廳排隊買票。

♪232-03 We're going to buy two movie tickets for *Dune*.
我們要買兩張《沙丘》的電影票。

♪232-04 How much is a movie ticket? 一張電影票多少錢？

♪232-05 Have you bought a ticket? 你買電影票了嗎？

♪232-06 I want to sit in the front row of the cinema.
我想坐在影廳前排。

How to Say

- **買電影票的數量**：I want two movie tickets. 我要兩張電影票。
- **看電影的種類**：I want to see a 3D movie. 我想看 3D 電影。
- **位置的要求**：I want to sit in the front row of the cinema.
  我想坐在電影院的前排。

Vocabulary

In the theater 在電影院 ♪233-01

type 種類 ♪233-02

- science fiction 科幻片
- comedy 喜劇片
- animated film 動畫片
- action 動作片
- documentary 紀錄片
- blockbuster 賣座鉅片
- independent (indie) film 獨立電影

screen 螢幕 ♪233-03

- special effect 特效
- dialogue 對白
- subtitle 字幕
- movie 電影
- film 電影
- video 影片

theater 電影院 ♪233-04

- open cinema 露天電影院
- wide-screen 寬銀幕
- row 排
- seat 座位
- curtain 簾幕
- projector 投影機
- cinema 電影院

concession stand 販賣部 ♪233-05

- popcorn 爆米花
- pop 氣泡飲料
- churros 吉拿棒
- sundae 聖代
- hot chocolate 熱可可
- cinnamon bun 肉桂捲

people 人物 ♪233-06

- actor 演員
- actress 女演員
- director 導演
- moviegoer 電影迷
- audience 觀眾

awards 獎項 ♪233-07

- Oscar 奧斯卡獎
- cinema industry 電影業
- nominate 提名
- nominee 被提名者

More to Know

面向愈來愈多元的奧斯卡獎

儘管受到 2020 年的疫情影響，全球的電影產業大受打擊，但電影業卻仍然在大量電影院關閉或倒閉的生存危機中，努力維持著與網路社群串流的轉機。而在 2020 年，有兩位女性獲得了奧斯卡獎項。她們分別是贏得最佳導演獎的趙婷，和最佳原創劇本獎的艾莫芮德。

情節故事 Story

Who You are a father of two kids.
♪234-01 你是兩個孩子的父親。

Where You are picking up your kids in the school.
♪234-02 你在學校接小孩。

When It's Friday. You want to have a movie night with your kids.
♪234-03 今天是禮拜五。你想要和孩子一起度過一個電影夜。

What You want to buy three tickets.
♪234-04 你想要買三張票。

How to Speak

在線上買票的優點：

- Buying movie tickets online will **save time**.
  線上買電影票可以省時間。
- We can also **choose seats online**. 我們還可以線上選座位。
- You can **see the ratings of each movie** online.
  可以看到每部電影的線上評分。

重點對話 Dialogue

票已售罄

♪235-08 對話練習！

♪235-01 I'd like two movie tickets for *Dune*.
我想要兩張《沙丘》的票。

♪235-02 Sorry. The tickets have been sold out. You can buy other movie tickets.
不好意思。票已經賣完了。你可以買別的電影票。

♪235-03 What else is on today?
今天還有什麼電影？

♪235-04 *Spiderman: No way home*. It's a great movie.
《蜘蛛人：無家日》，那是一部很棒的電影。

♪235-05 Sounds good. I'd like two tickets, please.
聽起來不錯。我要買兩張票。

信用卡折扣

♪235-06 Tina, have you seen any good films recently?
緹娜，你最近看過好看的電影嗎？

♪235-07 No, but the cinema will show some wonderful movies this week.
沒有，不過這週會上映幾部很棒的電影。

More to Know

到電影院當然要配爆米花！快看看下方例句，聽清楚店員在說什麼吧！

- We offer **two kinds of** snacks. 我們提供兩種小吃套餐。
- Snack B **includes** a bag of popcorn and a bottle of coke.
  套餐 B 包括一包爆米花和一瓶可樂。
- If you **order** this kind of snack, we'll also get you a cup of coffee.
  如果您點這種小吃套餐，我們還會送您一杯咖啡。

Sentences & Grammar

♪236-01 **1.** If you have a membership card, the **movie** ticket can be 20% off.
如果你有會員卡，電影票可以打八折。

movie、film、與 cinema 都指電影。 movie theater 和 cinema 則指電影院，所以去電影院可說「go to the movie theater」或「go to the cinema」。

- It's convenient to watch **films** on streaming platforms, but certain movies are much better to watch in the **cinema**.
  在串流平台上看電影很方便，但部分電影去戲院看更棒。

♪236-02 **2.** Please **show** your membership card before you buy the ticket.
買票之前，請出示您的會員卡。

片語「show A to B」及「show B A」都指把 A 呈現給 B。

- The teacher **showed** **his puppet** **to** **a bunch of curious children** who can't stop asking questions.
  老師把他的木偶展示給一群不停問問題的好奇小孩。

♪236-03 **3.** Can I **lend** my membership card to others?
我的會員卡可以借給別人用嗎？

lend 與 borrow 都指「借」，但用法不同：

A lend sth to B	指 A 把某物借給 B
A lend B sth	
A borrow sth from B	A 向 B 借某物

- The items were **lent** **to** us by the coach.
  東西是教練借給我們的。
- The items were **borrowed** **from** the coach.
  東西是向教練借的。

The best choice

電影院總是會上映各種類型的電影，而影迷也是百百款，大家都有自己喜歡的類型；請根據提示，為以下三位角色挑選適合他們的電影吧！

A	B	C
• science fiction	• comedy	• Action
• nominated for Oscars	• 3D movie	• Directed by Tim Brown
• 185 minutes	• 78 minutes	• 105 minutes

❶ I love laughing in the movie theater! I also feel happier when I hear others' laughter. And I love 3D movies because it's so exciting! Don' t you think so?
我很愛在電影院裡大笑！聽到別人的笑聲，我自己也會感到更開心。然後我很喜歡 3D 電影，因為很刺激啊！你不覺得嗎？

Which one should you recommend? 你該推薦哪部電影呢？ ______________

❷ I'm a big fan of director Tim Brown! I have watched every movie he directed, and I love all of them, especially action movies.
我是導演提姆・布朗的忠實粉絲！我看過他導的每一部電影而且也都非常喜歡，尤其是動作片。

Which one should you recommend? 你該推薦哪部電影呢？ ______________

❸ I really enjoy watching mind-twisting science fiction movies. Even if it's more than three hours long, I'll go to the theater and watch it!
我真的很喜歡看燒腦的科幻電影。哪怕片長超過三小時，我也會去電影院看！

Which one should you recommend? 你該推薦哪部電影呢？ ______________

解答

1. B 喜劇片／ 3D 電影／片長 1 小時 18 分鐘
2. C 動作片／提姆・布朗執導／片長 1 小時 45 分鐘
3. A 科幻片／奧斯卡提名／片長 3 小時 5 分鐘

UNIT 04

Customer Service

客服

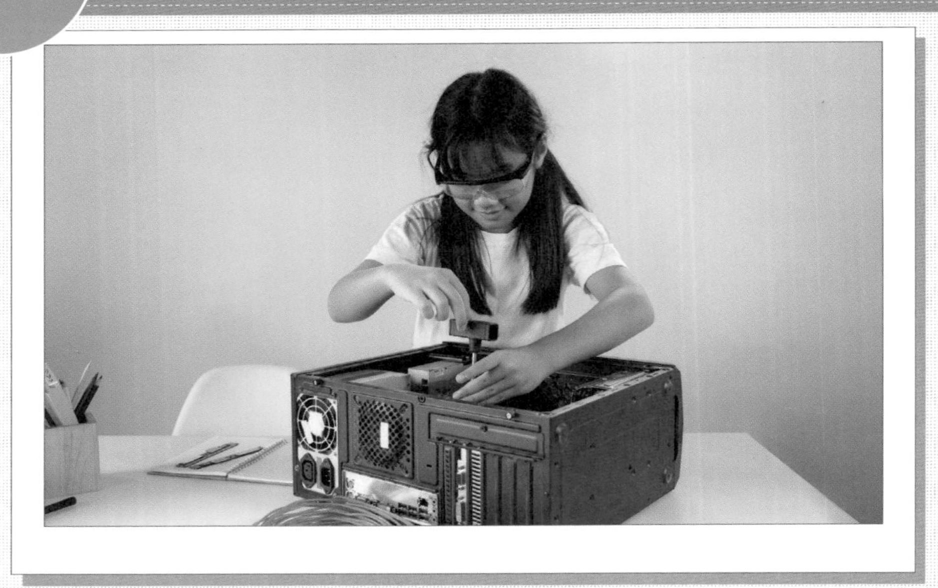

♪238-01 **The internet broke down. Would you please send someone to have a check?**
網路斷線了，請問能派人來檢查嗎？

♪238-02 The staff will check the Internet for your home this afternoon. 工作人員會在今天下午為你們家檢查網路。

♪238-03 Please speed up the Internet for us. 請幫我們提高網速。

♪238-04 Now the speed of the Internet is too slow.
現在的網速太慢了。

♪238-05 Will my mobile phone network be interrupted after I go abroad? 我出國以後，手機網路會中斷嗎？

♪238-06 Can I pay the net fee by phone? 可以在手機上繳費嗎？

How to Say

「年費、月租」該怎麼說？

- I suggest that you choose the **yearly package** because it is much cheaper than the **monthly package**.
  你可以選擇年費套餐，比月租方案便宜得多。

Vocabulary

♪239-01
about customer service 關於客服

♪239-02
about complaints 關於抱怨

- complain 抱怨
- product 產品
- poor 糟糕的
- unproperly 不妥善地
- out of date 過期

♪239-03
about praises 關於讚美

- fresh 新鮮的
- fabulous 完美的
- properly 妥善地
- completely 完全地
- on time 準時

♪239-04
process 流程

- change 更換
- packing 包裝
- 補 package 包裝
- seperate 分開
- support 支持，支援
- change 改善
- replace 替換
- receive 接收

♪239-05
about money 關於錢

- return 退款
- 補 refund 退錢
- charge 收費
- arrear 拖欠費用
- owe 欠款
- bill 帳單
- reissue 重新發行
- pay 支付

♪239-06
service 服務

- online 線上
- 24 / 7 全年無休（一天工作 24 小時，一週 7 天）
- center 中心
- customer service 客戶服務

♪239-07
other 其他

- fragile 易碎的
- sign 簽收
- glass 玻璃
- regerigerated package 冷凍包裹
- quality 品質
- quantity 數量

More to Know

跨國的客服中心

隨著物價上升，許多大企業為了降低人事成本，便在人力薪資相對低廉的國家成立客服部門，這樣一來，不只可以利用時差安排錯開的輪班，達成 24 小時專人在線，更能省下國內較高的人事成本和輪班的夜班加班費用，可說是一舉兩得。

情節故事 Story

Who You are an unlucky person with network problems.
240-01 你是個遇到網路問題的倒霉人。

Where You are in your house, sitting on the sofa.
240-02 你在你家，坐在沙發上。

When It's three in the afternoon. It's Saturday.
240-03 現在是下午三點。今天是週六。

What You are calling the service center.
240-04 你正在打給服務中心。

How to Speak

向客服表達你遇到的問題：

- Hi, my network is not working. 嗨，我的網路不會動。
- Hi. The network seems to have run into a problem. I can't fix it.
  嗨。網路好像遇到一點問題。我沒法解決。

重點對話 Dialogue

網路斷線

♪241-07 對話練習！

♪241-01 My home network is broken.
我家的網路斷線了。

♪241-02 Have you paid the bill on time?
請問您按時繳費了嗎？

♪241-03 I just paid the net fee last week.
我上週剛繳完。

♪241-04 Please fill in this form with your name, address, and telephone number. We'll send someone to your home to check it out.
那請您在這張表上填上您的姓名、地址和電話。我們會派人到您家去查看。

寄來的商品不符

♪241-05 I bought a red skirt on the Internet, but it is a yellow one.
我在網上買的是紅色的裙子，但是寄來的卻是黃色的。

♪241-06 I'm sorry, it's our fault. The refund would be completed within a week.
對不起，這的確是我們的失誤。一週之內將會退款完成。

More to Know

聽懂客服的回答：

- **無法退款，但可以換貨時：**Sorry, we'll get a new one for you right away. 不好意思，我們馬上給您換一件新的。
- **進行換貨，索取收件資料時：**Please tell me your name and your address. 請告訴我你的姓名和地址。

Sentences & Grammar

♪242-01 **1.** Your credit card's limit has been **exceeded.**
您的信用卡已經透支了。

exceed 在數量或品質上超出、勝過。 但若指銀行帳戶透支，則要用「overdraw 過度提款（動詞）」或 overdraft（名詞）。

- The performance has far exceeded our expectation.
  演出大幅超出我們的預期。
- It shows an overdraft in your account, ma'am.
  女士，這裡顯示您的帳戶超支。

♪242-02 **2.** Your credit card has been **declined.**
你的信用卡被拒刷。

decline 有婉拒、謝絕之意，用在信用卡或現金卡上指可能因凍結或餘額不足，使其在機器上刷不過。refuse 雖也指拒絕、不肯，但 decline 語氣更委婉。

- Diana respectfully declined the drink as she was the designated driver.
  黛安娜很有禮貌地婉拒邀酒，因為她是指定安全駕駛。
- He refused my invitation because he doesn't like me.
  他拒絕我的邀請，因為他不喜歡我。

♪242-03 **3.** What happens if I don't pay **on time**?
如果我沒有按時還款，會怎麼樣呢？

片語「on time」指準時，「in time」則表示及時。

- The tailored suit was delivered in time, allowing the groom to arrive at the wedding on time.
  修改的禮服及時送到，讓新郎能準時抵達婚禮。

♪242-04 **4.** You'd better pay the **bill** on time, or it will affect your credit limit.
您最好按時還款。逾時未還將影響你的信用額度。

例句中的 bill 是名詞，指帳單，當動詞時則有「給……開帳單、要……付款」之意。

Mission clear

回想本單元學到的單字，挑戰看看，你能答對幾個呢？

						s			
c	o		p						c
						n			
							q		n
			r						
		a					i		
q							y		

解答

						s			
c	o	m	p	l	a	i	n		c
	n		r			g			h
	l		o			n			a
	i		p				q		n
	n		e				u		g
	e		r	e	p	l	a	c	e
			l				l		
	p	a	y			b	i	l	l
							t		
q	u	a	n	t	i	t	y		

寫作練習

Review 7

A 填空練習

- What kind of ___________ would you like to have?
  您想開哪種帳戶？
  答案請見 P.220

- We can't send this ___________. These articles are ___________.
  我們不能幫您寄，這些是易燃物。
  答案請見 P.226

B 引導造句

- **I would like to... 我想要……**
  I would like to ____.
  我想買一張明信片。
  答案請見 P.229

- **sold out 售罄**
  ____?
  票已經賣完了。
  答案請見 P.235

- **fill in 填寫**
  ____.
  答案請見 P.241

C 引導寫作

標題	Internet Problems 網路問題
網路有問題	
打給客服	
請求支援	
提高網速	

參考短文：今天網路好像斷了，連不上網。所以我打給客服，請求他們協助派人來檢查。工作人員下午來檢查網路。我詢問他們可否順便提高網速。

Chapter 08

Traveling
旅遊

UNIT 01

Airport Check-in

機場報到

♪246-01 **Where is the boarding gate number 8?** 八號登機口在哪裡？

♪246-02 When can I check in? 我什麼時候能辦理登機？

♪246-03 When will I board the plane? 我什麼時間可以登機？

♪246-04 I have a suitcase and a handbag.
我帶了一個行李箱和一個手提包。

♪246-05 Please take your valuables with you.
請隨身攜帶您的貴重物品。

♪246-06 Can I carry this handbag on board?
我能帶著這個手提包登機嗎？

How to Speak

托運行李：

- How much do you charge for my **baggage**?
  托運我的行李要多少錢？
- Is my luggage **overweight**? 我的行李超重嗎？
- Where can I **check** my baggage? 請問我到哪裡托運行李？

Vocabulary

♪247-01
Check-in 報到

♪247-02
baggage 托運行李

- free baggage allowance 拖運行李重量限制
- goods to declare 報關物品
- personal belongings 個人物品
- scale 磅秤
- unaccompanied weight limit 重量限制
- carry-on bag 隨身行李；手提行李
- baggage claim 提領行李
- bonded baggage 存關行李
- baggage carousel 行李運輸帶
- baggage inspection 行李檢驗
- baggage tag 行李吊牌

♪247-03
Service Counter 服務台

♪247-04
departure and arrival 出入境

- emigration control 出境檢查
- embarkation card 入境記錄卡
- flight information board 航班顯示板
- international flight 國際航班
- timetable 時刻表
- time zone 時區
- jet lag 時差

♪247-06
passport and ticket 護照與機票

- destination 目的地
- domestic flight 國內班機
- flight number 班機號碼
- gate number 登機門號碼
- non-stop flight 直飛班機
- one-way ticket 單程機票
- round-trip ticket 來回機票

♪247-05
duty-free items 免稅商品

- dutiable goods 須課稅商品
- duty-free shop 免稅商店
- exchange and tax payment 兌換及付稅
- exchange rate 匯率
- extra charge 額外費用
- in-flight sales 機上免稅品販賣
- airport tax 機場稅

More to Know

看動時刻表與詳細資訊：

- estimated time of arrival (ETA) 預計到達時間
- estimated time of departure (ETD) 預計起飛時間

情節故事 Story

Who ♪248-01
You are the customs in the airport.
你是機場的海關。

Where ♪248-02
You are in the airport.
你在機場裡。

When ♪248-03
It's two twenty. The plane will take off in forty minutes.
現在是兩點二十。飛機 40 分鐘後起飛。

What ♪248-04
You are checking tourists' baggage one by one.
你正在一一檢查旅客的行李。

How to Speak

Oops! 這些東西不能上飛機喔！

- Your recharger **cannot be brought** to the plane.
  你的行動電源不能帶到飛機上。
- Something like lighters **is not allowed to** bring on the plane.
  有些東西像打火機不允許帶上飛機。

重點對話 Dialogue

金屬物品要拿出來喔

♪249-08 對話練習！

♪249-01 Do you have any metal things on you?
您身上帶有金屬物品嗎？

♪249-02 I have an electronic pen.
我帶了一隻數位筆。

♪249-03 Please take out your electronic pen. We have to check it.
請您把它拿出來，我們要檢查。

♪249-04 OK, do you have any other questions?
好的，還有別的問題嗎？

♪249-05 No, I wish you a pleasant journey.
沒有，祝您旅途愉快。

咦？金屬探測器怎麼又響了？

♪249-06 Please go through the security check here. What's in your pocket? The metal detector is ringing.
請到這邊過安檢。請問您口袋裡裝的什麼？金屬探測器在響。

♪249-07 It's my cell phone.
是我的手機。

More to Know

這些東西絕對不能帶到飛機上喔！

不是所有東西都能帶上飛機，一定要注意免得受罰喔。

- **Controlled Items 搭機違禁品：**box cutters 美工刀、knives 刀類、scissors 剪刀、guns 槍械、liquid over 100ml 超過 100ml 的液體、fruits & vegetables 新鮮水果蔬菜、meat 肉類。

Sentences & Grammar

♪250-01 **1.** Would you **mind** opening the bag for me?
請您把包包打開讓我確認，好嗎？

mind 當動詞時有介意之意。後接名詞、動名詞、及 that 子句，常被用來委婉地提出要求。

- Do you think Jack would **mind giving** me a ride?
  你覺得傑克會介意載我一程嗎？

♪250-02 **2.** Please remove the metal objects from your body. **Take off** your coat, please.
請您取下身上的金屬物品。請脫掉外衣。

穿脫衣服的動詞：

穿上	put on	put ＋代名詞＋ on
脫下	take off	take ＋代名詞＋ off

♪250-03 **3.** You may have prohibited **articles**, please cooperate with our work.
您可能攜帶的有違禁物品，請配合我們的工作。

除了物品、商品，article 也有文章、條款之意。

- Has everyone read this **article** on today's Liberty Times?
  每個人都有讀到今天自由時報上的這篇文章嗎？

♪250-04 **4.** I'm sorry, sir. You cannot take **these** things abroad.
抱歉，先生。你不能攜帶這些物品出境。

定冠詞	意思	搭配
the	這、那、這些、那些	單、複數可數名詞、不可數名詞
this	這	單數可數名詞、不可數名詞
that	那	單數可數名詞、不可數名詞
these	這些	複數可數名詞
those	那些	複數可數名詞

準備行李 Check your baggage!

出國旅行總是令人感到興奮！但興奮之餘，也要記得注意自己的行李是否裝了不該裝的東西。讓我們一起來檢查看看行李裡哪些東西該被拿出來吧！

Please put a cross on the controlled items. 請在搭機違禁品上打叉。

Your baggage:

你的行李：

- ☐ the passport
  護照
- ☐ a hat
  一頂帽子
- ☐ an apple
  一顆蘋果
- ☐ a bag of mask
  一袋口罩
- ☐ the ticket
  機票
- ☐ a pair of scissors
  一把剪刀
- ☐ a lighter
  打火機
- ☐ a pair of sneakers
  一雙布鞋
- ☐ a scarf
  一件圍巾
- ☐ a notebook
  筆記本
- ☐ a telephone
  一支手機
- ☐ a storybook
  一本故事書

解答

a pair of scissors 一把剪刀、an apple 一顆蘋果、a lighter 一支打火機

UNIT 02

Boarding

登機

♪252-01 **Good afternoon, welcome aboard.** 午安，歡迎登機。

♪252-02 You go to the wrong gate; you should board at gate number 9. 您走錯登機口了，你應該在 9 號登機口登機。

♪252-03 You will be frisked before you board the plane. 你在登機之前會被搜身。

♪252-04 The flight BA 125 to Beijing is now boarding. 英航 125 飛往北京的航班正在登機。

♪252-05 Sir, please show me your boarding pass. 先生，請出示你的登機證 .

How to Say

向櫃檯請教登機資訊：

- Has my fight begun **boarding**? 我的航班開始登機了嗎？
- When will I board the plane? 我什麼時間可以登機？
- At what time should I **check in**? 我該什麼時間辦理登機手續呢？

單字地圖 Vocabulary

boarding 登機 ♪253-01

incident 意外 ♪253-02

- turbulence 亂流
- delay 延誤
- ditching 水上迫降
- evacuate 疏散
- forced landing 迫降、緊急降落
- head wind 逆風
- hijack 劫機
- water evacuation 水上逃生
- out of order 設備故障

tool 工具 ♪253-03

- dry chemical extinguisher 乾粉滅火器
- slide 逃生用充氣滑梯
- smoke hood 防煙面罩
- fire extinguisher 滅火器

class 座艙等級 ♪253-04

- Economy 經濟艙
- Business 商務艙
- First class 頭等艙
- charter flight 包機

seat 座位 ♪253-05

- seatback 椅背
- headsets 頭戴式耳機
- airsickness bag 嘔吐袋
- blanket 毛毯
- break-in area 逃生窗
- life vest 救生衣
- seat belt 安全帶

service 服務 ♪253-06

- call button 呼叫鈕
- wireless internet access 無線上網
- bassinet 嬰幼兒睡床
- trolley 餐車
- wheelchair 輪椅

other 其他 ♪253-07

- facility and services directory 設施服務指南
- trash 一般垃圾
- waste bin 垃圾桶
- lavatory 洗手間

More to Know

看懂廁所的指示！

- 廁所的英文：
  - toilet 廁所
  - bathroom 多半是含衛浴設備的廁所
  - restroom 廁所
  - lavatory 飛機上的洗手間

情節故事 Story

Who ♪254-01

You are a passenger on the plane.
你是飛機上的一名旅客。

Where ♪254-02

You are heading to the U.S.
你正要前往美國。

When ♪254-03

The flight would take off within 15 minutes.
航班十五分鐘內啟程。

What ♪254-04

Suddenly, a woman pats your shoulder.
突然，有個女人拍了拍你的肩膀。

How to Speak

On the plane... 在飛機上，有時候會遇到有人尋求換位置的情況：

- Can I change seats with you, Sir? 先生，我能跟您換一下位置嗎？
- With pleasure. 我很樂意。
- Sorry, I don't want to change. 抱歉，我不想換。

Dialogue

坐錯位置

♪255-08 對話練習！

♪255-01 Your seat is here, Sir. Your seat number is F03.
先生，你的位置在這邊。你的座位號碼是 F03.

♪255-02 Really? I thought my seat is by the window.
真的嗎？我以為我的位置靠窗。

♪255-03 Excuse me, sir. You're sitting in my seat.
不好意思，先生，您坐的是我的位置。

請對號入座

♪255-04 Ladies and gentlemen, please take your seats.
先生、女士們，請對號入座。

♪255-05 Miss, can you help me find my seat?
小姐，能幫我找一下我的位置嗎？

♪255-06 Please show me your ticket, I will find the seat for you. Your seat is the first in the second row.
請讓我看一下您的機票，我幫您找位置。你的位置在第二排第一個。

♪255-07 Thank you so much. And can you help me to put my luggage in the averhead bin?
謝謝你。還有請問您能幫我把行李箱放到上面嗎？

More to Know

登機證的小秘密：你一定要知道！

- **登機證上面的訊息：**登機證上面有機場名稱、登機門號碼、航班號碼、艙等、旅客姓名、座位號碼、目的地、出發地等各種個人資訊。
- **登機證上面的條碼：**其實登機證上面的條碼亦存載著很多個人訊息，意圖不軌的人可能會藉此侵入你的帳號，將你帳號內的飛行積分轉到其他帳戶名下，還有可能會洩漏金融卡或信用卡的訊息。
- **使用完的登機證：**使用完的登機證最好投入碎紙機銷毀，以免個人訊息、資料等外洩。

Sentences & Grammar

♪256-01 **1.** Would you please **reconfirm** your seat belt? Thank you.
請您再次確認繫好您的安全帶，謝謝。

字根 re 即有重複之意，搭配動詞就是重複此動作或強調。以例句來看，可能之前已請乘客確認的情況下再請確認，或強調大家一定要確認。

- The client demands us to **redesign** the logo.
客戶要求我們重新設計 logo。

♪256-02 **2.** Please make sure that your carry-on items are properly placed in the overhead rack or **under** the seat.
請您確認您的手提物品是否妥善安放在頭頂上方的行李架內或座椅下方。

表達位置的有：

in front of 在前方	behind 在後面
out、outside 在外面	in、inside 在裡面
on、on top of、above 在上方	under、underneath、below 在下方
on A's left side 在 A 的左邊	on A's right side 在 A 的右邊

♪256-03 **3.** This flight is **non-smoking** all the way.
本次航班全程禁煙。

簡單的禁止祈使句寫成「no＋名詞／Ving ＋ allowed（可省略）」即可。

- No **pets** are allowed inside the park.
公園裡不能帶寵物進去。
- No **gossiping** in the church.
教會裡不准八卦。

該登機了 Who's first?

♪257-01 **吉米、喬伊、亨利、莎莉四人在機場準備登機。請掃 QR Code 聽機場的廣播，看看誰是第一位要前往登機的人呢？**

Jimmy's ticket
吉米的機票

AIRLINE Boarding Pass	AIRLINE	
Flight ______	Name	Surname
Date ______	Flight	
Gate ______	Date	Time
Seat ______	Gate	Seat

Joe's ticket
喬伊的機票

AIRLINE Boarding Pass	AIRLINE	
Flight ______	Name	Surname
Date ______	Flight	
Gate ______	Date	Time
Seat ______	Gate	Seat

Henry's ticket
亨利的機票

AIRLINE Boarding Pass	AIRLINE	
Flight ______	Name	Surname
Date ______	Flight	
Gate ______	Date	Time
Seat ______	Gate	Seat

解答

Jimmy 吉米
Your flight would be **MH330**, to London. Board at **gate 15**, your seat would be 11A.
你的班機是 **MH330**，飛往**倫敦**。請在 **15** 號登機口登機。你的座位是 **11A**。

Joe 喬伊
Your flight would be **B4315**, to **San Francisco**. Board at gate **4**, your seat would be **6C**.
你的班機是 **B4315**，飛往**舊金山**。請在 **4** 號登機口登機。你的座位是 **6C**。

Henry 亨利
Your flight would be **A2210**, to **Tokyo**. Board at gate **3**, your seat would be **23B**.
你的班機是 **A2210**，飛往**東京**。請在 **3** 號登機口登機。你的座位是 **23B**。

UNIT 03

On the Airplane

在飛機上

♪258-01 **What would you like?** 您要點什麼？

♪258-02 I'd like something to drink. 我想要點喝的。

♪258-03 I would like a cup of wine. 我要一杯紅酒。

♪258-04 Would you like some coffee? 你想來點咖啡嗎？

♪258-05 We serve bread and drinks. 我們提供麵包和飲料。

♪258-06 Coffee is gone, sir. How about tea?
先生，咖啡已經沒有了。喝茶可以嗎？

♪258-07 Wait a minute. Your drink will be sent to your seat.
稍等。你要的飲料會被送到你的座位上。

How to Say

有禮貌地詢問空服員你想要的物品或食物：

- **Would you mind** bringing me some tea? 可以給我一杯茶嗎？
- **May I have** a glass of water? 請問可以給我一杯水嗎？

單字地圖 Vocabulary

during the flight 航班中
♪259-01

seats 座位
♪259-02

- overhead compartment 艙頂置物櫃
- aisle 走道
- window seat 靠窗的座位
- aisle seat 靠走道的座位
- center seat 中間的座位

cabin crew 機組人員
♪259-03

- captain 機長
- co-pilot 副機長
- flight attendant 空服人員
- 補 attendant call 呼叫空服員
- ground crew 地勤人員
- navigator 領航員

aircraft 飛機
♪259-04

- belly 機腹
- flight deck 前艙
- undercarriage bay 貨艙
- wing 機翼
- panel 儀錶板
- runway 跑道
- retractable landing gear 伸縮起落架
- tank 油箱
- fuel 燃料

passengers 旅客
♪259-05

- connecting passenger 轉機旅客
- handicapped passenger 身障旅客
- transit passenger 轉機旅客
- no-show 誤機者
- departing passenger 出境旅客

other 其他
♪259-06

- take off 飛機起飛
- land 飛機降落
- tail wind 順風
- layover 外站過夜
- cruise 巡航

How to Say

國際機場大多都提供換錢的服務，若想換錢，請記得以下的關鍵字：

- currency declaration 貨幣申報
- Foreign Currency Exchange 外幣兌換

情節故事 Story

Who You are are a flight attendant on the plane.
♪260-01 你是飛機上的空服員。

Where You are on the flight to New Zealand.
♪260-02 你正在前往紐西蘭的航班上。

When It's time to serve meals.
♪260-03 現在是上餐的時間。

What You just received several questions from the passengers. One asks for the duty-free product, and the other asks for the specialized meal.
♪260-04 你剛收到旅客們的問題。一個想問機上免稅，一個想問特製餐點。

How to Speak

我要去免稅店！

- I'm going to buy a gift for my mother in the **duty-free shop**.
  我要去免稅店買給媽媽的禮物。

Dialogue

我點的是無牛餐，好像送錯了。 ♪261-07 對話練習！

♪261-01 Here is your lunch, sir.
先生這是你的午餐。

♪261-02 I think you made a mistake. I ordered no beef meal.
我想你搞錯了，我點的是無牛餐。

♪261-03 I'm sorry. It's my fault. Just a moment, please. I'll be right with you.
很抱歉。是我搞錯了。請稍等。我馬上過來。

耳機壞了，可以給我新的嗎？

♪261-04 What's up, sir?
先生，怎麼了？

♪261-05 My headphones are broken. Can you bring me new ones?
我的耳機壞了，可以給我拿個新的嗎？

♪261-06 Of course. Wait a moment, please. Here you are.
當然可以。您稍等。這邊給您。

More to Know

特殊飛機餐：

Religious Meal 宗教餐點	▪ Muslim Meal 伊斯蘭餐（清真食品）的認證 ▪ Hindu Meal 非素食印度餐 ▪ Kosher Meal 猶太餐
Vegetarian Meal 素食餐點	▪ Vegetarian Indian Meal 印度素食餐 ▪ Vegetarian Oriental Meal 東方素食餐 ▪ Vegetarian Vegan Meal 西方素食餐 ▪ Vegetarian Lacto-ovo Meal 蛋奶素餐
Dietary Meal 病理餐點	▪ Non-Beef Meal 無牛肉餐 ▪ Diabetic Meal 糖尿病餐 ▪ Gluten-Free Meal 無麩質餐

Sentences & Grammar

♪262-01 **1.** I'm a little **cold**. Give me a blanket, please.
我有點冷，請給我一條毯子。

天氣冷：形容自身感覺冷時，只能用 cold 與 freezing。

cool 涼快的	cold 冷的	chilly 冷到使人不舒服的
freezing 嚴寒的	frosty 結霜的冷的	icy 冰冷的

- He ate **cold** soup on a **cold** day. Of course, he felt **cold** and ended up with a **cold**.
  他在冷天喝冷湯，當然會覺得冷，結果還得了感冒。

♪262-02 **2.** Please help me get some tissue and a **garbage** bag.
請幫我拿些衛生紙和一個垃圾紙袋。

其他的垃圾說法：

單字	名詞	動詞
trash	垃圾	破壞
waste	廢棄物（統稱）	浪費
litter	徧散亂的物品	亂扔垃圾

♪262-03 **3.** Could you tell me where the duty free **shop** is?
你能告訴我免稅店在哪嗎？

商店規模比較：

stand	shop	store
小攤販	商店	大商店

- Rick bought cigarettes at the grocery **shop**, went to a shoe **store** to **shop** for sneakers, and stopped at a snack **stand** for azuki bean soup.
  瑞克去雜貨店買菸，進到一家鞋店買運動鞋，並停在一個點心攤吃紅豆湯。

機上問題 Problems on the plane

空服員總是會不遺餘力，協助解決飛機上乘客的各種問題；請你幫助這位空服員，將正確物品配對給對的人，滿足乘客的需求吧！

I'm a little cold. Give me a blanket, please.

Which one should you give her?
你該給她什麼呢？ ___________

B

My headphones are broken. Can you bring me new ones?

Which one should you give him?
你該給他什麼呢？ ___________

C

Could you please give me a cup of tea? I'm thirsty.

Which one should you give her?
你該給她什麼呢？ ___________

D

I feel like I have a fever. Do you have cold medicine?

Which one should you give her?
你該給她什麼呢？ ___________

解答

A blanket 一條毯子	A pair of headphones 一副耳機
A cup of tea 一杯水	Some pills or medicine 一些藥丸或藥

UNIT 04

Arrival

抵達

♪264-01 **Can you tell me how to fill out this single entry?**
你能告訴我怎樣填寫入境單嗎？

♪264-02 Is here the immigration counter? 這裡是入境審查處嗎？

♪264-03 Please show me your passport. 請出示你的護照。

♪264-04 I will check your documents and identification.
我將要檢查你的證件和身份。

♪264-05 May I see your papers? 我可以看看你的證件嗎？

♪264-06 Do you come here alone? 你是一個人來的嗎？

♪264-07 No. My parents are here with me.
不是，爸爸媽媽跟我一起來的。

How to Say

過海關必經的問答：

- **How long** will you stay here? 您將在此逗留多長時間？
- I will stay about one month here. 我會待在這裡一個月左右。

單字地圖 Vocabulary

In the airport 在機場中

♪265-^01

airport 機場

♪265-^01

- air bridge 登機廊橋
- cabin crew 空勤人員
- air current 氣流
- air traffic control 航路管制
- aircraft 飛機
- Airline Check-in Counters 航空公司報到櫃台

airlines 航空公司

♪265-^01

- airport fire service 機場消防隊
- airport information 機場業務答詢
- Animal & Plant Quarantine 動植物檢疫局
  - 補 animal quarantine 動物檢疫
- airport office 機場辦公室

arrival and departure 入出境

♪265-^01

- arrival lobby 入境大廳
- automatic door 自動出入門
- baggage claim area 行李提領處
- baggage delivery 行李托運
- carousel 旋轉行李輸送帶
- departure lobby 出境大廳

place 地方

♪265-^01

- Customs 海關
- Disabled Customer Service Counter 無障礙服務台
- immigration 移民局
- information counter 詢問處
- lost and found 失物招領
- medical center 醫療中心
- baby care room 育嬰室
- baby nursing room 哺乳室

More to Know

認識更多機場周遭相關的英文指示！

- airtel 機場飯店
- apron 停機坪
- greeting area 到站等候區
- entrance 入口
- escalator 電扶梯
- exit 出口

情節故事 Story

Who You work in the tourist center in the airport.
♪266-01 你在機場的旅客中心上班。

Where You are at your counter in the airport.
♪266-02 你在機場裡，你的櫃檯前。

When It's time for the plane B737 to take off.
♪266-03 現在是該是機次 B737 起飛時間。

What A man comes to you. He looks anxious.
♪266-04 有個男人走向你。他看起來很焦慮。

How to Speak

終於抵達目的機場！現在，去領行李吧！

- Excuse me, where to take my **baggage**?
  不好意思，我在哪裡可以領行李？
- Excuse me! Where is the **baggage carousel**?
  不好意思！請問行李運輸帶在哪邊呢？

Dialogue

輕鬆通過海關

♪267-09 對話練習！

♪267-01 Could you please tell me the reason why you come here?
請告訴我你為什麼來這裡？

♪267-02 I want to travel here.
我想來這裡旅遊。

♪267-03 How long will you stay here?
您將在此逗留多長時間？

♪267-04 Around one week.
一週左右。

♪267-05 Ok. Have a nice trip.
好的，祝您旅途玩得愉快。

行李不見了怎麼辦？

♪267-06 Excuse me. My luggage has been lost. What should I do?
不好意思，我遺失了我的行李。請問我該怎麼辦？

♪267-07 Don't worry, sir. Do you remember the tag's number?
不要著急，先生。您記得行李上行李牌號碼嗎？

♪267-08 I can't remember the exact number. My baggage is a red middle-sized of trolley case.
我忘了行李號碼。是個中等型號的紅色皮箱。

More to Know

填寫入境卡！

飛機降落之前，**機組人員（screw）**都會發放該**目的地入境卡（arrival card）**。建議可以事先在飛機上完成，才不會在落地之後還要找地方填寫。畢竟，入境審查常常都大排長龍，如果能提早完成，也能節省一些時間。

Sentences & Grammar

♪268-01 **1.** You must **declare** this article, or the article may be taken away.
你必須申報這件物品，不然這個物品可能會被沒收。

declare 有申報、宣告之意。

- The customs officer will confiscate cigarettes and alcohol that are not **declared**.
  海關人員會沒收沒申報的菸酒。

♪268-02 **2.** Can I **leave** the airport after I take my baggage?
提取行李後，我可以走出機場了嗎？

leave (A) for B 從 A 離開前往 B。

- Immigrants **left** their hometown **for** the New World.
  移民離開家鄉去到新大陸。

♪268-03 **3.** You can take back your **luggage** after we check it.
等我們檢查完，你就可以取回行李了。

行李的說法：

不可數名詞	luggage 行李的總稱	baggage 行李的總稱
可數名詞	suitcase 行李箱	duffle bag 行李袋

♪268-04 **4.** Excuse me. My bag has been **lost**. What should I do?
不好意思。我遺失了我的包。請問我該怎麼做？

遺失相關的單字：

lose	lost	loss	missing
動詞	**形容詞**	**名詞**	**形容詞**
遺失	不見的	損失	不見蹤影的

- My key is **missing**! I can't believe I **lost** the key again! As if the previous **loss** of my wallet isn't bad enough!
  我的鑰匙不見了！我不敢相信我又把鑰匙弄丟了！好像之前我皮夾遺失還不夠慘！

Go through customs

出國旅遊總是令人感到興奮，而下飛機之後一定會需要通過海關；請試著完成對話並通過海關，開始你的旅行吧！

Please show me your __________. 請出示您的護照。

護照是以下哪個呢？

☐ luggage　☐ arrival card　☐ passport

Here you go. 在這邊。

Could you please tell me the reason why you come here?
請問您為什麼來這裡呢？

I want to ________ here. 我想來旅遊。

旅遊該怎麼說呢？

☐ travel　☐ work　☐ study

How long will you stay here? 您將在此逗留多長時間呢？

Around _________. 一週左右。

一週該怎麼說呢？

☐ one month　☐ one week　☐ four days

解答

- 行李／目的地入境卡／護照
- 旅行／工作／讀書
- 一個月／一週／四天

寫作練習 Review 8

A 填空練習

- When can I ______________________?
  我什麼時候能辦理登機？ 答案請見 P.246

- You go to the wrong ___________. You should ___________ at gate number 9.
  您走錯登機口了，你應該在 9 號登機口登機。 答案請見 P.252

B 引導造句

- **excuse me... 不好意思**

  _________________, sir. You're ________ in my ________ .
  不好意思，先生，您坐的是我的位置。 答案請見 P.255

- **broken 故障**

  ____?
  我的耳機壞了。 答案請見 P.261

- **the reason why 為什麼、……做某事的理由**

  ____.
  答案請見 P.267

C 引導寫作

標題	Take a Plane 搭飛機
出國旅遊	
機場報到	
清點行李	
候機	

參考短文：上週，我第一次搭飛機出國。我到機場的櫃檯報到。也清點了行李。然後，我被告知登機門號碼，順利地到達登機門候機。

Topic 1 詞性：名詞

• 何謂英文單字？

「word 單字」意思是個別的英文詞語，通常單一存在狀態下就有自己的意義。

• 片語：

「phrase 片語」是形成某個慣用意義的一組字，可長可短。如單字「run」最為人所知的意義是「跑」，含run的動詞片語有「run into 偶然碰到」、「run through 瀏覽」、「run amok 亂竄」、「run errands 跑腿」等。

> My secretary ran into his ex-boyfriend when running errands for me.
> 我的祕書幫我跑腿時碰到前男友。

> She ran through the report of a man running to stop the kids from running amok in the playground.
> 她正在瀏覽某位先生跑去制止小孩在操場橫衝直撞的報告。

• 名詞：

名詞有兩種，分別是可數名詞及不可數名詞。可以數出來、計量的名詞，通常是可數名詞，如：book 書、key 鑰匙。

無法計量的、怎麼數都數不清的，就是不可數名詞：hair 頭髮、water 水。

A. 一個可數名詞是單數，超過就是複數，通常加「s」。

> Here are three bowls of cereal.
> 這裡有三碗穀片。
> 「bowl 碗」為可數名詞，「cereal 穀片」是不可數名詞。

B. 字尾若為「y」，則去「y」加「ies」。

> I read ten stories to you last Saturday.
我上週六唸了十個故事給你聽。
「story 故事」變成複數時，去「y」加「ies」。

C. 字尾若為「s」，則再加「es」。

> I bought a red dress. I love dresses.
我買了件紅色洋裝。我喜歡洋裝。

- **代名詞：**

若一個名詞重複在句子中出現，我們會用代名詞用來代替原本要講的名詞。

單數人稱：

	我	你／妳／您	他／她／牠／它
主格	i	you	he / she / it
受格	me	you	him / her / it
所有格	my	your	his / her / its
所有格代名詞	mine	yours	his / hers / its
反身代名詞	myself	yourself	himself / herself/ itself

複數人稱：

	我們	你們／妳們	他／她／牠／它們
主格	we	you	they
受格	us	you	them
所有格	our	your	their
所有格代名詞	ours	yours	theirs
反身代名詞	ourselves	yourselves	themselves

> She wants to do her assignment by herself.
她想要她自己來做自己的功課。

> That book is ours. Give us the book.
那本書是我們的。把書給我們。

Topic 2 詞性：動詞

• 動詞：

表達動作或存在狀態的詞，通常在句子主詞後，可單獨使用，或和普通助動詞或情態助動詞連用。動詞分及物動詞及不及物動詞，及物動詞在句子中需後接受詞。很多動詞同時是及物與不及物動詞，使用上要小心。

> The suspect ran.
嫌犯跑了。
「ran」是不及物動詞「run」的過去式。

> I like it.
我喜歡。
「like」表達「喜歡」時是及物動詞，後面的「it」不可省略。

• 助動詞：

能與主要動詞一起出現的動詞，「do」、「have」、及「be」都是常見的助動詞。助動詞能有助於表示時態、時間、和可能性。另外，上述提及的三個助動詞也是一般動詞，能與句中其他助動詞搭配使用。

• 情態助動詞：

「can、will、should、must」等在功能性及詞性則與上述普通助動詞有所差別，本身也可能會因情境或時態改變。情態助動詞後接原形動詞。

> We have had lunch already.
> 我們已用過午餐。
> 「have」是助動詞，為複數主詞在現在完成式的型態。「had」是一般動詞「have」，以過去分詞型態出現。

> You might not enjoy this TV drama.
> 你可能不會喜歡這個電視劇。

- **不定詞：**

是動詞的基本形式，通常為「to＋原形動詞」，可當主詞、受詞、受詞補語、或副詞等。

> To see is to believe.
> 眼見為憑。
> 「to see」的「to」與「to believe」的「to」都是不定詞，前者為主詞，後者為補語。

Topic 3 詞性：動詞

- **何謂動詞變化？**

在簡單現在式中，動詞會因為句子的主詞不同而改變。在中文中，「我喝飲料」和「她喝飲料」，動詞「喝」並無不同。但是，在英文中，動詞「喝」就需要依據主詞做變化了。

> I drink coke. She drinks milk.
> 我喝可樂。她喝牛奶。

- **一般動詞變化的原則為第三人稱單數為字尾加 s。例如：**

我	I	eat
你／妳	you	
他／她／牠／它	he / she / it	eats
我們	we	eat
你們／妳們	you	
他／她／牠／它／們	they	

另外，be動詞的變化較為特殊，詳參下方表格。

我	I	am
你／妳	you	are
他／她／牠／它	he / she / it	is
我們	we	are
你們／妳們	you	
他／她／牠／它／們	they	

> She is awesome!
> 她好厲害！

> You are awesome!
> 你們好厲害！

> I work in IT, my husband works in public relation, and his parents work in energy sector.
> 我在電子產業工作，我先生從事公關，他爸媽就業於能源部門。

• 時態分詞（三態變化）

A. 規則變化

動詞有三個時態，分別是現在式、過去式、及過去分詞。

第一種，是動詞變化有規則可循，也就是「過去式」及「過去分詞」兩個形態變化一樣，皆以「ed」結尾。

	一般動詞	字尾為 y 的一般動詞	字尾為單母音＋一子音的動詞
變化原則	後加 d 或 ed	去 y 加 ied	重複最後子音後加 ed
動詞	煮	研讀	停止
現在式	cook	study	stop
過去式	cooked	studied	stopped
過去分詞	cooked	studied	stopped

這類的動詞也有例外，如：「play 玩耍」的過去式及過去分詞都是「played」。

> Jack listened to the radio last night.
> 昨晚Jack聽收音機。
> 「listened」是「listen」的過去式。

> Mia hadn't cried for 20 years until last year.
> 直到去年，Mia已經有20年沒哭了。
> 「cried」是「cry」的過去分詞。

B. 不規則變化

不規則變化的動詞一樣有現在式、過去式、及過去分詞。後兩者非ed結尾，且無特定變化模式。

變化原則	動詞	現在式	過去式	過去分詞
三態相同	放置	put	put	put
三態相同但發音不同	閱讀	read [rid]	read [rɛd]	read [rɛd]
過去式及過去分詞相同	有	have	had	had
現在式及過去式相同	打、揍	beat	beat	beaten
現在式及過去分詞相同	成為	become	became	become
三態都不同	唱	sing	sang	sung

變化原則	be 動詞現在式	過去式	過去分詞
I	am	was	been
you	are	were	
he / she / it	is	was	
we	are	were	
you			
they			

C. 另外，be動詞過去式與過去分詞之變化較特殊。

> Gina hasn't spoken to her mom for a long time. The last time she spoke to her was when she left for college. Now she speaks to her dad only.
吉娜已經很久沒和她媽媽説話了，最後一次她與媽媽説話是離家上大學時。現在她只和她爸爸講話。

> He was the team captain, and all members were good friends.
他曾是隊長，所有隊員都是好朋友。

> Things had been smooth until that day.
直到那天之前事情都很順利。

Topic 4 詞性：形容詞

- **何謂形容詞：**

用來修飾名詞及代名詞的字。描述抽象特質的形容詞語。

> You are angry.
> 你很生氣。

> Elena has a good heart.
> 伊蓮娜有顆善良的心。

> The baker makes delicious croissant.
> 麵包師能做美味的可頌。

- **何謂形容詞比較級：**

表達程度更高一級時，需使用比較級形容詞。表現方式有兩種，一是將字尾改「er」，或形容詞前加「more 更加」。

> I am smart. She is smarter than me.
> 我很聰明。她比我更聰明。

- 比較級可單獨使用，也可與他人或事物比較。若要比較，要寫成「比較級形容詞＋ than」，意指「比……更……」。

> The shouting guests became angrier when denied entrance.
> 那位尖叫的客人在被拒絕入場後，變得更火大了。

> Greg is a better listener than his siblings.
> 是個比其他兄弟姊妹更好的傾聽者。

> Food is more delicious with fat.
> 添加脂肪的食物更美味。

- **何謂形容詞最高級：**

  最高級形容詞表達最大的程度，表現方式有字尾改「est」，或形容詞前加「most 最」。

  > Bruce Banner turns into Hulk when in the angriest state.
  > 布魯斯班納在最生氣的狀態時會變成浩克。

  > My mom's pasta is the most delicious in the world.
  > 我媽做的麵條是全天下最美味的。

- 形容詞原形、比較級、與最高級後接名詞時，原形與比較級可前接不定冠詞或定冠詞，但最高級必須前接定冠詞。

- 另外，「good 好」與「bad 壞」是少數「形容詞－比較級－最高級」三者都不規則變化的形容詞。

形容詞	比較級	最高級
good 好	better 更好的	best 最好的
bad 壞	worse 更糟的	worst 最糟的

> Jimmy is one of my best friends.
> 吉米是我最好的朋友之一。

> Lying is bad, getting caught lying is worse, and getting caught lying in front of everyone is the worst.
> 撒謊很糟糕，被抓包撒謊更糟糕，在大家面前說謊還被抓包是最糟糕的。
> bad的比較級是worse，最高級是worst。

• 副詞：

A. 副詞用來修飾動詞、形容詞、副詞，及整個句子。

Apparently, Mr. Wallace works extremely hard.
很明顯地，Wallace先生工作極其認真。
三個副詞，副詞「apparently」修飾整句，副詞「hard」修飾動詞works，副詞「extremely」修飾副詞hard。

> Cockroaches are really annoying.
> 蟑螂有夠煩人。
> 副詞「really」修飾形容詞「annoying」。

B. 英文有四個疑問副詞，分別是「when 何時」、「where 何處」、「why 為什麼」、及「how 如何」。

> When did you finish college?
> 你什麼時候念完大學的？

> Where have you been?
> 你們去哪了？

> Why are they moving to south?
> 他們為何要搬到南方？

Topic 5 其他詞性

- **冠詞：**

共有「a 一（個）」及「an 一（個）」，後接非特定的單數可數名詞。an僅用於母音開頭的名詞。

> There is an apple in the basket.
> 有一顆蘋果在籃子裡。

> A dog followed us home.
> 有一隻狗跟著我們回家。

- **定冠詞：**

the後接單數可數名詞、複數可數名詞、及不可數名詞。該名詞可能先前已提過，或有清楚的脈絡讓讀者知道是特定的。

此外，the的發音為[ð]，若後接母音開頭的名詞則改[ði]。唯一例外是，當強調該名詞是非常特別、獨一無二時，口語也發音[ði]，書寫上也常全大寫，讓受眾能心領神會。

> The wine is disgusting.
> 這那酒好噁心。
> 若去掉the，代表對講者而言，所有的酒都很噁心

> A dog followed us home. We later adopted the dog.
> 有一隻狗跟著我們回家，之後我們領養了狗。
> 句中的「a」意指是某一隻狗，後句用「the」就代表是狗是前句提到的、是特別指定的。

> A dog followed us home. We later adopted a dog.
> 有一隻狗跟著我們回家，之後我們領養了狗。
> 後句也用「a」，那被領養的狗和前具提及的狗可能是同一隻、也可能不是。

> Helen of Troy is not a great beauty. She is THE great beauty.
特洛伊的海倫不僅是一個美人，她是獨一無二的美人。
表達不僅是眾多美女的其中之一，而是唯一舉世無雙、名垂千古的美女。

• **介系詞：**

用來顯示名詞間的相互關係，後面需接受詞（名詞、代名詞、動名詞、及名詞子句）。介系詞很多，常見的有「in、to、of、at」等，且就不同狀況有特定用法。

> Vicky has been on my mind for a long time.
我掛念薇琪很長一段時間。

> The group went to Osaka from Tokyo by train.
該團搭火車從東京去到大阪。

• **連接詞：**

A. 對等連接詞：
有「and、but、or、nor、for、so、yet」等，連接兩個重要性對等的單字、片語、或子句。

He wants fries. 他要薯條。	+	He wants coke, too 也想要可樂。
用對等連接詞 連接兩個單字		
He wants fries and coke. 他要薯條跟可樂。		

<table>
<tr><td>He wants fries and coke.
他要薯條與可樂。</td><td>+</td><td>She wants rice or noodle.
她要飯或麵。</td></tr>
<tr><td colspan="3">用對等連接詞
連接兩個單字</td></tr>
<tr><td colspan="3">He wants fries and coke, but she wants rice or noodle.
他要薯條與可樂，但她要飯或麵。</td></tr>
</table>

B. 附屬連接詞：

附屬連接詞則含「after、before、when、because、if、as、as long as、even though」等，將主要句和修飾主要句的從屬句，連結成一複合句子。

> Rose refuses to work before the managers arrives at the store as long as she's paid minimum wage.
> 只要還是拿最低時薪，Rose就拒絕在經理到店前工作。

> When in Rome, do as the Romans do.
> 入境隨俗。

Topic 6 句子的結構：句子組成的基本句式

- **五大句型：**

① S＋V

「Subject 主詞」＋「Verb 動詞」。為最基礎的句子結構，需使用不及物動詞。

> Dad cooks.
> S ＋ V
> 爸爸煮飯。
> 此句採「cook」的不及物動詞形式。

② S＋V＋C

「Subject 主詞」＋「Verb 動詞」＋「主詞補語」。此句型使用的動詞為be動詞，而主詞補語為形容主詞的名詞或形容詞。

> Dad was a cook.
> S ＋ V ＋ C
> 爸爸曾是一名廚師。

③ S＋V＋O

「Subject 主詞」＋「Verb 動詞」＋「Object 直接受詞」。需使用及物動詞。

> Dad cooks dinner.
> S ＋ V ＋ O
> 爸爸煮晚餐。
> 此句採「cook」的及物動詞形式

④ S+V+O+O

「Subject 主詞」+「Verb 動詞」+「Object 間接受詞」+「Object 直接受詞」。需使用及物動詞。

> Dad makes us dinner.
> S + V + O + O
> 爸爸煮晚餐給我們吃。
> 此句「make」意指「製造、做」。

⑤ S+V+O+C

「Subject 主詞」+「Verb 動詞」+「Object受詞」+「受詞補語」。受詞補語為形容受詞的名詞或代名詞，說明受詞經動詞影響而變成了什麼。

> Dad makes us strong and health.
> S + V + O + C
> 爸爸讓我們強壯健康。
> 此句「make」有「使成為……」之意。

國家圖書館出版品預行編目（CIP）資料

寫給過了30歲才要開始好好學英文的你我：邁向雙語國家的成人英文基礎課/Raymond Tsai著. -- 初版. -- 臺北市：易富文化, 2022.10
面； 公分
ISBN 978-986-407-191-3 (平裝)
1.CST: 英語 2.CST: 會話
805.188 111006952

寫給過了30歲才要開始好好學英文的你我

[邁向雙語國家的成人英文基礎課]

書名 / 寫給過了30歲才要開始好好學英文的你我：邁向雙語國家的成人英文基礎課
作者 / Raymond Tsai
發行人 / 蔣敬祖
總編輯 / 劉俐伶
執行編輯 / 林宜彤
英文錄音 / Terri Pebsworth、Jacob Roth
中文錄音 / 劉家燕
校對 / 蔡曉芸、楊易
圖片資訊 / pixta.com、unsplash
視覺指導 / 姜孟傑、鄭宇辰
排版 / 陳涓
法律顧問 / 北辰著作權事務所蕭雄淋律師
印製 / 皇甫彩藝印刷股份有限公司
初版 / 2022年10月
出版 / 我識出版教育集團──懶鬼子英日語
電話 / (02) 2345-7222
傳真 / (02) 2345-5758
地址 / 臺北市忠孝東路五段372巷27弄78之1號1樓
網址 / www.17buy.com.tw
E-mail / iam.group@17buy.com.tw
facebook 網址 / www.facebook.com/ImPublishing
定價 / 新臺幣 399元 / 港幣133元

總經銷 / 我識出版社有限公司出版發行部
地址 / 新北市汐止區新台五路一段114號12樓
電話 / (02) 2696-1357 傳真 / (02) 2696-1359

港澳總經銷 / 和平圖書有限公司
地址 / 香港柴灣嘉業街12號百樂門大廈17樓
電話 / (852) 2804-6687 傳真 / (852) 2804-6409

2011 不求人文化

2009 懶鬼子英日語

2005 意識文化

2005 易富文化

2003 我識地球村

2001 我識出版社

2011 不求人文化

2009 懶鬼子英日語

我識出版教育集團
I'm Publishing Edu. Group
www.17buy.com.tw

2005 意識文化

2005 易富文化

2003 我識地球村

2001 我識出版社